WHAT THE RAIN REVEALS

ADVANCED PRAISE

WHAT THE RAIN REVEALS

by Ken Brosky

"***What the Rain Reveals*** is a work of visceral description, well drawn characters and carefully constructed plot which quickly pulls the reader in and doesn't let go."

—**Jessica Hamilton,** best selling author of ***What You Never Knew***

"Sharp, smart and wonderfully ambitious. A bold debut from a thrilling new voice."

—**John Fram,** author of ***The Bright Lands*** and ***The Midnight Knock***

KEN BROSKY

WHAT THE RAIN REVEALS

For my family.

WHAT THE
RAIN REVEALS

Prophecy

WITNESS A BODY.

Witness the rain, hard and loud, pounding cracked concrete, washing away blood. Millions of drops landing on pitched roofs made of flimsy sheet metal, screwed into place without washers so rust has formed dark halos.

Witness shadows moving in the darkness.

Witness a flash of lightning that illuminates the flood. Water spilling over eaves in heavy streams, slipping into the cracks in the concrete.

Witness a second body, the rain washing away mud, baptizing bloated flesh and tender skin, one clawed hand reaching up to the sky for salvation.

SUNDAY

1

The Root of All Evil

REVEREND ANTHONY JENKINS holds up the hundred-dollar bill for the congregation to see. He puts one corner in his mouth, gripped tightly in his yellow teeth. With his right hand—his only hand on his only arm—he strikes a match across his black leather belt and brings the flickering flame to the bill. In one smooth, practiced motion, he tosses the match and pulls the bill from his mouth, holding it up.

The blend of cotton and linen burns away, scorching the face of Benjamin Franklin. The orange flame travels up to Jenkins' thumb, desperately licking his skin black before dying out.

Eyebrows are an instrument of expression

Eva allows a look of surprise to pass over her face. None of the thirty or so parishioners has made any move to stop their clergyman from destroying the money. Eva is sitting in the last row of folding chairs and can only see the backs of their heads, but she can see nodding, can see stiff backs leaning forward. She can feel a fire burning, as if the flame from the hundred-dollar bill has magically transferred itself to the gasoline-like hatred stored in her stomach.

"I've just committed a crime," the Reverend says in a heavy baritone voice. "You cannot burn money. You cannot deface it. You cannot destroy it. Why? Because it doesn't belong to you. Think about that. You work for money. You toil for money. You save it. You spend it. You leave it in your pockets and run it through the wash. But it's never yours."

Nods. Amens. Reverend Jenkins feeds off their affirmation—Eva can see it in the way the large man carries his weight with each step as he paces in front of the pine altar. His suit coat has been modified so that, instead of an empty left arm sleeve, it's been carefully sewn as if all suitcoats came like this, as if no reverends in the world have two arms.

The Reverend continues with a wry smile: "I read that there are some cities where it's illegal to help the homeless. Think about that: your own money can't be given to someone in need. What would Jesus say, if he was *arrested* for washing the cracked, blistered feet of a man who can't afford shoes?"

More nods.

"Now, I know you've heard this homily before. But, see, I was sick last week. And when I'm sick, I like to watch TV. So I'm watching TV and lo and behold, on comes a preacher! He's in this big mega-church with all these giant stained-glass windows and he's preaching the gospel of *prosperity*! He says, Pray to God, live a good life, and God will reward you with wealth. God will reward you with pieces of paper that you *do not really own*. That's not a reward. That's a curse. We have been taught to cherish wealth as if it's the answer to all our problems. Earn it, spend it, worship it."

He walks in front of his congregation. His eyes land on Eva, lingering. She feels her heart begin to race. She's an intruder here. Not part of his flock. He knows this.

"We have been lied to," he continues. "Trump lied to us.

Biden lied to us. Our high school economics teacher lied to us. Money doesn't free us, it *shackles* us. A gift from God? No. God offers you only one gift: salvation. And the only way to earn that gift is to purge the evil from your life in Jesus' name."

"Amen," the congregation affirms in one voice. Almost scripted. And Eva can feel the passion behind the Reverend's words. He's practiced this monologue the same way an actor practices for an audition.

Eva watches the collection plate go around. Bills enter so fast that it's soon overflowing, fives and tens and twenties hanging over the tarnished brass like the leaves of a plant. She hadn't considered bringing cash, but this will work in her favor. When the bald man in front of her turns and holds out the plate, she sheepishly looks away and shakes her head. This is good. It draws attention to her and adds to her mystery.

"Even right now, the value of these dollar bills is changing," the Reverend says, his eyes watching the collection plate move from hand to hand. Counting, maybe. Taking notes on how much each person is giving. "Currency flows like the streams that cut through the Driftless, disappearing from one person's bank account and reappearing in someone else's. But the value never stays the same."

The Reverend reaches out to the front row. Eva cranes her head, looking over the shoulders of middle-aged couples—and one whining toddler half-asleep on his mother's shoulder—to see a woman in the front row hand the Reverend a Bible. He opens it to a page marked with a red linen bookmark that hangs like a strip of meat, glances at it once, then shuts the book and recites from memory:

"Jesus said *Again, I tell you, it is easier for a camel to go through the eye of a needle than for someone who is rich to enter the kingdom of God ... And everyone who has left houses or brothers or sisters or father or mother or wife or children or fields for my sake will receive a hundred times as much and will inherit eternal life.* This is the Gospel of the Lord."

"Amen," says the congregation.

"Page three, please," Jenkins says. The woman in the front row gets up and walks over to the portable organ beside the Reverend. Eva recognizes her immediately: Tina Jenkins, the Reverend's wife. Eva can remember, as a child, seeing Tina around the town of Carthage—at the grocery store, at the hardware store, sometimes at the Citgo gas station. Now Tina's eyes find Eva, and here is the first major test. Does Tina recognize her? Eva holds her breath, staring ahead, feeling her heart thump against her chest.

Tina's eyes drop to the organ keys. She starts with a thundering A chord.

The congregation sings a song from their hymnal, an old book published by a Methodist church in Missouri. It's a dull, lifeless tune praising Jesus for being so selfless and forgiving. Eva mouths the words but does not contribute to the off-key performance.

She remembers Mass as a child. She remembers the chapel, its nave adorned with beautiful paintings of angels. She remembers the polished steel pipes of the thundering organ, the way the light streamed in through stained-glass windows of two-dimensional saints who had flat, pale faces. She remembers being surrounded by Latino farmhands and their families, feeling the music deep inside her chest and thinking it must be the Holy Ghost.

She doesn't feel that here in this stuffy, cramped one-room building that was once a schoolhouse. The wooden floorboards are worn, and black dirt gathers in the quarter-sawn oak grain. Raindrops land on the west-facing windows; water finds its way through cracks in the frame because water always finds a way. It slips through a hole in the ceiling, running down a chalkboard nailed to the wall, eroding Bible passages written there in big, bold letters.

The Reverend grabs a bottle of red wine and pours it into a silver chalice. He holds it up. "Debt is sin, and sin is debt. Why did Jesus wash away the sins of the world? Because during the time he was alive, debts were recorded on clay ledgers. To clear a debt was to wash it away. Jesus understood that people in debt were demonized and maligned. He stood up and said no, debt and sin are nothing more than etchings. And giving yourself to Christ is like a pounding rain that smooths out the clay. So give yourself to Christ."

Communion begins and at least this is familiar. The congregation walks up to the altar one row at a time. They kneel on the hard floor. The Reverend places a wafer in their mouth—the kind of Christ's body that comes in sealed packages of a hundred. Then he takes his chalice full of wine and brings it to each person's lips, distributing Christ's blood in the portion he sees fit. As they walk back to their seats, they steal glances at the trespasser. Eva feels their eyes on her, like biting black flies she wants to swat away.

Take the time to center yourself between takes. Find your character.

Eva closes her eyes for a handful of breaths, imagining herself floating in the empty blackness. While no one's attention is on her, she's free to reset and gather her thoughts. Stifle the anxiety and fear hitching a ride on her red blood cells, pumped through her body by a frantic heart that feels like it might burst.

When the second-to-last row has finished, Reverend Jenkins meets eyes with Eva again. He gestures her forward. She can feel the magnetism of his invitation and it sickens her, but she pushes that feeling deep down to maintain the appearance of shy apprehension.

Embody your character.

She shakes her head.

Reverend Jenkins motions again. Warm. Inviting. No judgment. No suspicion.

Now is the moment to feel pressured. Pushed against a corner. Scared. Eva thinks back to her childhood cat, Buttons. She remembers the afternoon he wouldn't come home when she called, and how she stayed up all night with a feeling of dread. She had at first called for him playfully, and then with a growing desperation until her throat was raw. She remembers the next morning, finding Buttons lying in the road, and the feeling of utter heartbreak at losing a family member.

Tears form in Eva's eyes. She hiccups, wipes the tears, and shakes her head again.

"All right," says the Reverend. He sets the chalice on the altar and extends his right hand. He smiles, radiating love for his congregation. "This Eucharist is complete. Please remember that we're setting up a search party this week for Elliot Stone, so keep your schedules open."

The congregants file out. Eva keeps her head lowered, staring at a black knot in the floorboards. She can hear voices murmuring, talking to each other about the recent storm that passed through, about the flooding, about the Stone boy who's gone missing. Eva half-listens, unable to concentrate on their voices, feeling the growing anxiety and dread gnaw at her stomach. It's only a matter of time now.

Nothing is certain yet.

Reset.

She breathes deep and waits.

Finally, the Reverend sits down beside her. His weight tests the folding chair. He's a big man—not fat, but tall and heavy. He could overpower her. He could kill her with his bare hand, grabbing her throat and squeezing tightly until the world went black. He could smash her head in with a rock.

"You're not from around here, are you?" he asks.

Eva blushes. The question sets her mind at ease, just a bit. It's a clichéd question, the kind someone asks to be nice but without actually having much experience being nice. It's the kind of question you ask when you're *not* suspicious. The kind of question a character might ask in the first draft of a screenplay.

Train your voice. Learn how to breathe and modify the resonance. Find the tone and rhythm that fits your character.

"I'm from Milwaukee," she whispers after a beat.

"Are you passing through, or …"

Eva lets the unfinished question hang in the air for a moment, pretending to consider whether to answer him at all. She licks her lips, still looking down at the floor, concentrating on a blackened burl like it's a camera mark. "I'm staying at the Sunshine Motel on Highway O."

"Ah. We call that intersection The Crossroads."

Eva knows this. She knows about the village of Carthage to the east of the Crossroads and the college town of Fayette to the west.

"So are you …" He clears his throat. "The strip club, I take it?"

The strip club is across the street from the motel. Last night, Eva could see its neon lights through the flimsy red curtains in her room. She'd considered being a stripper, but decided that might be too scandalous for the Reverend. Or, worse, he might see it as an opportunity to reach out sexually.

"No," Eva says between heartbeats. She can barely think straight. What was her story again? Her mind recalls the notes she'd written, the colors she'd used to memorize different details. She takes a deep breath.

Don't give him anything. Make him ask.

"Are you planning on staying at the motel for long?"

She could kill him. She has a knife in her purse.

"I don't know," she answers. Her skin tingles. He knows who she really is. She has to run, now, while she still can.

No. He can't possibly know. If he did, he would have thrown her out and cursed her to Hell.

"Well, you're welcome to attend Bible study on Tuesday, if you're still around. It's very informal. We meet right here at seven o'clock."

"OK," Eva mumbles. She can sense his curiosity now, the way his voice is growing patronizing and higher in pitch. He wants to know more, but he's careful with his questions. Eva thinks about Buttons again. She thinks about how unnaturally twisted his body looked and how much she loved cuddling with him every morning as a child.

"Are you OK?" the Reverend asks.

The cat would nuzzle her chin with his chin, like a kiss. He would purr in her ear.

Eva bursts into tears. She covers her face with her hands, desperate to hide from the world. Embarrassed at her weakness. She is a proud young woman and breaking down like this in front of a stranger is a humiliating surprise.

This is her character.

A hand lands on her back. Warm. Gentle. Just above the bra line. Not the Reverend but his wife, who's taken a seat to Eva's right. She thinks about the stained-glass image of Jesus in her childhood church, flanked by angels, radiating morning sunlight.

"I don't know what I'm doing," Eva sobs. "I just can't go back."

"Go back to what, sweetie?" coos the Reverend's wife.

"All of it," Eva says. She pushes memories of Buttons to the back of her mind to stop the tears. "I don't trust myself," she continues between wet hiccups. She talks into her hands. "I give in every time. They pressure you to live this, this lifestyle that you can't afford."

"Of course," says the Reverend. "Money doesn't buy you happiness, does it?"

Eva shakes her head. She pulls her hands away from her face. She can feel the sting in her eyes, the puffiness of her cheeks.

The terror of what might come next. Stick to the script, a voice inside her head urges.

"I don't want to go back," she says. Firmly. Stubbornly. The butterflies in her stomach cease fluttering as she takes control.

"You don't have to, sweetie," says the Reverend's wife.

"It's just like they …" Eva pauses, pretending to search for the right words. But she's practiced this moment. This pause. "It's like they give you bonuses just so you can waste it all. You have to buy a fancy car. You have to buy the nicest clothes. And the worst part is, we don't do anything to deserve it. All we do is sit in our little office and move clients' money around and pretend we're doing something good for the world."

She takes a deep, shaky breath. Raindrops patter the windows. She's expecting the Reverend to ask more questions and she's ready with more half-answers. He can ask about her job. He can ask about the parties, the money, her broken life. She's ready. Her character is ready.

Instead, he offers his right hand. "My name is Anthony. This is my wife, Tina."

Eva takes his hand and gently shakes it. "I'm Sofia," she says. "Sofia Lopez."

2

Heifers

DEPUTY MASON TAYLOR honks his horn. The three escaped Jersey heifers promptly make an about-face in the road, scurrying back to the Jenkins driveway. Mason knows they're Jerseys because of the black noses, the black around the eyes, the soaking wet brown coat of fur.

He turns onto the driveway, honking again to keep the Jerseys moving before they can nibble on the bed of flowers around the Jenkins family mailbox, its rusted red flag hanging like a broken limb. The corn crops ten feet beyond the flowers are submerged in flooded water that darkly reflects the heavy gray clouds, like spilled mercury. The corn has just emerged in the past few days, nothing more than single green leaves in neat rows, desperate for just a day's respite from the wet weather.

Ahead is the Jenkins house in all its dilapidated glory, a two-story farmhouse that's seen better days. Missing gutters so that rain drips down the peeled, white aluminum siding. Stone foundation with holes in the mortar, perfect hiding places for earwigs and box elders. A dozen old gardening tools laying on the soggy grass. A metal bird feeder hanging from a tree branch at a violent angle, its contents moldy and brown.

Beyond the house are another twenty or so escaped cows, lingering behind one of the massive loafing sheds, a half-open structure with white and blue aluminum paneling peeling off in strips.

"God damn it," Mason mutters. He's about to call it in when he sees the Jenkins boy turn the west corner of the shelter, bringing with him another half-dozen heifers.

Mason parks the Kane County Sheriff SUV sideways so the cows are less inclined to head back toward the driveway. He gets out and gives the boy a wave. What was his name again? Jake? Jerry?

Josh.

"How about a hand?" he asks.

The teenager stops next to the electric pole that holds a jumble of black wires leading to each of the farm buildings, as if he's not sure what to do next. Everyone in the Carthage police department calls him *retarded*. Too many concussions when he played a year on the Carthage High football team, they joke. Judging from the boy's size, Mason would put him at tight end or maybe offensive tackle. He's only sixteen years old but he's big, just like his father the Reverend.

Mason can tell just by looking at the boy's green eyes that he's working things out in his head. Trying to figure out the easiest way to get these escaped cows back into their pen. Weighing Mason's help vs. the very real possibility of the Reverend coming home from Sunday service and seeing an officer of the law on his property, and the consequences of that.

Josh looks exhausted—how long has he already been trying to round up all these escapees? His gray t-shirt is torn near the armpits, soaked through with rainwater and sweat. A real "work shirt." Chocolate-colored manure stains his rubber boots, his bare legs, his Nike shorts.

Finally, the boy nods.

"Where'd they come from?" Mason asks.

"West group. We can take them down the driveway."

"Where do you want me?"

Josh gestures vaguely toward the big shop building on the other side of the concrete lot. It has a tall garage door, big enough for million-dollar John Deere equipment to get through, although according to everyone in the Carthage government building, the Jenkins family hasn't owned any big farming equipment since the dairy shut down ten years ago and the bank came calling.

A pair of cows have found some grass growing in a crack near the garage door. Their Barbie-pink tongues curl around a few blades, cutting the clump with their lower incisors.

Mason shoos the cows down the driveway while Josh gets the rest of the herd in the right direction. Mason walks past a heap of blue scrap metal sitting between the big shop and another building. It runs along the driveway on the left, made of the cream-colored bricks that are famous in southern Wisconsin. There's a steel hopper bottom grain bin near the front door and a pair of yellow pails sitting underneath.

"That where you raise the calves?" Mason asks, gesturing to the cream-colored building.

Josh gives Mason a strange look, then finally nods.

Across the driveway is the north group. Heifers ready to be impregnated watch behind a fence that's been cobbled together. Broken wooden posts have been replaced with four-by-fours held in place by cement in old tires. Some remnants of the wood fencing remain but most has been replaced with wire fencing and steel gates that are tied together with orange bale twine and metal wiring. It's not the worst fence Mason has seen in the county, but it's close.

The cows moo.

"They're just mad they can't escape, too," Josh mumbles.

Mason walks carefully on the cracked concrete, avoiding where rainwater and manure have puddled. The stench has a hint of sweet to it because the cows are fed corn silage. Josh moves ahead of the group, cutting them off where the driveway forks. Off to the left is a cul-de-sac with a pair of gas pumps. To the right is a driveway that leads along the west group feed panels, flanked on one side by a single silo and four more foundations where silos once stood, now nothing more than concrete stumps. Mason figures the last one remains only because it's too expensive to take down. It looks in bad shape: the steel wire wrapped around the concrete brick exterior has snapped in places, and the rusted black ladder hangs by a thread about halfway up.

"Don't step there," Josh says, pointing to the brown manure sludge around the silo. "It's way deeper than it looks."

"Good to know. Thanks." Mason stands a few feet away, shooing the cows so they follow the path along the feed panels, where they stop to pick at the piles of sweet silage. Mason doesn't know much about dairy cows, but the basics have been pretty easy to put together since he first started his job in Kane County, Wisconsin: mature heifers poke their heads through to eat the silage, panels are locked in place, cows are inseminated.

Then, apparently, they're marked. He can see some of the cows standing behind the metal panels have green symbols on their hindquarters. They pull back as Mason passes, knocking the back of their heads on the metal bars.

"Go on!" Mason says to the escaped Jerseys. He gives one a hardy slap on the rump. The muscle and mass, the very sound of his hand hitting something so heavy and solid, is a good reminder to keep an eye on his feet and make sure none of their hoofs find his toes.

Ahead is a small shed just big enough for a single vehicle, and beyond that is the west group's pen. Josh has opened the old gate and parked his truck next to it so the cows don't go veering left toward the big, open-sided barn where all the hay and feed is stored. Josh walks to the other side of the open gate while Mason keeps the cows moving forward. They fall in line to the very last one, who skittishly tries to get past Josh but he quickly gets his hands on her shoulder and gives her enough of a push to turn her around. Yeah, definitely an offensive line-man, Mason decides.

Mason closes the gate. There's manure on the metal bars, and now it's smeared across his palms.

"Thanks," Josh says, locking the gate with a chain. "They pushed the feed bunk forward. I gotta push it back in place."

"I'll stay right here."

Josh walks to the little vehicle shed and hops in the skid steer, which looks like a miniature bulldozer. He throttles up the growling engine and brings it to the feed bunk just to the left of the west group gate. The bunk is old, with peeling green paint and rust along the corners. Empty, too. Maybe the cows were hungry. Maybe the boy shouldn't be running this opera-tion. Maybe he should just go to church with his daddy.

Josh uses the skid steer's bucket to push the bunk back into place so it's flush with the rest of the fencing. The west group's perimeter is now, once again, closed. But if the cows want to get out, there's a couple places along the wire fencing where they could probably push and do it. At the far corner, Josh has simply tied an old wooden pallet to two posts. Not quite what Mason would call a "fence."

Josh dumps fresh hay into the feed bunk, then parks the skid steer as a brace against it so the cows can't move it again. He hops out, tests the chain on the gate to ensure it's tight. "The Jerseys like to lick the lock open," he says. "I lost a chain the other week and some got out."

"They wouldn't eat it, would they?"

Josh shrugs and looks down. "Probably just got lost in the manure."

Mason takes a deep breath. Here, away from the north group headlocks where the wet silage sits, he smells only the shit. At least it's not hog shit. He's very quickly learned the difference, living out here in southwest Wisconsin.

"What about her?" Mason asks, nodding to a big cow lying on a bed of straw next to the truck. A Guernsey, with pretty white spots and a pink nose. On the other side of another rough-shod fence, very large, very pregnant cows watch with curiosity. They stick their heads between steel gates held together with bale twine.

"She fell," says Josh. "Slipped in the manure a few days ago. Did the splits. Hasn't gotten back up since."

Mason cringes. "She gonna be OK?"

Josh's eyes glance at the large mound of dirt piled between the two pens, at the edge of a field of very waterlogged yellow corn leaves. There's a smaller mound, and a spot beside it where wet, dark brown wood chips have been laid out.

"You compost the corpses?" Mason asks.

Josh nods. "Rendering plant doesn't pick them up for free anymore. So I was reading how you compost. And it's really easy, actually. You just lay a bed of wood chips to start. Then you gotta lance the abdomen so it doesn't bloat. Then you cover it with dirt."

Mason stares at empty bed of wood chips, not fully listening. All he's thinking about now is Elliot Stone, thirteen years old, missing two weeks now. Elliot Stone, who belonged to the Reverend's church. Who may have disappeared somewhere in this valley. Mason isn't going to get another chance to converse with the Jenkins boy like this. The Reverend hates police officers and wants nothing to do with them.

Keep him talking.

"You lose a lot of cows?"

"Heck no, sir. My cull rate is two percent."

"Is that good?"

"Average is six. My grandma taught me a lot before she had her stroke. And I've been reading, too."

"You get a lot of those farming magazines?" Mason's been getting them in the mail ever since he moved to Kane County.

"Yes, sir."

"Wilson's must like you." Mason doesn't know much about the massive dairy operation, except that a lot of local farmers raise calves for them. Farmers who used to have their own dairies and now are overburdened with debt and have to work for a CAFO.

Once the heifers are pregnant, Wilson's Dairy will pick them up and take them to its milking facility. Mason sees trailers full of them on his patrols.

Josh wipes sweat off his forehead. It drips from his fingers. He looks exhausted. Stressed. Maybe Mason can build a rapport with him.

Then ask a few hard questions.

He checks his watch. Church just got out. The Reverend and his wife will no doubt stay afterward for a while to speak with congregants, then they'll come home. Mason can't be here when they arrive.

But he won't get a chance like this again.

"How about I help you get caught up with chores?"

Josh shrugs. "I guess we could finish the feeding."

They take buckets of grain pellets to what Josh calls the "new group" on the south end, around the other side of the dismantled silos. Mason tosses pads of hay into a rusted metal feeder that's been squeezed like a barricade into an old vehicle entrance of the loafing shed; Josh goes inside, gently yelling at the cows to get out of the way so he can dump grain into the feed bunk inside. His boots make a *sluck-sluck-sluck* sound in the manure. When he gets back out, his hands are smeared black.

Mason takes the push broom from inside the vehicle shed. He pushes the sweet-smelling grain up to the headlocks of the north group. Heifers stick their heads through, lapping greedily at the silage. The metal hinges squeak. By the time he gets all the way to the other end, every headlock is occupied. Josh walks down and locks the row in place just as a white truck makes its way down the driveway and parks at the north group gate.

A middle-aged man steps out, glancing warily at Mason's uniform. He has a pockmarked face, brown hair tucked under a Milwaukee Brewers baseball cap. "Uh oh. Josh OK?"

"He's fine," Mason says. "Just some cows loose."

"That's Steven," Josh says. "He inseminates the cows for Wilson's Dairy."

"Steven Brown," says the man, giving Mason a quick shake. Thankfully, it's clean.

"I gotta take care of one before you start," Josh mumbles.

Steven slips off his shoes and pulls a pair of rubber boots from the trunk. "Bummer. 3145?"

Josh nods.

"Better get it done now." He removes a vat of bull semen from the truck, then gestures with the AI gun over Mason's shoulder. "He warn you about the manure moat by the silo?"

Mason smiles. "Yup."

"Almost fell in once," Steven says, climbing over a section of the old fence that's made of wooden two-by-sixes. "Slipped on the edge. My whole leg went under."

The north group pen, like the other pens, has a loafing shed where the cows can take shelter from the elements and rest on dry bedding composed of manure and straw. Creosote posts hold up the structure with impressive resolve, given how old everything else looks. Mason remarks on this as they walk back up the row of headlocks.

"They're older than my grandmother," Josh says. "The cross-beams need repair. So do those." He points to the blue aluminum sheets making up the west-facing exterior wall that are bent and damaged, hanging by a couple rusted screws in some places. "Strong wind storm blew a few panels off the roof and one corner actually caved in. But I think I can fix it when I get the time."

Mason examines the teenager. Not so dumb, after all. "Ever think about hiring someone to help you out?"

He shakes his head quickly. The question has made him uncomfortable for some reason. Mason didn't expect that. He searches his mind for something else to ask, something friendly that will disarm the boy.

Then he remembers: the game store. He'd seen Josh there once a month ago, buying a pack of *Magic: the Gathering* playing cards. Josh hadn't seen Mason standing near the board games; Mason had watched him walk in, go for one of the packs next to the register, pay with a handful of one-dollar bills, then scurry out. "Pick up any good *Magic* cards lately?"

Josh looks at him uncertainly. Is the boy embarrassed about his interest in the game? Maybe the football team made fun of him. He was never actually enrolled at Carthage High. Apparently, home-schooled kids can still play for the local high school's sports teams, and that's what Josh did for a year until the Reverend put the kaybash on it.

They return to the area just past the vehicle shed, where the pregnant cows are still watching the injured Guernsey. She hasn't moved. Her bloodshot, bulging eyes follow Mason; her breaths come fast. Mason holds out his hand and lets her lick his fingers with her long, sandpaper tongue. "I hear your dad's putting together a search party for Elliot Stone."

Josh looks up sharply, his eyes suddenly filled with curiosity. "You think Elliot's OK?"

Kids don't disappear for two weeks and turn up alive very often. Mason doesn't want to just out and say this, but maybe if he broaches the possibility, he can get Josh talking a bit. "I'm holding out hope."

"Sometimes people just leave without saying goodbye," Josh says glumly. "That's what my sister did."

"Miriam moved out?" It seems like a simple follow-up question. But something about it clearly makes the boy uncomfortable.

Josh wipes his hands on his shorts, smearing manure.

Mason takes a deep breath, watches the injured heifer try to get up, only to roll back onto her side. He doesn't know anything about Josh's sister; the Reverend's entire family is notoriously reclusive.

"Hey Josh. You ever talk to Elliot? Maybe at your father's church services?"

Josh whispers something to the injured Guernsey, one hand running along the white spots on her torso.

"Did Elliot ever stop here?" Mason knows he's pressing but he can't help himself. "Maybe him and his parents stopped by to see the Reverend?"

"No," Josh mumbles. He gently scratches the cow behind her ears. Mason feels uncomfortable seeing it, as if he's spying something personal and intimate.

"Do you think it would be worth it to give your sister a call?" he asks. "Maybe see if she ever talked to Elliot?"

Josh's face contorts. He sniffs in so hard Mason can feel his own sinuses reacting, then goes back to the vehicle shed and pulls out a box, setting it on the tire of the skid steer. He opens it and pulls out a silver revolver. Mason's hand automatically goes to his service piece, but he stifles the reaction. *He's just a boy*, the voice in his head soothes.

Sometimes people just leave without saying goodbye.

"Did Elliot ever talk to you at church?" Mason asks. "Can you try and think back for me?"

Josh checks the chamber, snapping it back into place. A profound shadow has fallen over his features; Mason doesn't know what to make of it.

The pregnant big breds edge their way to their fence to get a better look. If they wanted, they could push on the fence and knock it over. The posts are so old and rotted that they won't hold nails anymore, so Josh has stacked two old, rusted feed bunks and tied them to the neighboring wire fencing with bale twine.

"Josh," Mason tries again, "we don't have any leads. Your family's practically the only one in the county that hasn't given the sheriff a statement. If you know *anything* …"

Josh walks over to the heifer and kneels beside her. He runs a gentle hand across her forehead.

"I'm sorry, girl."

Mason realizes what he's about to do now. He squats beside Josh. "You have to do this?"

"She's in pain," Josh says. "Her weight is pinching her nerves and cutting off her blood supply."

"Can't give her another day?"

Josh shakes his head. "She's suffering. My grandma taught me to never let them suffer."

Mason watches the boy press the barrel of the gun to the center of the heifer's forehead. One bulging, bloodshot eye rolls toward the steel. Her heaving chest draws in slower breaths, as if a cooling relief has washed over her. Here is a coming mercy, Mason knows. Still, the trauma of his past cools the sweat on his neck, a heavy shadow that reaches through his back and squeezes his heart.

Josh pulls the trigger. The cow's body collapses onto the wood chips, blood seeping out of the hole in her head.

And Mason can't help but wonder how many bullets are left in that gun.

3

Rehearsal

EVA GRABS A CUP of coffee at Crossroads Coffee, Bike and Ski, across from the dumpy old motel on the west end of Carthage. The café has the quaint façade of an old-fashioned general store. Inside is a pastry case and espresso machine and a handful of coffee tables in one corner. Old hardwood floorboards creak and groan. An open doorway leads to a little shop filled with bike supplies.

The pastries are delicious. The coffee is fresh. The woman behind the counter has lived in Kane County all her life and served Eva and her college theatre friends all the time back in their senior year of high school. The perfect test.

Eva pays with cash.

The woman makes change, looks up at Eva. Eva can feel her ears grow hot—thankfully, she's let her hair down. This woman wouldn't remember Eva's wavy brown hair; in high school, Eva dyed her hair all sorts of colors and kept it short. One of the many ways she attempted to torture her dad, only to learn— with typical irrational teenage frustration—that her father had no qualms whatsoever about what she did with her hair. Having a cool dad could be the *worst*.

"Stay dry out there," the woman says.

Eva holds her breath until she's safely inside her rental car, then sighs with relief. The woman examined Eva and saw nothing familiar, no vestige of her past. She feels the same high that nearly overwhelmed her when she gave the Reverend her fake name, when he and his wife accepted it, accepted her—not Eva, but *Sofia*.

In the 10 years she spent in Los Angeles, she went out of her way to avoid watching herself in any role. Skipped the parties her bit-part actor friends threw in their apartments when films appeared on Netflix, never took the plastic off DVD's sent to her by her agent, and always, always changed the channel if that awful L'Oréal shampoo commercial ever came on.

Still, self-reflection is important. She shouldn't have tried so hard to make eye contact with the woman in the café. How could she have admitted she was looking for someone? Because he disarmed her with his kindness.

Definitely shouldn't have cried so much in front of the Reverend. She laid it on too thick. It felt too melodramatic. Luckily, it had only made her seem more pathetic, warranting an extreme act of kindness from the Reverend's wife: dinner. At the Jenkins family house.

Inside the dragon's lair.

Eva pulls out of the café parking lot and takes the highway road back toward the town center of Carthage. She can't make any mistakes at dinner with the Reverend. She has to know the character of Sofia Lopez as intimately as she knows herself. It's more than simply reading lines—any serious actor can attest to that. It's about disappearing into the role. Convincing the audience that Sofia Lopez isn't a character at all—she's a person.

It's about deception.

She passes farms whose budding corn crops are contoured

to the rolling land and rattles off the family names by heart, a census. She knows them because her father knew them. She knows the land growing corn now grew soy the year before. She knows the pools of standing water in the fields will eventually drain through the tiles, into the ditches, to the nearest streams, carrying the rain to the Kewaunee River and eventually the Mississippi, draining into the Gulf of Mexico.

She sees the yellowed tips of infant corn stalks desperately breaching the pools of water and knows they're doomed. She's seen flooding in Kane County before.

In Carthage, Eva slows to the 25 MPH speed limit. She travels down Main Street. Beyond the town are the bluffs, tall like castle walls. Eva used to climb them with her father, looking for evidence of ancient sea creatures left in the layers of stone. She remembers how the afternoon sun shines down on the bluffs and gives Carthage a natural beauty that California just can't capture. When she was a girl, this would have been enough to set her head right.

But now, Carthage feels different. Rain runs darkly down the exposed sandstone. Streams of water drown Main Street's old sewer system. The ancient buildings look as if their bricks are made of bread that's grown soft and spongy. A Hollywood façade, filming finished, the sets waterlogged and abandoned.

The appliance parts store is gone. The fine clothing store is gone. Janet's Cake Shop has been replaced with the Kane County Republican Party headquarters.

Eva turns left on Milwaukee Avenue, passing a Mexican restaurant she doesn't remember and the old Carthage Theatre where she acted in family-friendly plays put on by the local thespians. On the marquee is a call for auditions for *Beauty and the Best*—the "a" has fallen off, carried away on the flood like a child's discarded paper boat.

The street takes her past a few blocks of two-story homes. She passes a pizza parlor, and—across the street—a hardware store. Beyond that is a small building with wet, dark brown bricks and shaded windows and no signs. Eva knows this is the women's shelter, intentionally indiscreet. Next to it was once a furniture store, now empty, its filmy windows offering only a dark glimpse of cracked tile flooring.

Eva pulls into the Piggly Wiggly supermarket parking lot, taking a spot near the adjoining McDonald's where a line of cars is queued all the way to the street. It's funny—she always thought "Piggly Wiggly" was such a normal name for a grocery store chain. Then she moved to Los Angeles and realized how absolutely ridiculous it is, right down to the winking pink pig mascot.

She hurries under the drizzle of rain to the entrance, casually running a hand through her wavy hair as she enters, pretending to not know where the shopping baskets are. She looks around. The market's layout hasn't changed: eight cashier stations near the front, produce to the right, bakery to the left. All the cashier stations but one are manned by teenagers. Eva was once one of those teenagers, scanning barcodes, memorizing Shakespeare lines, dreaming of leaving this shit hole town.

Put on what weary negligence you please, you and your fellows. I'll have it come to question.

Eva spots Meredith Holtz at Register 5. Meredith Holtz, a Piggly Wiggly lifer, a divorcee, a heavy smoker. Always timed Eva's breaks. Always complained about the immigrants who worked the Kane County farms. Always called the police when kids left their bikes in the rack outside overnight.

Eva grabs a bag of apples, a bag of chips, a couple boxes of energy bars, a six-pack of lime-flavored seltzer. She got used to drinking warm seltzer water on movie productions, where actors playing bit roles are expected to stick around between shots and can't always get to the food tables set up by the craft services crew. She gets a can of almonds, then swings by the bakery to pick up a little container of cinnamon donut holes to satisfy a very specific, nostalgic hunger.

She pretends to look at the rotisserie chickens while an older man with lots of groceries checks out at Station 5. Eva sets items on the black conveyor belt. The rubber is clean, still streaky from whatever cleaner Meredith keeps under the register. A decade has passed and she still has the same habits.

"How are you today?" she asks.

"Wonderful," Eva says, forcing down the butterflies in her stomach.

Meredith glances up when she reaches the donut holes. In this moment, they make eye contact. Meredith is short, her back slightly hunched over, her curly dark red hair hiding a scar above her right ear that she got from a drunk driving accident near the Crossroads. "There's a sale on these if you buy two."

"One is plenty." Eva gives her a practiced smile. It's not the type of smile a moody 17-year-old Eva would have flashed while working here. This is a smile—slightly crooked, slightly forced—that only Sofia Lopez would share, an effort to put on a brave face even though her life is spiraling out of control.

"Are you driving through town?" Meredith asks, weighing the bag of apples. Eva knows she has the four-digit code for Gala apples memorized, but the woman pretends to look it up instead. She wants conversation, desperate even a decade later for any human contact.

"I'm heading to Fayette," Eva says. "I got my degree there. Thought I'd visit some of my old teachers."

Meredith glances up again. Eva feels the butterflies rise; the woman is trying to place her. Searching her memory for someone who resembles Eva. She's struggling, though. Eva's body is skinnier, thanks to Hollywood's impossible beauty standards. Her eyebrows are thicker because she stopped plucking more than a month ago in preparation for this role. Even her eyes are darker, the result of brown contact lenses.

Her skin is darker, too. The first time in years she's allowed herself to go more than a day without heavy sunscreen. Eva remembers a callback audition for a movie role two years ago. She'd been so close. She'd read for the part of a scientist partnering with a mathematician to develop a new vaccine that would change the world. But instead of winning the main part, she was offered the role of *Hispanic Bartender*. She'd been out in the L.A. sun too long the previous week, sending her melanin production into overdrive.

"That's a nice thing to do," Meredith says finally. She sets aside the apples and scans the boxes of energy bars. A bored-looking blond boy ambles over and starts putting everything in a plastic bag. "Not enough people thank their teachers."

"I owe them a lot," Eva says. "I almost majored in History. Came to my senses and switched to business."

Meredith simply smiles and announces the total: $35.76.

Eva reaches into her black leather purse for her wallet, pulling out two twenties.

"Are you from around here?" Meredith asks as her fingers slide coins out of the till. The subtle meaning of her question is obvious: *Were you born here?*

"No," Eva says, and the word comes out too sharp. She swallows hard, forcing herself to maintain eye contact. "I grew up in Evanston, just north of Chicago."

"That makes sense." Meredith hands over the change and looks Eva up and down.

She always used to intimidate you. Don't let her do it now.

Eva patiently waits for her receipt, staring into Meredith's eyes, pushing aside memories of a thousand petty exchanges.

"Don't be a stranger," Meredith says, handing off the receipt.

Eva thanks her, takes the plastic bag from the boy, and walks to her car. Her words play over and over in her head. What could she have done better? The "No" came out too defensive and fast, as if she'd been hiding something. Sofia Lopez doesn't care about what these small-town rubes think of her. When talking about her education, she should sound proud; she graduated summa cum laude, after all. And Eva must remember the most important part of Sofia's story: she's not really here to reconnect with old teachers.

Sofia Lopez is *struggling*.

Eva pulls out of the parking lot, back onto Milwaukee Avenue. She turns left on Main Street, which terminates three blocks up where the old Carthage Elementary sits, surrounded by dark green grass and tall pine trees. She turns right on Jefferson Street. These side streets are the real Carthage, full of hidden pieces of history mixed with modern amenities. An ancient service station with old-fashioned gas pumps. A *Super Mercado* where immigrant farm laborers shop for fresh sour cream and Duvalín and Gansito. A little cream-brick factory building where the Swamp Angel cannon was constructed for the Civil War, now home to an antique store world-famous for its hundreds of cookie jars.

In her mind, she's racing through Sofia's character again— deeper now, plumbing the depths of her fears and anxiety and sorrow.

She parks at St. Patrick's Catholic Church. One more rehearsal.

The marquee sign on the grass outside invites people to an English service Sundays at 9:00 and a Spanish service Sundays at 11:00. Above the replaceable lettering is the priest's name: Father Emilio Del Toro, the same priest from Eva's childhood.

She sits in the car for a moment, watching a robin land on the marquee board and survey the lawn. The drizzle of rain has stopped but there's no sign of blue sky in any direction. She debates whether to walk in wearing her sunglasses. She fears Father Del Toro will recognize her, even though she hasn't been to Mass since she was in her early teens. He was always supportive of her acting dreams. Sometimes, when she per-formed at Shakespeare in the Park, she saw him in the audience.

Eva checks the clock: one p.m. She digs through her purse for her little black diary, filled with both Eva's and Sofia's secrets and desires and failures and dreams.

She gets out and walks up to the heavy front doors of the church, pulling open the right one because it was always the door she pulled open as a child. Cool air kisses her skin as she steps into the dimly lit cathedral. Eva looks around nervously, her eyes passing over the beautiful stained-glass windows, the empty wooden pews, the beautiful altar covered by a silvery white frontal, before landing on the confessionals off to her right. Eva remembers the confessional being warm in the sum-mer. She remembers feeling suffocated inside, uncomfortable. She remembers it feeling so pointless.

Now, there's a point.

She steps inside the left confessional and pulls shut the red curtain. She sits on the wooden bench, heart pounding.

Deep breaths.

The wooden panel between the confessionals slides open. Through the black screen, Eva can see Father Del Toro's face. Her knees tremble.

Center yourself between takes.

"In the name of the Father, and of the Son, and of the Holy Spirit," she begins. Her voice comes out stronger than expected. She tempers it ever so slightly so that the vowels come out shaky and soft. "My last confession was more than a year ago."

"Why so long, if I may ask?" His voice, raw and silky, just a hint of his Hispanic accent, brings back a flood of memories for Eva. Mass with her mother, sitting in the second pew on the right. Singing along in the hymnal, listening to her mother's beautiful voice, her perfect pitch.

Eva sets those memories aside. Sofia doesn't have those memories. "I've lost my way," she says. The words come out too easily. Not humble enough. She clears her throat, continuing: "I let greed turn me into someone I don't recognize in the mirror."

"We're all tempted to possess more than we need," Father Del Toro offers.

The black diary in her lap now, Eva quietly opens it to her character notes. "I took a finance job right out of college. They do wealth management for rich clients. I thought I'd only be there for a few years, but ..." She leaves it hanging, expecting Father Del Toro to chime in with an empathetic homily. Instead, he stays silent, forcing her to continue: "All of my co-workers are so ... slimy. They act as if money is the most important thing in the world."

"I have a book for them to read."

Eva smiles. Father Del Toro's sense of humor hasn't changed. "Being around them for so many years has changed me, father. I feel like I've tried so hard to fit in with them that I'm not the person I used to be. And I loved the person I used to be. She cared about other people. She was kind. She fostered stray cats and volunteered with her church."

"You can still be that person."

Eva takes a deep breath, preparing to venture delicately away from her prepared remarks. Let his comments guide her to new places so she can flesh out the character of Sofia Lopez. So she can ad-lib during her dinner with the Reverend. "I don't know how to go back. They pressure me, father. They spend money like water. We went on a retreat to Vegas a month ago. My co-workers were spending thousands of dollars every night. I couldn't keep up but I had to try so I could fit in."

"Why do you have to fit in?"

"Because," she says quietly, conjuring the whole of her experiences with a little Hollywood improv troupe whose Golden Rule was *And then.* "People who don't attend the expensive dinners or the retreats or the trips ... they become outsiders in the company. They're shut out like pariahs. If you don't act like them and if you don't believe what they believe, you're nothing."

Father Del Toro exhales gently. Eva, head still lowered, notices in her peripheral vision that his hand has brought a handkerchief to his forehead, gently dabbing sweat. Eva, too, can feel the warmth inside the confessional. She can smell the aristocratic blend—jasmine, Black Currant, Oud—of perfume favored by the Mexican women. The same perfume Eva's mom sprayed twice on her neck each Sunday morning.

"We all wear masks sometimes," Father Del Toro says. "You're an actor in a great morality play."

Eva's heart nearly stops. Her hand clutches the pen before it can slip out of her grip and land on the floor. Does he recognize her voice, after all these years?

"What matters is there's no script for us to follow," he continues. "We're free to choose our own paths."

He knows. Eva is sure of it now. Needles run down her arms. No. He *can't*. She shakes the thought away, centering herself again. "What do I do?"

"You must find the strength to locate the part of you that feels lost. She's still inside you. And I suspect she is anxious to meet you again."

"But how?"

"Penance," Father Del Toro says, "alleviates the severity of the sins in God's eye, but it does so much more. It allows us to achieve peace with our own mistakes. To allow ourselves a second chance."

"I want that," Eva whispers. She digs deep, imagining not just Sofia's fictional mistakes but her own, too.

"May I ask your name?" His voice is so gentle that it breaks Eva's heart.

"Sofia."

"Sofia. I feel as though I know you." A pause. Enough time for Eva's muscles to stiffen. For sweat to trickle down her left temple. "Maybe," Father Del Toro continues, "I recognize your situation. And I empathize with it. We're all pressured to fit in."

"I feel guilt for all the money I've wasted just to keep a job I hate."

"I would never encourage someone to quit their job." Father Del Toro clears his throat. "I know that we all must earn a living. But as a penance, I want you to take some time searching for the version of you that you so love. Find her in your acts and deeds. Embrace her when she appears and go out of your way to find her when she does not."

"Yes, father." Eva gently closes the diary and puts it back in her purse. "Thank you."

She opens the curtain and walks quickly to the entrance of the church. She gets back into her car just as the rain picks up again, pelting the windshield in fat drops. She takes the car around the block, passing a gas station and a pair of taverns. She turns onto Main Street. She forces down the guilt, telling herself it was necessary.

Behind her, a Carthage Police car pulls behind her.

4

A Promise

"SHIT," EVA HISSES, checking her speed. She's not over the limit. Was she earlier? Her mind races, searching for any infraction that could have occurred in the span of three blocks. Was it the stop sign? Did she not make a complete stop before she turned?

She passes the Kane County government building and holds her breath, glancing in the rear-view mirror. The police car doesn't pull in. It's close enough that she can see the man driving—older, alone, both hands on the steering wheel.

Eva rolls down the window a crack. Raindrops pelt the plastic interior of the door, staining it a dark black. Could she use her fake ID? It looks real and it has Sofia Lopez's name on it. But no, it wouldn't scan. She'll have to use her real ID. There will be a record of her in town. Odds are, someone in the department will recognize her real name. Older officers will share one of the many stories of Eva, busted for truancy on Senior Skip Day, busted for misdemeanor pot possession, busted for punching a boy in high school who grabbed her bare thigh.

They'll wonder why she's returned.

"Shit," she whispers. Her mind races. Should she park, pretend she lives around here? Should she make a couple turns and force the officer's hand?

Now she's at the western edge of town and the police car is still following her.

Heart racing, Eva puts on the blinker. She turns right on Hickory Drive, a north-south road that cuts across the Kewaunee River north of the old lead mine. Ancient oak trees mark the property lines between waterlogged fields. Many have stood over a hundred years, silent sentries of a century of changes in the Driftless Area, helpless to intervene. They watched miners dig their tunnels. They watched cows overgraze. They watched tillers erode layers of black soil, carried away by an unforgiving southern wind. They watched farmers' grandchildren pay the price of these mistakes. They watched FOR SALE signs pop up along the road—first one, then five, then dozens.

The police car follows her onto Hickory Drive.

"*Fuck.*" She slows where the road curves around a crop of winter wheat contoured over a steep slope with exposed dolomite rock, black and glistening.

The police car stays close. Nearly riding her bumper.

Eva turns west on Badger Road, passing an old ruined stone cottage and white, two-story farmhouse located precariously close to a series of steppes where rows of green corn stalks have just sprouted. Eva's foot falls off the gas pedal as she glances nervously in the rear-view mirror.

The police car drives past without turning.

Eva exhales. It takes a moment to settle down and get her bearings. These side roads twist and turn with the streams, slipping in and out of dissected valleys. She remembers that the first lead miners were nicknamed "Badgers" because they dug holes to mine lead and slept in them at night. Off to the right is a single Cornish cottage, still standing amidst tall grass and abundant weeds; wet, green moss on its stone roof catches a few rays of sunlight shining like spotlights between heavy gray clouds.

Off to the right, flooded cropland gives way to rising earth and white pines that find a way to grow strategically on the eroded bedrock. Eva realizes she's heading toward the college town of Fayette. She can take this road another two miles and approach it from the northeast. There's a cheese factory at the edge of town—Fayette's last crucial connection to Carthage. Farmers raise cows for Wilson's Dairy. Wilson's Dairy sells milk to the Fayette Swiss Factory. Eva has no idea why someone decided on Swiss cheese so long ago, but she does know that the move from mining to dairy was made easier because the prairie grass was perfect for cattle grazing. She knows the first crops were corn because cornmeal was a sought-after commodity in the lead mining regions across southwest Wisconsin.

Carthage and Fayette used to look identical. Carthage's financial rock was the lead mine, Fayette's was the university. Both had a single theatre. Both had a supper club. Both had an antique store, a restaurant, an Ace Hardware. When Eva passed through Fayette before attending the Reverend's church service, she was surprised to see how much it had grown up. There are shops that sell olive oil and soaps and cheese. The university's new Arts building. Bike lanes. A rainbow flag outside the library. An art installation in the center of town. Signs advertising a Saturday farmer's market. The old Opera House, now a whiskey distillery.

She turns left onto Chestnut Road, which winds around a tall, forested hill. The rain picks up for a moment, then just as quickly stops. The car's tires crunch on wet gravel. The road leads to the entrance of Trengrouse Cemetery: a wrought-iron gate, locked by a heavy chain. But the security measure is only for cars—to the left and right of the gate is a quaint picket fence that runs all the way around the property. Eva parks and gets out, climbing over the fence.

Standing water floods the cemetery in murky pools reflecting the orange afternoon sunlight. Eva follows the route by memory and finds the grave of her mother next to headstones etched with familiar Carthage family names and ancient birthdays. Anderson. Heisner. Bauer. Cox. Stone. Cranston.

Eva's mother has been laid to rest at the edge of a sloping hill whose entire existence owes a great debt to the roots of a massive oak tree, its gnarled limbs barely able to hold more than a few dozen leaves. Other oaks stand like cracked incisors, assassinated one by one over the years by stray bolts of lightning. Summer downpours have erased the grass, leaving dark mud that seems to be oozing out of the earth and sliding down toward the tombstones.

She remembers coming here when she was in high school to memorize her lines. She imagined the spirit of her mother was with her, listening. Back then, the grass was always cut and at least a few of the tombstones were always adorned with fresh flowers. Eva would recite her lines here among the dead—first high school productions and then, her junior and senior year, Shakespeare. With the tombstones as mental markers, she could memorize even the most complex soliloquies. Her own macabre memory palace. Her quiet audience, listening to her recite the lines of Goneril from King Lear. Her mother would have loved to see Eva play the conniving shapeshifter.

Now, her mother's tombstone is as abandoned as the others. She doesn't fault her father for it; he's always been a hard-ass about sentimentality. Part of growing up in a rural area, she thinks, remembering all the farmers in her father's life who couldn't vocalize their darkness. Men who hid their sadness behind sunken eyes. Maybe, Eva thinks, she has a little of that in herself, too.

Rainwater drips down the carved I's of Jori Heisner's tombstone like tears.

The ground is uneven here, in the oldest part of the cemetery. The gravestones have no clear pattern. Some sit in the soft ground at violent angles. Moss stains the old stone. Eva stops at the edge, where the picket fence runs along the bank of the river. It's engorged, high, running fast. Beyond it, the earth rises up, revealing black dolomite that hangs out like the upper jaw of a hippo. A rogue sliver of sunlight penetrates the maple and pine trees higher above the exposed dolomite, casting shadows across the soggy graves.

Eva finds the gravestone of Donald Jenkins, father of Reverend Anthony Jenkins, in the southwest corner of the cemetery. Here there is a row of tombstones of increasing levels of decay, a row of cow teeth with room enough at the end for another. The wet grass here is mown; green clumps lay scattered as evidence. Flowers are arranged at each tombstone, their yellow petals curling ever so slightly. The oldest gravestone is that of Henry Jenkins, born 1816, died 1902.

Eva wonders what the Reverend's ancestors would think, to know what a disgustingly vile creature he's become. She wonders how much of the Reverend's evil was passed down and how much of it grew in the nitrate-rich manure of his religion.

"I'm going to find Miriam Jenkins," she whispers. "No matter what it takes."

Eva to presses her foot to the gravestone of Henry Jenkins …

… and kicks it over.

5

Carthage

MASON REACHES THE END of the Jenkins driveway just as the Reverend and his wife are returning from church. He turns off his podcast about cults, as if the Reverend might overhear it, then gives a wave and turns the Kane County Sheriff SUV onto Swamp Angel Road.

It isn't until he's back at the station that he realizes he should have explained his presence on the Jenkins property.

"Reverend called," says Patricia as he walks past the secretary's desk. "Wants to complain about a trespasser."

"For Christ's sake—"

Patricia holds up a manicured fingernail. "Christ's on the Reverend's side, Mason. Don't forget that."

"Sheriff want me?"

"He sure does," she says, going back to typing up a report on her computer. Everything in the sheriff's station is a little older than what Mason was used to when he worked for the Milwaukee Police Department. Computers a little slower. Filing system a little more dated. Desks a little more scraped up and dinged on the corners. Coffee a little staler. Tile floors a little more scuffed by black boots. Ugly eggshell walls that are covered with framed photos of elected sheriffs dating all the way back to the early 1900's.

Mason stops off in the bathroom to wash his hands, then walks into the sheriff's office, giving the open door a knock. "Escaped cows," he says. "That's it. No shenanigans."

Sheriff Henderson looks up from his laptop. There's a 50-50 chance he's either writing up a drunk driving report or surfing the web for information on missing persons. Mason's caught him a couple of times browsing a popular site that details what to do after the crucial first 48 hours have passed. Elliot Stone is the first missing person case in Kane County in almost a decade and by all accounts the sheriff has failed. Two weeks missing. Locals questioned. No hard leads. No evidence, no witnesses. Privately, Henderson is holding out hope that the boy just ran away from home.

"Don't piss off the Reverend, please."

"All I did was corral the cows with the son so they wouldn't go traipsing down Swamp Angel."

"Doesn't matter. Reverend's exactly the kind of asshole I can't piss off right now. Stone family belongs to his church."

"Did you know Miriam Jenkins moved away?" Mason asks, his tone sharp enough that Henderson looks up from his computer. The sheriff's bloodshot eyes scrutinize the deputy.

"Yes I did. David Bauer mentioned it when I was questioning him."

Elliot Stone had been painting Bauer's porch the day he went missing. Just up the road from the Jenkins property. Mason remembers from the sheriff's report that Bauer had claimed Elliot left that afternoon in the direction of the Jenkins property.

"Did you ask the Reverend if he's heard from his daughter at all?"

"Of course. He said they got into a bad fight months ago and she moved out."

"You don't think that's suspicious?"

"She's 29 years old. The hell do you want me to do?"

"Why was—"

"Am I a suspect?" Henderson snaps. His eyes circle the room. "Or am I your God damned superior?"

Mason clears his throat. "Sorry, boss."

Henderson leans over the desk and nods. "You tracked manure into my office."

Mason looks down at his boots. Sure enough, there's a trail of dry shit crackers all the way back to the entrance.

"Get Henry a Starbucks card," Henderson murmurs, going back to his laptop. "Just cause he's the janitor doesn't mean he deserves extra work."

Mason goes back to the locker room and changes into jeans and a t-shirt, then leaves an apologetic note and a tenner for Henry. He's about to leave when he remembers what the sheriff said about Bauer. He walks back into the office in his civvies, casually thumbing through a pile of red folders sitting next to Patricia's desk. He grabs the one marked "Bauer-Jenkins" and takes the hallway leading to the rear exit, past a slew of other offices in the old Kane County government building. The morning rain has added to a pair of big puddles that Mason made the mistake of parking next to the previous evening, when he started his night shift. There are no other deputies' cars nearby—they know where the bad puddles form and have parked a few spaces away.

Mason walks to his lonely white Chevy and opens the door, awkwardly hopping in to keep his boots dry.

The Kane County government building sits in the dead center of the town of Carthage. Wrapped tightly around the it are streets with 25 mph speed limits and lots of storefronts located in two-story brick buildings. He hasn't explored it all yet, but the Chinese restaurant is pretty good. There's a uniquely small-town shop that sells Amish candles and fireworks.. Four bars and one pub that serves great burgers. A Republican Party headquarters. A huge, two-story antique shop. A laundromat tucked away down one of the side streets. An old dairy supply store with the original faded sign still hanging by a single screw. A Mexican grocery store. A bunch of empty storefronts whose windows are slowly gathering film. Towering hills to the north and east.

190 miles west of Milwaukee, where Mason started his career.

He screeches his car to a stop at the Main Street stop sign. A pair of kids on bikes go past without looking. Mason turns right, passes a bar called Lucky's, then a couple blocks of houses with rows of "For Sale" signs—big houses whose first floors were once zoned for commercial use: accountants, dentists, realtors. He passes more than a few properties bold enough to put WE BACK THE BADGE signs on their yards. Mason scoffs at the incredulity of it. What the hell do these people back, exactly? The local law enforcement are just four months removed from one of the biggest scandals in Kane County history.

Mason's Bluetooth connection kicks in.

"Cult leaders are authoritarians," says the podcast host, a popular philosopher from the University of Wisconsin-Fayette. "Emmanuel Kant said it's not simply where you end up that matters, it's *how* you get there. He argues that being a good person is tied to the actions you take. But cult leaders want trust in a higher power. This allows them to tie goodness to submission."

Main Street turns into Highway O just beyond the stop sign next to Carthage High School, its football field bumping up against brown farmland too muddy to plant. In another half-mile, the two-story houses and maple-lined boulevard on the north side of the road are gone, replaced by expansive hills and a sea of brown earth waiting for corn seeds. Hundreds of acres, inundated with rain, muddy and impossible to till. Farmers are worried—the planting deadline for crop insurance is May 31st. It's already May 29th. People are constantly checking the weather app on their phone when they should be driving.

The road dips into a shallow valley where sandstone bluffs rise up like cresting waves. To the left are hundreds of acres of winter wheat, carefully plowed on contours along each hill, maximizing soil use. They look to Mason like artistic green brush strokes, mirroring the patterns found in the roadcuts of sandstone. The wheat is supposed to be dark green, but the rains have washed away so many nutrients that entire rows are a dark shade of yellow.

Mason passes Wilson's Dairy on the right; the cool air coming in through the truck vents brings with it the smell of methane. A tanker truck is ambling past the row of buildings, and through the openings Mason can see hundreds of cows behind steel stalls. Four long rows of barns that are each capable of holding five hundred cattle each. Next to them is a lagoon of shit, its ramparts built up so the offending excrement is hidden from the adjacent highway road. The sign at the entrance is flanked by two beautiful Holsteins and a little sign in Spanish offering work.

Beyond the dairy is an old family farm with a pen holding a pair of horses. Chickens with brown feathers peck at the grass next to a white fence, oblivious to traffic. Behind the two-story house is an old barn whose roof has collapsed, revealing rotten, cracked beams like a broken ribcage. Red paint peels from the ancient wood exterior.

Mason passes more farms, an old family dairy operation with a three-bay barn lined with basement windows to let in natural light. He passes a road that leads north into another valley where streams carved through the sandstone rock a million years ago, now tributaries to the Kewaunee River. An old lead mine used to operate just north of here. It sits right in the middle of the county, between the towns of Carthage and Fayette.

Mason knows this because it's mentioned on a plaque that hangs on the exterior of the Kane County government building.

Welcome to the Driftless Area, a region of southwestern Wisconsin that was spared from the Ice Age glaciers. Rivers dissect dolomite and sandstone formations, carving out beautiful bluffs and valley walls. Streams disappear into holes in the fractured dolomite bedrock, reappearing miles away in the form of cold springs.

Mason loves the scenery of the Driftless Area, the way the highway roads cut through the hills, twisting and turning, revealing new valleys of towering stone pared by streams that serve as the region's circulatory system. It's why he chose this place to make his new life. To start over.

He follows County Highway O another mile, where it intersects with Highway 15. The Crossroads. It was once a small, unincorporated town with a couple little shops, back when the railroad line was still transporting lead and zinc. Now it's home to a pub, a café, a strip club, and a motel, one on each corner. The Sunshine Motel is Mason's home. The café is where he gets his coffee. The pub is where he gets a beer sometimes. And the strip club is where he's not allowed to go, ever, under any circumstances.

Mason parks in the little weed-encrusted Sunshine Motel lot and gets out, sees a young Hispanic woman at the Pepsi machine on the other end of the one-story building. He's surprised anyone else is here. This place is a complete dump. Dark green paint flaking around the windows. Old A/C units whose vents are painted with mildew. Curtains that belong in a 1980's porn. Carpet that stinks like cigarettes.

He gives the woman a nod and opens his door, then stops.

"Just checked in?"

"Last night," she says.

"Working at the club?"

The woman cocks her head and smiles. "I'm not a stripper."

"Oh, that probably came across—"

She crosses her arms.

"Hold on. I've got an idea." He fumbles in his pocket for a few dollar bills. He uses them in the soda machine that stands between their two rooms. He buys two 7-Ups. Each can clangs through the machine's guts before it's spat out.

"Cheers," Mason says. "I'm Mason."

"Sofia."

They sit on a pair of plastic lawn chairs and drink their 7-Ups, watching vehicles come and go at the gas station across the street. Finally, to break the uncomfortable silence, Mason says, "Gonna move here?"

Sofia shakes her head. "Nope. Just looking for someone."

"Me too." He clears his throat. "Not romantically. Sorry. I'm looking for a missing kid. I work in the sheriff's department."

Sofia sips her soda. What's she thinking?

"I hope he's safe," she finally says.

Mason doesn't respond. Her words have turned the sweat on his forehead cold. He's lost all hope that the word "safe" applies to Elliot Stone.

"Thanks for the soda." She gets up and returns to her room.

He unlocks his door and goes in and sets his shoes near the bed. At least the shitty curtains are dark enough to hold back most of the sunlight. Problem is, they give the entire room a reddish tint. This already feels enough like Hell, thank you very much. He opens one curtain and gets a water from the mini fridge he purchased at the Carthage Wal-Mart, adding a packet of cherry sweetener. He takes his Escitalopram, 20 milligrams. Across the street he can see the Sapphire Lounge, open every day. He knows his brain is tired and he knows he's not at his best after a long third shift, but he can't help but wonder if Sheriff Henderson put him up in this motel on purpose.

Testing him.

He walks to the space on the big dresser where a flatscreen

TV used to sit. Mason has moved it all the way to the right side to make room for his extensive collection of board games, which he prefers to play alone rather than watching TV. He has *The Deadliest Night* game board laid out on the carpeted floor, next to a plastic cup holding an inch of bright orange juice. In *The Deadliest Night*, players have to solve a cold case before sunrise, while all the suspects are convened for an event. Players pick a character - and there are no heroes in this bunch - jaded family seeking revenge, amateur sleuths, nosy reporters, and of course shady detectives who drink too much.

Mason examines the cork board hanging on the wall. Elliot Stone's picture is in the middle—the last photo the family took of the boy, smiling with a Milwaukee Brewers baseball cap on, his black hair tucked behind his ears, playing in Carthage Park in April on a warm, dry day. His parents had used the same photo for the MISSING flyer they'd put up around town, a misguided attempt that forgot to include an email address and mistakenly said the sheriff was offering a reward for information, which was news to Henderson. The black-and-white copy obscures Elliot's dark face, blurring it and softening any distinguishing features. Next to the flier is a pinned copy of the adoption papers courtesy of the Ho-Chunk nation. Signatures of both parents, legally turning Elliot over to the Stones.

The NCIC report sits on the edge of the dresser, thinner than a high school essay. Mason's notes are scribbled in pencil all over the manila folder. Gaps in the sheriff's initial interviews with anyone connected to Elliot. Theories. Questions. Any thought that's come to Mason in the past two weeks. He sets the red "Bauer-Jenkins" folder on top of it, next to a detailed map of Kane County with all its side roads, streams, valleys and farms clearly labeled. Mason's highlighted all the roads Elliot could have taken on his bike to get home after painting David Bauer's porch the evening he went missing. The straight shot along Swamp Angel Road passes the Ramirez property, the

Jenkins property, and the Anderson property. The roundabout way takes him through Carthage; there are red marks denoting stores he was seen in the week he disappeared: the Piggly Wiggly supermarket, Early Rising Bakery, and Wonders Collectibles.

And now Mason adds something new: a sticky note with the words "Miriam Jenkins, 29" written in black marker. It might mean nothing, but all he has left are nothings.

Mason's cell phone rings. He answers with a gruff hello.

"Mason Taylor? This is Robin Wells from the *Kane County Courier*. We need to talk."

MONDAY

6

Skeletons

MASON FINDS ROBIN WELLS sitting in the back of the Maple Street Café, keeping her distance from the UW-Fayette college students who have taken over all the couches around a small fireplace, their wet shoes drying on the stone hearth. Robin is sitting underneath a painting of swirling colors that feels like the entrance to a surrealistic void. She watches Mason approach, legs crossed, her heels dripping muddy water onto the tile floor.

Christ, she already has a little notepad out on the table, next to her half-eaten red velvet cupcake.

"Why here?" Mason asks as he sits down.

Robin gestures to the cupcake. "That's real cream cheese frosting, Mase. Everything on the menu's made from scratch. Ever eat at Carthage Café across the street from your work?"

"Of course."

"Pancakes made from Bisquick. Frozen sausage patties. Frozen veggies. What's the point in eating out if it's just expensive shit?"

Mason takes a drink of his decaf coffee. He has to admit, the brew definitely tastes good. Too bad it doesn't sit well; Mason's stomach is in knots. It's been hurting ever since Robin called him out of the blue. He knew someone from *The Kane County Courier* would come after him eventually. It's not the *New York Times*, but regional newspapers always have a hidden gem on their staff.

Robin is that hidden gem.

"Sleep well?" she asks.

"I'm on third shift. Just got off." Hence the decaf, he hesitates to add. She's not here to chit-chat, and he has the sneaking suspicion she scheduled their meeting a day after her impromptu phone call to give him time to think. *Worry*.

Robin takes a sip of her latte, using one finger to gently brush a little foam off her upper lip. "Right. So let's put our cards on the table. I know what you did in Milwaukee three years ago."

Mason folds his hands in his lap to keep them from shaking. He can feel his eyes getting glassy; he takes a deep breath to hold it together. He won't give her the satisfaction of seeing him crumble. Just come out with it and be honest, his inner voice tells him. There's no point in lying or being cagey. Robin wouldn't have called this meeting if she didn't already know it all.

"I have a proposition for you."

"I don't have any money."

"What?" Robin's eyes widen in an expression of pure surprise. She laughs hard enough to startle the group of college students drying their feet by the fireplace. "No. Jesus Christ, no. What the *hell* have you heard about me?"

"Local law enforcement don't like you," he offers delicately. There's no point in being more specific, given the nasty names they have for her around the sheriff's department. Mason looked her up after she called him yesterday morning. She's worked for *The Kane County Courier* for twelve years. She was the one who broke the stripper scandal wide open.

Robin rolls her eyes and uses her fork to tear off a piece of her cupcake. It's infuriating to see how cool and collected she is while Mason feels like he's about to break down and have a heart attack. "Yeah, well maybe your fraternal brothers shouldn't have been running their own private brothel at the Sapphire Lounge." She gives him an appraising look. "Or do you think it's OK for officers of the law to fuck strippers in the middle of every shift?"

"No," he says honestly. His leg bounces anxiously under the table.

"You can tell your friends they got lucky," she mutters. "I had that asshole deputy Tim Clark dead to rights before my source recanted and refused to go on record."

"I haven't spoken to anyone about it," he says. "All I know is a couple guys got fired."

"Is that how you got this job?" she asks. "You've been a deputy for what, a few months now?"

Mason nods.

"That would make sense—my first story on the scandal hit four months ago. Shit, the sheriff must have been desperate if he hired you."

Mason offers a forced smile. "He said as much."

Robin studies him as she uses her fork to scrape a little cream cheese frosting off what's left of her cupcake. She stirs it into the latte. "You know where I went to college? UW-Fayette. Graduated middle of my class. I was a super senior. I got a D in my public reporting course and had to retake it because it was required for my Journalism major. Then I graduated and poof! The harsh reality of my chosen profession revealed itself to me. The best reporting jobs went to the best students. And all that was left for me was a gig at my shitty hometown newspaper that barely paid enough to cover student loans."

"You've won some awards."

Robin smiles. He's revealed something important to her: he's done his homework, and now she knows this. "I turn thirty-five this year, Mase. I'm running out of time to get a plum position at a metro newspaper." She leans forward, pressing her finger onto the table surface. "I need another good story for my portfolio. Something I can put on my resume to leapfrog all the goody two-shoes straight-A fuckers right outta college."

"I don't know if writing about me is juicy enough," Mason says. "I mean, it was already written about in Milwaukee's newspaper."

Robin grins. "Of course your story isn't good enough, dummy. I'm thinking way bigger. I'm thinking a multi-week feature. *Cops With Shady Pasts.*"

When he set up *The Deadliest Night* in his motel room, Mason had randomly selected the "shady detective" character. Robin would probably find this hilarious.

"There's half a dozen like you all over Wisconsin who just can't quit criminal justice," Robin says. "No matter how many times they fuck up. Drunk drivers. Wife beaters. Killers."

Mason feels his stomach tighten. He wants to throw up. He wants a sip of hot coffee, but his hands won't stop shaking under the table.

Robin's eyes study his posture. She knows. Of course she does. "Or maybe you can give me something better."

"Like what?"

"Like an inside look into how you solve Elliot Stone's disappearance."

Mason exhales slowly. His mind is whirring to the point that he feels dizzy. The sound of the espresso machine has gotten so loud, hissing and frothing. "I haven't solved it."

"Not yet." Robin leans back. Just increasing the distance between her and him makes Mason feel more at ease, like they're a pair of magnets. "I know you've been sniffing around when the sheriff is busy."

His look betrays surprise.

Robin winks. "Carthage government building's got gossipy secretaries."

"Then you know there aren't any leads."

"So let me help," Robin offers, "in exchange for an inside look into the investigation." She leans forward again. "Mase, this is the perfect story for both of us. I can portray you as the tainted officer seeking redemption. The guy trying to do right to make amends for his past mistakes. The public will eat it up."

"And so will newspaper editors?"

Robin taps her nose. "What makes it even better is that Elliot was Native American. Adopted by white parents. Is there a hate crime here? Something deeper, gnawing at the soul of Kane County?"

"I don't know."

She finishes her cupcake, then dips her fork in the latte to dissolve the last of the cream cheese filling stuck between the prongs. "So decide."

Mason finally takes a sip of his coffee. The nervous energy has subsided enough to bring the cup to his lips. Redemption. Isn't that why he's trying so hard? Isn't that why he took another job in law enforcement? To make up for what happened in Milwaukee?

"OK."

Robin beams, toasting him with her latte. "All right, lay it on me. What do you got so far?"

Mason hesitates. All the far-fetched leads and flimsy evidence hardly even seem worth bringing up. "The sheriff thinks he ran away, got lost, maybe drowned in a flooded stream."

Robin waves that thought away with her fork. "I don't give a shit what that old goat Henderson thinks. He's out there spinning this like Elliot just decided to go live off the land. Henderson doesn't want to look like a failure before November's election." She points the prongs at him. "Tell me what *you* think."

"I think someone killed him."

"Why?"

"Because Swamp Angel Road isn't a thoroughfare. It's a side road of a side road tucked inside a little valley in the Driftless."

"Who are your suspects?"

"There's the Anderson family," he begins. "Their teenage son worked on the Stone farm last year. There was an accident."

Robin nods seriously. "Jon Anderson died inside a grain silo. Seventeen years old."

Mason nods, recalling from memory everything he's researched in the past week. The police report mentioned farming terminology that made it difficult for a city slicker like him to picture the scene. "He was digging some piece of broken equipment out of a grain silo and the chute carrying fresh air to him got plugged somehow. The Anderson boy suffocated."

"And you think his parents might have killed Elliot Stone … what, as revenge?"

Mason shrugs. It actually feels good talking this through with someone. "I did some digging and there never was an OSHA investigation over Jon Anderson's death. No fine. Just labeled an accident."

"Small farms are exempt from OSHA regulations," Robin murmurs, jotting down a note in her notepad. "Deaths on small farms are hardly ever investigated. But revenge is a stretch."

"People want justice. When the law doesn't deliver, people take it up themselves."

"But the Andersons? Really? They're passive as lambs."

"They refused to talk to the sheriff," Mason says. "Wouldn't answer the most basic questions about the night Elliot died until Henderson threatened to haul them in."

"Fine, put a pin in it. Who else?"

"So then there's Edgar Ramirez. He owns a house on the east end of Swamp Angel Road. Says he saw Elliot pass on his bike at 6:30 p.m."

"And?"

Mason makes a drinking motion with his hand.

"Ah," Robin jots down a note. "Who else?"

"David Bauer."

Robin looks up and smiles. "You're kidding. Gentle David? The guy's a teddy bear! I wrote a story on him years ago because he was volunteering at the battered women's shelter. In *Carthage*. Most of the men in Carthage don't even think spousal abuse is a *crime*."

"Elliot Stone was painting Bauer's patio the day he disappeared. Says Elliot left at 6:40 p.m. So either he's lying, or Ramirez is lying."

"That's it? Did the boy do a shitty job or something?"

Mason ignores the gallows humor. He pulls out his phone, checking the notes he'd taken yesterday evening from the sheriff's "Bauer-Jenkins" file while he sat in his squad car on Highway O, lasering late-night speeders. "There's more. Apparently, Miriam Jenkins was doing morning calf chores at Bauer's place for about a year. He raises a small group for Wilson's Dairy."

"Ah yes ... the *bovine enslavement facility*. Scourge of family farms." Robin jots something down in her notebook. "I'm surprised Ol' One Arm farms out his own kids. I thought he only took his congregation's money."

"Miriam disappeared five months ago."

Robin's grin fades. "What do you mean, *disappeared*?"

"Stopped coming to work. And David Bauer didn't tell Sheriff Henderson until *this week*."

"That's a long time to sit on important information."

"Right. So the sheriff paid Anthony Jenkins a visit. The Reverend said Miriam moved out after they had an argument. Didn't elaborate."

"No shit." Robin sips her latte, thinking. "So, hypothetically, what's your imagination building here? You think Miriam returned one evening and stole away Elliot Stone? Why?"

"I just think it's suspicious for two of Bauer's employees to disappear."

"And two people connected to the Reverend." She jots down another note. She has horrible handwriting. Fast, though. Probably good for interviews. "So the sheriff questioned Bauer?"

"In the sense that he asked some basic stuff that Bauer could answer with a yes or no. Didn't ask follow-up questions."

"Typical Henderson," Robin mutters. "David Bauer inherited a hundred acres and a dairy from his parents. Fell in love with the first female farmhand he hired. It was pretty big joke around Carthage for a long time."

"The land is the other weird thing," Mason says. He leans forward so he can lower his voice. "I looked into him yesterday, and it turns out Bauer sold all his acreage *right after* Miriam went missing."

Robin's hand stops jotting notes. She fixes him with an inquisitive glare. "Farmers don't sell land unless they're in trouble. It's a huge tax hit. If Bauer owed any money to the bank, the bank would get first dibs."

Mason watches her jot down another note. This one he can read pretty clearly: Badger Credit Union. She knows where the local farmers go for loans.

"What about the Cox family? The Cranstons?" She knows the other families on Swamp Angel Road by name.

"Airtight alibis. I can't find any connection to Elliot or his parents."

"You dismissing the Reverend?" she asks.

"Home with his wife and son, playing *Uno*. Didn't see Elliot Stone that evening."

"You trust him?" she asks with an eyebrow raised.

"I don't know."

"He makes all his congregants' children work to protect the *sanctity of their souls*," Robin says, letting the last few words drip off her tongue. "You might want to check on the rest of them, just in case. Lots of lead kids, like Elliot."

"Lead kids?"

"Yup." Robin looks up. She has striking blue eyes with pupils like black holes. "Is that news to you?"

"Do you mean their parents worked in the old lead mine or something?"

Robin shakes her head. She finishes her latte. "OK, I'm going to give you the quick and dirty story. Ready? The lead mine polluted. A lot. All the pollution went into the Kewaunee River and ended up in Kewaunee Lake. No one ever cleaned it up, but no one cared because all the pollution settled at the bottom of the lake. Not a problem."

"Seems like a problem."

"Not a problem," Robin says, holding up a finger, "until about fifteen years ago, when Wisconsin's summers started getting hotter. Do I need to explain to you how Global Warming works, or are you mildly intelligent?"

"I know how it works."

"Good. So the hotter-than-average summers stimulated plant growth in the lake. Plant growth disturbed the settled lead pollution. Kids who swam in the lake year after year started getting sick. Doing bad in school. Getting in trouble. Lots of blue herons and swans died, too, but nobody gave a shit about that except a few biologists at UW-Fayette. It all got traced back to the lake."

"But people still swim there," Mason says.

Robin, wide-eyed, gives him a faux-shocked expression. "Yeah, even after I wrote a feature about it! Go figure."

"I knew Elliot had a learning disability." The boy's parents gave the sheriff all his academic records. Reading and math scores dropped every year. No one put him in a special ed program right away because, well, they didn't have a good reason.

Mason suspects it's because the boy is Native American and they just assumed he was naturally rebellious.

"The lead kids all have learning disabilities," Robin says. "That's how the Reverend ropes in a lot of his congregation. He finds the people who've been shat on the most. Parents with poisoned kids. Farmers on the verge of bankruptcy. People in Carthage watching their town die while Fayette thrives."

"Did you ever meet Elliot?"

Robin shakes her head. "I've talked to a lot of people, though. Seemed like a sweet kid. Loved his bike. Once got his shoelace caught in the gears and scraped his knee pretty good. Some teenager working at the gas station on Main Street saw it and came out to help him. From that point on, Elliot always stopped during the summer to drop some dimes in the Take-a-Penny dish, like he was trying to pay it forward or something."

"Ever get the sense he might try to run away?"

Robin points her fork at him. "Don't buy into that bullshit Wild Indian stereotype. He was a good kid, even if he stole candy corn from the Piggly Wiggly once in a while. Didn't make him a felony-level thief. I used to steal makeup all the time as a kid."

Mason smiles, despite himself. He used to steal quarters from his dad's change jar when he was young. "Reverend Jenkins and his congregation will be hard to investigate. They aren't big fans of police officers, on account of the whole stripper-fucking thing."

Robin grins. "Any other suspects?"

"The sex offender living in that trailer park in west Carthage. Owen Murphy."

Robin nods. "I'm surprised Henderson hasn't made him a focal point."

Mason shrugs. "Henderson questioned him. Alibi sounded good."

"You just think there's something he missed," Robin says.

Far-fetched leads and flimsy evidence. But the trick to

winning *The Deadliest Night* is thinking outside the box. "You know anything about Murphy?"

"Only the child porn crime he got convicted of." She hums to herself, glancing around the café. Her keen eye is observing the place, maybe checking to make sure no curious college students are eavesdropping. "Still, Murphy's probably your best suspect."

"Usually, the simplest answer is the right one. Unless it was a random abduction."

"Ugh. Let's not even think about that. I'd hate to realize how much time I wasted on this whole project."

Not wasted, Mason thinks. Because he knows if he doesn't solve this case, Robin still has a story. Only instead of a feel-good redemption story, it'll be an exposé about *him*.

7

Supper

EVA TURNS ONTO the driveway, windshield wipers brushing aside rain and a few light green leaves falling from the weeping willows that stand in a neat row to the left.

She feels a panic attack wash over her. She's on the Jenkins property. She's finally here.

"Sofia," she whispers to herself, setting her sunglasses on the dashboard. "Your name is Sofia Lopez. You grew up in Chicago. You work in finance. You won the audition. You nailed the rehearsals. Now play the part."

She checks her purse one last time to make sure it's just as she prepared it at the motel. It's big and bulky and fancy, with a silver clasp. Eva would never carry a purse like this, but Sofia does. Eva has carried it around for weeks, getting a feel for it.

You can always tell an actor who's never touched a prop before the day of filming.

Eva can unlock her purse with a flick of one finger. Each pocket inside serves a purpose: one for her wallet, one for her emergency tampons and pocketknife, one for her phone, one for receipts. She knows where everything is and she prefers to sling it over her right shoulder.

She gets out of the car and looks around. The backyard forms a semi-circle of soggy grass. Beyond that is a concrete lot where a beat-up white truck sits parked next to a blue compact car and a silver livestock trailer. At the other side of the lot is a loafing shed paneled with rusted blue aluminum siding. A calf barn sits next to the vehicle garage, its cream-colored bricks stained dark by rainwater. Old pieces of wire fencing rest against one of the electric poles, beside a pile of orange bale twine. Wild grape infiltrates everything, its dark green leaves hiding the most neglected junk.

The back of the loafing shed is missing a few panels near the ground, revealing wooden posts and oozing wet manure. A few newish two-by-sixes have been hammered into place but it looks like the project was abandoned. The exterior is made of mismatched aluminum panels—some white, some blue, some yellow. Eva knows there's a guy in Kane County who disassembles barns and then repurposes the materials. He probably repaired these barns, just as he'd done on Eva's childhood farm.

Pieces of twisted aluminum panels sit discarded next to the vehicle garage on the cracked concrete; weeds are poking out between them, nearly three feet high. Behind the loafing shed stands a lone concrete silo, an artifact of an older generation of farmers. Eva knows that newer silos are made of fiberglass bonded to sheets of metal—sturdier but twice as expensive. "Never pass up a chance to put a farmer in debt," her father would always mutter while reading his farming magazines every Saturday morning.

The Jenkins house looks in bad shape, too. Old plastic plant pots sit littered everywhere around a tall oak tree growing dangerously close to the house. Plants sprout from gutters. White siding has been eroded in places to reveal the aluminum dermis.

Weeds grow out of the stone foundation. In the corner of one gable is a massive wasp nest, bulging like a tumor.

Eva walks into the closed patio. An orange cat is sitting on a pile of newspapers, next to a heap of old ducting whose edges have gathered lint and dust. The front door of the house is made of some cheap veneer that's peeling off like sunburned skin.

The Reverend's wife, Tina, answers the door in a pale dress and stained polka-dot apron. Unlike her husband, she's thin, so thin that Eva is shocked at the sight of her bare arms. Her elbows are bones covered by pink cellophane.

"Sofia, welcome! Come in."

Eva steps into an open hallway that leads into a quaint living room with a pair of brown couches arranged in an L-shape, facing a cast-iron fireplace framed in by a red brick hearth. She's shocked at the beauty of the place. The wooden flooring looks high-end. The couches have the kind of heavy, thick cushions that are perfect for napping. The drapes in the tall windows on the other side of the room look expensive, if mismatched. Two red, two brown, two beige, all drawn.

"Please take your shoes off, sweetie."

Eva does so, feeling her anxiety rise at the simple gesture. Every part she's ever played has required a full wardrobe. She always avoided the risqué roles like "Hooker #4" and "Naked Female Corpse" where certain articles of clothing are left in the dressing room and actors walk around in robes on closed sets. Taking her shoes off intimately binds Eva and Sofia together. Leaving will require her to put them back on or flee barefoot to her car.

"Hello Sofia!" Reverend Jenkins calls out from the adjoining kitchen. He's sitting on a stool at a white marble countertop peninsula that divides the little kitchen in half. The left sleeve of his button-down shirt has been very carefully hemmed with a pick stitch.

Beside him sits a much older woman with curly white hair

and a pair of red-framed glasses. She bears a striking resemblance to Tina.

"Ma, this is Sofia. Our guest," says Tina, walking with Eva into the kitchen. The woman turns her entire body. She's wearing a sweater that reads, "Wisconsin Dells". She half-smiles. Her pale skin is sallow and heavy around her left cheek. Her left arm hangs from her side.

"Well, how is it?" she asks.

"I'm well, thank you." Eva doesn't stare. She's had friends with grandparents who'd suffered strokes.

Tina goes back to cooking something on the stove, hidden by a glass cover filmed with steam. It smells like broccoli. "Did you find the place all right?"

"Yes," Eva says. "You have a very interesting farm."

Don't act too impressed. Sofia's supposed to be a city girl.

"Do you raise those cows out there for meat?"

Reverend Jenkins chuckles. "Lord, no. Those are dairy heifers. Our son Josh raises them for Wilson's Dairy. That's the giant farm on the west end of Carthage."

"They don't raise the cows themselves?" Eva asks, feigning confusion.

"Oh, some. But they can only squeeze so many onto their property. So they hire local farmers to keep production at full capacity. Please." He gestures to the plate of cheeses and crackers sitting on a silver tray. Sitting behind them is a porcelain cookie jar shaped like a Holstein cow.

Eva puts together a sandwich of herbal crackers and what looks like an asiago cheese of some kind. She can't admit it out loud, but she missed Wisconsin cheese. "Seems like a lot of work for just one person. Or does your son have help?"

"Nope, nope." The Reverend uses his pitted fingernails to break off a chunk of aged cheddar. "He likes it, though. Hard work is good for the soul."

"He's excellent with the cows," Tina says without turning

around. She lifts the lid off the little pot on the stove. Eva was right: broccoli. *Overdone* broccoli. "Ma taught him everything. He could have run a dairy if things had turned out different."

"I don't understand," Eva says. It sounds a little too forced, like she's being intentionally dense. She grabs another cracker, feeling the tips of her ears warm.

Reset.

"Did you used to milk cows here?" she asks.

"We did," Tina says. "But milk prices …" She leaves it at that. Something holds her back from saying more. Maybe some bull-shit *don't complain* rule set by her fanatical husband.

"Lots of family dairies have gone under around here," the Reverend says.

"Lots of splintered families," Tina adds. The tone of her voice has changed ever so slightly; Eva glances at the Reverend to gauge his reaction, but he seems not to have noticed.

"Your cooking smells wonderful." Eva grabs another cracker, looking around, anxious about finding that middle ground between curious and nosy.

"We're having ham," Tina announces. "And broccoli. And Hawaiian bread. I didn't make the bread."

"Ma insists on Hawaiian bread with every meal," the Reverend says brightly.

Wilma, smiling, neither affirms nor denies this.

The Jenkins family is the type of family that posts things on the fridge—pictures, notes, reminders. Eva's too far away to get a good look and her stressed brain can't think of a plausible excuse to step closer. Then she spots something familiar. "Is that an apple orchard?" she asks excitedly.

The hardest part of an actor's job is the walk. What are your character's intentions? Hands in the pockets or swinging at the side? The moment you become aware of it is when you realize how difficult pretending to walk truly is.

Eva takes quick steps to the fridge so she can admire the

photo, her feet padding gently on the tiles. No one questions her gait. She stands in front of the photo, admiring the family sitting on a picnic table next to a red, round-roofed barn.

There, sitting next to the Reverend, is Miriam Jenkins. His daughter. Smiling. Happy. Her beautiful brown hair tucked behind her ears.

"That's the Apple Barn," Tina says. "On Cobblestone Drive."

"My dad used to always take me to an apple orchard," Eva says, veering off-script. She can't pass up this chance to bond with them. "Every single summer."

"Where are you from, originally?" the Reverend asks.

"We lived in a suburb in Chicago when I was a kid."

"So you visited an apple orchard in Illinois?"

No. The Apple Barn. Eva's father used to take her to the fucking very same place in the photo. And now she realizes her mistake, because it's the *only* apple orchard her father ever took her to. Her heart thumps nervously against her chest. "There was one near Rockford, actually. I don't think it exists anymore."

"There are always pink ladies," says Wilma.

"That's right, Ma," the Reverend says. "The Apple Barn is the best. A whole paper bag for five bucks! You can't beat a deal like that."

"I hope your father didn't spoil you with cider," Tina tells Eva. "There's a lot of sugar in it."

Eva's dad *always* spoiled her at the Apple Barn. They started with a cider donut, grabbed a bag, and went out to the vast orchard. He held her up so she could grab the best apples that no one else could reach. He complained about the spoiled ones on the ground and told Eva that you could finish a couple hogs on all the waste. Just bring 'em out and let 'em gobble the fallen apples right up! And then he'd chase Eva around, tickling her when he caught her.

As she got older, the trips grew more serious. No more donuts because she wanted to lose weight for potential roles in

Fayette's summer Shakespeare series. No more tickling because that was embarrassing. But they still made a habit of it because they loved having apples sitting in a bowl on the kitchen table. Once in a while, Eva's dad would still help her get the best ones from the highest branches. Only instead of holding her up, he'd let her stand on his bent leg.

"We were a good team," she says. "My dad knew all the varieties of apples." A thought comes to her. Just a blip of a memory of something she'd once seen mentioned in the *Kane County Courier*, years and years ago. An article about a popular apple orchard near the city of Madison. She decides to use it. "I remember there being a different corn maze every year. They were always in the design of animals. But one time, I got ahead of my dad and I got lost. It was pretty traumatizing for a twelve-year-old."

"We never used to let the kids out of our sight. Too much can go wrong." Tina finally turns off the stovetop. The broccoli is beyond overcooked.

Eva pretends to examine the rest of the fridge. There's a to-do list (groceries, cleaning, gardening) that has items crossed off with "TJ" initialed by each one. There are magnets of happy sheep and cows holding up business cards for a well drilling company, a furnace specialist, and Wilson's Dairy. There's another photo, just below a calendar for the month of May that has a calf feeding schedule scribbled in each box. It's a portrait of Miriam, no longer a teenager, her face soft and her smile reserved, as if she's no longer sure of her future.

I'm going to find you.

The sound of a knife slicing through warm ham sends a shiver down Eva's spine. She turns. The Reverend is looking at her. So is Wilma. Eva's been examining the photos for too long; she has to say something. But it can't sound forced or suspicious. It has to sound right, and the only right thing to do is just come out and ask the most obvious question.

"Is the girl your daughter?" she asks. She's suddenly aware of her hands, limp at her sides. She fights the urge to put them in her pockets.

The Reverend smiles and nods. "Miriam."

"Moved away?" Eva says, stepping away from the fridge as if she's not interested at all in the answer. Surely her anxiety is visible on her face. Surely they can hear her heart beating between syllables when she speaks.

The Reverend nods, but says nothing.

"I was supposed to meet Miriam somewhere tomorrow," Wilma says.

Eva feels electricity course through her body. She reaches for another cracker, then stops herself when she sees her hand begin to shake. She grabs the edge of the countertop instead and watches the Reverend turn to Wilma.

"No, Ma. You have dinner tomorrow with your friend Patty. Remember?"

"But we meet at the supper club," Wilma says, confused. "We always, yes, and then there are the … the … we do the Jumble."

Tina uses the knife the saw through the soft meat. Again and again, quick and determined.

"No, Ma. We're going to do Bible study tomorrow and Tina is taking you to dinner with Patty."

Wilma makes a surprisingly disgusted face when he mentions Bible study.

"Would you like to help me set the table, Sofia?" Tina asks. She puts the broccoli into a big bowl with a single square of butter melting on top.

"Absolutely." Eva grabs the stack of plates sitting next to the cheese tray, letting her eyes track the entire kitchen as if she's a director making sure the scene is properly blocked. A beautiful carved credenza sits against the wall next to the entryway to the dining room that looks like an antique, refurbished, and on the top are stacks of mail and a row of religious books.

Speaking in Tongues: The Purpose and Meaning.
The Attributes of God.
The Beast of Revelation.
The Burning Wheel.
He Shall Have Dominion.

Tina has moved to the sink to wash her hands. Wilma's arthritic hands are folded as if in prayer, her eyes on the fridge but her mind somewhere else entirely; lost in a memory of Miriam.

The Reverend is looking directly at Eva.

He's suspicious. Something she said.

He's not suspicious. He can't be suspicious.

The Reverend stands up. Eva flinches in terror, frozen. He walks past her to the sink, holding his right hand under the faucet. Tina squeezes green soap into her hands, then gently massages the soap between the Reverend's fingers.

Eva, embarrassed at the intimate moment, walks into the adjoining dining room. Her mind methodically goes through the conversation in the kitchen. Nothing she said was out of place. Nothing was forced. It was Wilma who'd mentioned meeting Miriam. But the stroke. Was it possible Wilma met Miriam somewhere *before* the stroke? Would the supper club staff remember the last time they saw Miriam?

She places plates in front of each old and mismatched chair. The table is beautiful, its honey stain scraped in places where the grain runs parallel to the edge. Real oak all the way through.

There are five plates for five chairs.

Eva goes back into the kitchen. "Silverware?" she asks cheerily. She imagines Sofia getting excited about having a home-cooked meal and being away from all the stress of her job and her life, oblivious to the tension simmering between the Reverend and his wife.

"Top drawer," Tina says, pulling glasses of varying sizes from the cabinets above the sink. The cabinets are beautiful, painted a dark green—but the ones above the counter are a shaker style, different than the inset style below.

Eva opens the drawer and grabs five forks, five knives, and five spoons, doing her best to avoid scrutinizing the décor any further. She's realized something important: everything in this house is beautiful and expensive ... but none of it *matches*, not even the silverware. The butter knife handles are shaped like fish. The forks have sleek, curved handles. Each spoon's bowl curvature is a little different.

"Are you a cook, Sofia?" the Reverend asks.

"I have few good dishes," Eva says. She takes the silverware back into the dining room and mentally curses. Sofia was supposed to live on take-out. Sofia was supposed to be a helpless adult. "Nothing that smells as good as your meal tonight," she calls out as an afterthought. It feels forced in her head. If she could do another take, she would have just left it unsaid.

The front door opens and shuts.

"How are the girls?" comes Tina's voice. A dull, quiet voice answers. Eva returns to the kitchen empty-handed and nearly bumps into a tall teenage boy. She immediately smells the cow shit; it conjures memories of growing up on her father's farm. The way he would always come in wearing socks stained with manure, the way her mother would always yell at him, the way he'd jokingly explain that the whole point of socks was to pick up dirt from the floor, like a feather duster for your feet.

Eva pretends to be mildly disgusted at the boy, wrinkling her nose and offering a forced smile. He's big, built like a tank, wearing a dirty pair of shorts and a gray t-shirt. Little whiskers poke out along his chin and nowhere else.

"Joshy, *please* remember to change out of your work clothes," Tina says.

"A little dirt won't hurt the floor," says her husband. Tina's face hardens; she turns away, fiddling with the stove knobs.

"This is Sofia," the Reverend tells his son. "She's our dinner guest tonight."

"Hi," Josh says, his quiet voice squeaking out. His elevator eyes are even less conspicuous than a middle-aged producer's. He notices Eva noticing and blushes, then turns to walk down the hall. The first thing Eva thinks is *How should I exploit his attraction?*

"What would you like to drink, Sofia?" Tina asks her. "We have milk or filtered water."

"Water is fine."

Tina and her mother take water as well. Josh gets milk. The Reverend gets a can of cream soda. "It's my guilty pleasure," he explains, taking his seat at the head of the table. Behind him, on the wall, is an assortment of animals that have undergone the taxidermy process, frozen in unapproved postures. A coyote. A racoon. A turkey vulture, its wings spread wide above the arching window overlooking swampy rows of corn leaves illuminated by the setting sun.

Josh joins them at the table wearing fresh clothes: baggy sweatpants and a red Wisconsin Badgers t-shirt. He sits next to his mom. Wilma gives him a disapproving look, her lips tight and her eyes narrowed. Eva pretends not to notice, instead glancing around the dining room with the admiration of a career woman who's been living in a too-small apartment. Tall windows. The sight reminds Eva of growing up, sitting outside on the porch with her father, playing card games after dinner.

She sheds the memory, grabbing a piece of Hawaiian bread and taking a bite.

"Let's pray first," says the Reverend.

"Right, sorry." Her carelessness accidentally plays right into Sofia's personality. She sets down the roll and folds her hands together. Everyone at the table does this except Wilma. She simply begins eating.

"Lord, thank you so much for a wonderful day," the Reverend

says. "Thank you for all the happiness you've brought us. Thank you for testing us and trying us, and helping us become better human beings. We're none of us perfect, but with your guidance we can always find our way. Amen."

"Amen," Eva whispers. Sofia may like the humble small-town charm of this kind of humble prayer, but Eva thinks it's a load of bullshit. She lets everyone else take their food first, giving the rest of the dining room a closer look. A grand piano sits behind the table. It's old, made of dark red mahogany. The China hutch has real China in it, filled to bursting.

Tina takes a single slice of ham and three crowns of broccoli. Her spare plate is a direct contrast to the loaded plates belonging to her son and husband. "Sofia, did you belong to a church as a child?"

Eva nods, using a knife to cut into the ham. "Saint John the Apostle Church."

"Catholic?"

"Yes. My mother's influence."

"Not your father?" the Reverend asks.

Eva takes a calculated bite of ham to search for her lines. She covers her mouth with one hand. "My father worked third shift while I was growing up. He was always late to Mass, but he never missed it."

"He sounds like a hard worker." The way the Reverend says this, it almost sounds pitying.

"Were your parents both born in the states?" Tina asks.

"Yes." Eva waits, half-expecting one of the follow-up questions she always gets at auditions.

Could you tan a little bit?

Can you do a Hispanic accent?

Will you read for the part of Gangster's Girlfriend?

Will you read for the part of Cartel Whore?

Will you read for the part of Drug Gang Initiate?

Will you do nudity?

And in a moment of distraction, she's fucked up. Her mother was supposed to be a Mexican immigrant.

"How did you ever keep track of all those saints?" the Reverend asks with a patronizing grin.

"I didn't!" Eva says, laughing. This gets a better response than expected. Nothing dispels tension like a good Catholic joke. And now is the moment to become serious again, to indulge in their curiosity and reveal a bit of Sofia's vulnerabilities. "I spoke with my priest a week ago. It … didn't go well."

"What do you mean?" the Reverend asks, his curiosity piqued.

Eva offers a calculated shrug. Her fork slides a piece of ham through a puddle of grease. "I told him how sad I was at my job, and how working with money all day has made me into someone I don't even recognize anymore. He didn't understand how that could happen."

"He took a vow of poverty," the Reverend says, not kindly. "You can't fully understand sin unless you experience it yourself. You have to feel it to respect its power over us."

"I told him about a trip to Vegas." She takes a calculated pause for a bite of mediocre ham, "Everyone was throwing money around. I had to do it, too, because that's how you network at these events. You waste money. You party. You buy status symbols like watches and necklaces and outfits that are more expensive than my college tuition. All my priest did was tell me to pay a *penance*."

"What do you mean?" Tina asks.

Eva is ready for this with a real memory. "I sat in the church and said forty Hail Marys. I lit a candle and searched inside for forgiveness, just like I was told. But I didn't feel better, and you know what the craziest part is? That's a sin, too! It's a sin of pride to feel guilty after confession!"

"You'll find our church …" the Reverend clears his throat

and glances at his wife. "That is, if you'd like to join us again, you'll find our church is less concerned with *frills*."

"We're more traditional in our beliefs," Tina says quietly. The Reverend gives a subtle nod and she continues: "Trust in God's word and accept his plan for you."

The Reverend nods, stuffing ham in his mouth. "Carthage's first churches were started by travelling preachers, you know."

Eva has heard this story before. But Sofia wouldn't have, so she encourages him to continue. "That's very interesting."

"This area was settled by miners," the Reverend explains. His wife cuts the ham for him. He eats in larger and larger bites, filling his mouth so that he can't seal his lips while he chews. "Travelling Methodist preachers used to just hold service in the largest home in the neighborhood. Eventually, Carthage and Fayette grew large enough that preachers started settling."

"Keeping the Sabbath holy was very important to the miners," says Tina. "People would walk from miles away to attend church, bible study, and an evening prayer all in one day."

"Family and God. That was all people needed."

"Those were hard times," Tina says quietly. "The old cemeteries tucked away in these valleys have a lot of children's tombstones."

Eva eats another slice of ham. It's as bland as can be. No honey glaze, no seasoning. "You said there was a Bible study tomorrow?"

"That's right. Seven o'clock."

"Are you going to talk more about the Gospel theme from Sunday's service?"

The Reverend nods enthusiastically. "I tailor every study group around the context of the Gospel passages I pick for Sunday service."

"I'd like to come."

"Everyone is invited." He gives her a solemn look. "I'm being especially careful to ensure we're supportive of the Stones during this difficult time."

"Are the Stones the parents of that boy who went missing?"

The Reverend and his wife nod. "Horrible thing," he says. "God knows it doesn't help that they're blaming themselves."

"The Stones adopted Elliot from a Ho-Chunk family," says Tina. "They raised him from when he was just a baby."

"Amazing, amazing work," says the Reverend. He sighs. "We were hoping for the best—you know, maybe he got lost or ran off."

"We can still hope for the best." Tina chokes up a bit. Eva watches the muscles in her face tighten, constraining tears that want to flow. The lines around her eyes deepen.

"The Stones are good souls," the Reverend says gently. His hand sets down the fork and rests gently on his wife's. "They don't deserve the pain of losing a child."

"No one does," Tina says.

The Reverend's hand slips away from hers.

"What souls?" Wilma asks suddenly. She turns to her grandson. "Not his. Not after what he did."

"Mommy," says Tina. "Please, not tonight."

The boy sitting beside his mother only looks down and blushes.

"Killer," Wilma growls at him. "You killed her."

Eva feels a chill run down her spine. She turns to Josh.

"Mother!" Tina says, throwing her napkin on her plate. "That's Joshy! Your *grand*son!"

Wilma's glare breaks, and Eva can see a weight fall off the boy's shoulders. His face is flushed red. Wilma looks around, her eyes landing on Eva. "You're not Miriam."

"Shhh," Tina soothes. "Mom, this is our guest, Sofia."

"Where did Miriam go?" Wilma's wide eyes look around. "I was supposed to make her breakfast today. Do we have enough eggs?"

"We had breakfast, Ma."

The Reverend's jaws violently work on a piece of ham.

"You killed her," Wilma says to her grandson. Josh's eyes have grown glassy, and in them Eva senses a deep concentration, the way an actor would stay in character during a particularly difficult scene. She feels a twinge of pity for him.

"Mommy," Tina says, helping the woman out of her seat. "Come. Let's get you in the bath and I'll read you a Gospel. That always makes you feel better."

"God," Wilma snaps. "What is this all for, anyway?"

Eva feels her heart skip a beat. Her hands, hidden under the table, fold tightly together.

The Reverend waits for his wife and mother-in-law to disappear down the hall. "Pray your parents are spared the trial of dementia, Sofia. Ma doesn't live in this reality anymore. She …" He sighs heavily, composes himself. "The Stone family. I'm arranging a search on Wednesday for Elliot, if you find yourself free. Could use all the help we can get."

The Reverend goes back to eating, his lips smacking loudly as if he's punishing the slice of ham for some pent-up frustration. His son sits, head down, face still burning. Something has just happened. The mood has permanently changed, dark and quiet with only the dim chandelier light above and the sound of rain pattering glass. The Reverend and his son wear the same grim, hardened expressions.

And Eva wonders if Miriam has disappeared … or if she's dead.

TUESDAY

8

Geology

DR. BERNIE LEFTWICH is late. Mason and Robin wait outside his office door on the second floor of UW-Fayette's Natural Sciences building. It's one of the oldest buildings on the campus, and the inside has the feel of an old high school: walls made of half glossy tile and half sheet rock painted blue, old wooden doors leading into offices and classrooms, and gray tile floors that will no doubt need to be treated for asbestos if they're ever replaced.

Bernie's door is paneled with political cartoons. The cartoons are dire and full of gallows humor: global warming will kill us all, but at least our collective action managed to bring the Twinkie back from extinction.

"Sorry, sorry," he says, emerging from the stairwell. The man looks in his forties, balding, wearing an untucked dress shirt and a pair of slightly wrinkled trousers. He has dark brown skin and black freckles on his cheeks. "I got a summer class and there are always questions about fossils. Ignatius rocks bore students but dino bones always perk 'em right up."

"I never took a geology course," Mason confesses.

"I did," Robin murmurs, and makes a silent hacking noise behind Dr. Leftwich's back. She and Mason follow him into his office. It's tiny and cramped, just wide enough for a single window overlooking UW-Fayette's green space where a handful of students are navigating puddles on their way to lunch in the Student Union. Bernie takes a seat at his desk; when he plops in his office chair, momentum carries it back and it bumps up against the antique bookshelf along the opposite wall. The desk is cluttered. Not enough room for a computer and monitor—just a Macbook and lots of stacks of papers.

"I didn't know the sheriff was even searching for the Stone boy anymore. This mean you got a new lead?"

"We're … exhausting every possibility." Mason has to stand because Robin has very quickly commandeered the only spare seat.

Bernie swipes away papers, revealing a topographical map of Kane County the size of a pillowcase. Streams run like a circulatory system into the Kewaunee River. Twisting roads follow the streams, disappearing into dead ends the way the streams disappear underground. Between them is elevated terrain where the trees grow in clusters that remind Mason of brain wrinkles. He's relieved to see that Bernie has marked up the southwest edge of Carthage significantly.

"The reason this took me so long," he says, flipping the map so Mason can see, "is I wanted to identify the older farms that don't drain well. I tried to pull as much from the county land use department as possible, but I have to admit I ran out of time."

"That's an incredibly detailed map," Robin says. Her natural snark has temporarily disappeared.

Bernie grabs a green pen sitting on a stack of papers. "I'll walk ya'll through my thought process based on the research I could compile. I'm estimating rainfall a little bit, especially since I did the bulk of this last night and we got another half-inch of rain that I didn't take into account. Too many frog stranglers this week to be super accurate."

"Say what?"

"It's an Alabama saying. Means too many hard rains. This is the wettest spring in a century."

"I've heard that," Robin says. "Lots of farmers worrying about getting everything planted before the crop insurance deadline."

Bernie nods. He clears his throat. "I'm operating under the assumption that Elliot Stone's dead."

"That's fair," Mason manages, hiding his disappointment. The truth is he'd wanted Dr. Leftwich to offer some last-ditch hope. Now, Mason can only pray it was a *humane* death.

"You can discard a number of the nearby farms," Bernie explains. His pen lands on various plots in the Carthage-Fayette area, crossing them off by scribbling his pen inside each property line. His dark brown eyes glance at a page of notes taped to his laptop screen. "According to the land use department, these farms don't have adequate tiling for their crops. That means lots of water that isn't draining efficiently. No way to bury the body on these properties."

"Is drainage a big problem in this area?"

Bernie exchanges a knowing smile with Robin. "Yes. Bedrock is near the surface here because there's no silt deposited by glaciers. Erosion causes flooding, too."

"We're looking for areas the initial search parties might have missed," Robin reminds him.

"Any places where a shallow grave might be a possibility," Mason adds.

"Too wet around here for that," Bernie says. "Rains would wash it up right quick. You're better off looking at places where the body could be *hidden*."

Mason feels dread hang in the pit of his stomach. At least with a burial, the boy could have been granted some dignity in death. A hidden body, a discarded body, is at the mercy of nature, deprived of any innocence.

Bernie points to one of the places on the map circled in red. Mason can kind of recognize the area. It's north of Swamp Angel Road, just beyond the Anderson farm. "That's the Grant Boyd Wilderness Preserve," Bernie says. "It's remote enough to hide a body, and a car parked at the preserve wouldn't attract suspicion."

"Sheriff searched it a couple days after the boy disappeared," Mason says. He remembers that day because he'd spent it with the Stones at the designated Command Post—City Hall. Stone family members weren't allowed to join the search, which is typical protocol but try explaining that to the Stones and their hyper-religious Reverend who already thinks the local police are corrupt.

Meanwhile, at the preserve, Sheriff Henderson had conducted the first ground search of his career.

"Henderson needs to go back," Bernie says stiffly. "I'm not gonna sit here and tell you how to do your job, but ten people searching a thousand-acre preserve ain't gonna cut it."

Mason had the same thought. But it hadn't been the sheriff's fault so few people turned up. "Reverend Jenkins is putting together a new search party. Maybe he'll play nice with the sheriff for a day."

"I'll put a bug in his ear." Robin puts her cell phone to her ear. "Henderson? Robin Wells, *Kane County Courier*. Some people are saying you didn't thoroughly search the wilderness preserve. Care to comment?"

"Some people!" Bernie leans back in his chair, hands behind his head. "Devious."

"That's one way to put it." Mason scans the map, running along the property lines dividing each farm. The side-roads run all lead to Highway O. "Anything else I should be focused on? Any other spots?"

Bernie points to another circled area, where a copse of trees runs between a residential property and a farm. Mason recognizes it immediately. The residential property belongs to Edgar Ramirez, the man who said he saw Elliot Stone pass by on his bike the night he went missing. The narrow forest is technically owned by the Cranston Family, Edgar's neighbors to the west. The Cranstons run what Sheriff Henderson calls a "hobby farm." Just a few dozen beef cattle and fifty acres of land waiting to be planted with corn. Not enough to make a living anymore. Just enough to keep a family tradition alive while the Cranstons pull second jobs to pay bills.

"You said your witness lives here," says Bernie, pointing to the Ramirez property.

"That's right," Mason says. "David Bauer owns the farm east of the Ramirez Property, where the boy was working that afternoon." Cropland zig-zags like wet noodles, acquiescing to the topography of hills and streams, the properties fitting together like a jigsaw puzzle.

"This little forest is deceptively large," Bernie says. "It runs all the way up to the next east-west road. No one may have seen a car parked here," he points to Swamp Angel Road. "But what if someone driving down Swamp Angel Road hit the boy on his bike, then put him in the car, maybe to get him to a hospital?"

"But he died en route." Mason traces the path west. It would turn north on Highway G, just past the Anderson farm, because there's a hospital with an ER in that direction. Mason stops at the next intersection and turns right on Lost Grove Road. "So the driver panics, makes the next available right turn, and ends up at the north end of the forest." He runs his finger down the road, until it reaches the forest. Nearly parallel to where the last person saw Elliot Stone alive.

Both roads are local, meaning there would be little chance of random cars passing by. Sheriff Henderson took deputies along both roads, but found nothing.

"So the driver panics and dumps the kid's body in the forest," Robin finishes. She shudders dramatically. "That's fucking cold-blooded."

"I did some research in this little forest, years ago. There's a sinkhole where the land just sorta …" Bernie drops his hand quickly, making a sucking sound.

"Is it dangerous?" Mason asks.

Bernie shakes his head. "Water dissolves the bedrock, forming honeycomb structures that can eventually break. It's really fascinating." He smiles. "If you're a geologist. There's an Algific talus slope in this forest, too. Absolutely beautiful. No one knows about it."

"What is that, exactly?" Mason doesn't want to ask the real question on his mind: *can you hide a child's body there?*

"It's a hill made of heavily fissured bedrock. Warm air enters through fissures near the top, and as it travels inside, it cools, exiting through fissures near the base. Big enough to hide a kid." He takes off his glasses and rubs his eyes. "I gotta confess, when my mind began to feel comfortable with these dark thoughts, it was difficult to stop. I'm not sure how you can handle this."

The antidepressants help. Mason knew a lot of detectives in the MPD who drank heavily. For now, obsessing over every single detail of the case has kept his mind constantly moving, avoiding the obvious: Elliot Stone is dead. Mason *has* to start looking for a body.

"Why do you think he's around this area?" Bernie asks. "If you don't mind indulging me."

Mason points to Swamp Angel Road. The eastern end terminates half a mile beyond the Bauer property, where two steep hills meet. He traces the path west, past the Ramirez property and the Cox property and the Jenkins property and the Anderson property, to Highway G. "At this intersection, Elliot would have turned south, and then it's a straight path home.

This road is active." He points back to Swamp Angel Road. "This road isn't."

"Have you considered," Bernie says slowly, "the possibility that Elliot Stone was attacked because he's Native American?"

"I have," Mason says. "But the sheriff considered this a small possibility."

Robin scoffs at this.

Bernie cleans his glasses with a green cloth. "I spent a decade studying Kane County's geological history. My office was in the back of an Ace Hardware, if you can believe it. It took … a long time for locals to accept a black scientist in their community."

"I'm sorry to hear that."

"The Ace Hardware is gone now," Bernie continues. "Family couldn't make the minimum purchase orders to maintain the franchise. They were nice, but I'm not naive enough to miss the resentment they had toward a black professor with a cushy job. Can't imagine they care about a kid like Elliot Stone."

"If it was a blonde girl," Robin mutters, "there'd be National Guard combing the county."

"What about this?" Mason asks, pointing to another circled spot to the northwest, near the Kewaunee River.

"Ah, that's a bit of stretch, but I had to include it." Bernie points to a big square next to the Kewaunee River. "Here's the lead mine." He slides his finger to the circled spot. "This is a historic landmark called Russel Shot Tower."

Robin leans back with a knowing nod. Mason has to ask: "What's it for?"

"Shot towers were used to make lead bullets for the Civil War," Bernie explains. He laughs. "I had to ask someone in the physics department, so please don't grill me on specifics. But the way it works is you pass molten lead through a strainer at the top of the tower. As the lead drops pick up speed, each drop becomes spherical and solidifies. The lead balls land in a pool of water at the bottom of the tower, finishing the cooling process."

"And then you have bullets," Mason says.

Bernie turns on his laptop. He pulls up the Russel Shot Tower website. The bright green Kane County Parks logo sits next to a slideshow of pictures. People standing on a makeshift staircase carved out of a sandstone and dolomite bluff. A wooden tower built into the sheer side of the hill where the rock has been partially carved away. The inside of the top floor of the tower, where visitors can pose next to the old lead melting equipment and the hole leading into the shaft.

"The base of the tower isn't open to visitors," Bernie says. "But I think you could persuade them to make an exception." He puts his glasses back on. They're old and familiar—the anti-scratch coating has come off in places on the lenses. "Obviously I don't want you to think of me as some monster harboring dark thoughts. But …"

"It would be possible to dump the boy's body down the shaft," Mason finishes, saving Bernie the awkward trouble of imagining another murder scenario. The poor academic probably just wanted to grade papers today.

"It would be entirely possible," Bernie says with a grateful smile. "And I can state with one hundred percent certainty that any light shined down the top of the shaft wouldn't reach the bottom. At least, any light that a visitor or tourist might bring with them on a whim."

"It's a pretty long shot," Robin murmurs. "Pardon the pun."

"Hey, what do I know about hiding a body?"

"It's appreciated," Mason says. "Really. And I'm glad you're thinking outside the box. We need that."

"I did a study," Bernie continues with a smile, "tracing the paths of streams in the Driftless Area. Used tracer dyes. Streams would bubble up from the earth, go a couple miles, slip back down under the earth, pop up another few miles away. It was amazing. It was like mapping out the blood vessels of a living creature." His smile fades. "One of the streams passed underneath Russel Shot Tower. There's no telling what's under it."

Mason shakes the professor's hand. "Thank you so much for your help."

Bernie grimaces. "Thank *you*, deputy. I'm glad you're still looking for Elliot."

Mason follows Robin out of the building with a sick feeling of dread in the pit of his stomach. None of these possible leads are an answer to Mason's prayer.

Wherever he is now, Elliot Stone was not granted a humane death.

9

Prayers

EVA ARRIVES at the little schoolhouse at 7:05 p.m. She's disheveled—purposely. Sofia isn't sleeping well, she's decided. And she's used to showing up late to places because she's bad at keeping track of time.

When she was a child, this schoolhouse was a historic marker. How did the Reverend get control over it? Who did he manipulate to turn it into a church? Does anyone even *know* it's being used as a church? The schoolhouse is down a forgotten street—aptly named Schoolhouse Road—that lost its usefulness about fifty years ago when the busier roads were paved for the family dairies. Still, the Jenkins family must have pulled some strings. It's shocking; when Eva was in high school, the Jenkins family wasn't worth more than a few passing jokes.

Eva barges into the schoolhouse, ready to rudely apologize. To her surprise, they haven't started yet. They're just standing around a folding table set up along one wall. There's apple cider and a pitcher of water and bread and cheese arranged in little half-circles on paper plates. Everyone's eating, but Eva notices immediately that all the men have cider and all the women have water.

The Reverend sees her and smiles. "Sofia, just in time! Steven here was just regaling us with a story about an overflowing waste lagoon at Wilson's Dairy."

The ugly man standing next to him grins awkwardly. "It's less gross than you'd think. Just getting too much rain lately."

"Yuck." Eva mugs a grossed-out face, purposely taking a glass of cider.

"More rain in the forecast," says the Reverend. "This is the wettest planting season in a hundred years."

"The Hughes family is gonna need to replant about a hundred acres of corn," says Steven. "Big loss."

"I'll reach out to them," the Reverend offers. "See if we can be of service."

Everyone around him nods. Tina stands beside him, looking up at her husband. Eva thinks she catches a look—not a nasty one, but something bordering on anxious. Eva glances at the Reverend's son, Josh, who's very discreetly sneaking cheese and bread by stuffing them whole into his mouth. He's picked up a terrible eating habit from his father.

"Let's begin," the Reverend says. He turns to the others mingling by the little snack table. "Take a seat, everyone."

Eva takes a seat at the far end of the circle, across from the Reverend and Tina and their son, sitting between the man named Steven and an older man with a dark gray beard. Seated beside the older man is his wife, one hand on his knee while the other fans her face with the Bible study's pamphlet. None of the windows are open. The air inside the schoolhouse is stifling and thick. Eva is the only woman *not* wearing a dress.

The Stones are here. Eva recognizes them, remembers seeing them around town when she was younger, although their features are considerably more haggard than she remembers. Henry Stone's face is pale and dirty, his unwashed brown hair pressing down against his skull. Linda Stone's anxious thumbs run along the rim of her cup. Her dress is wrinkled and stained green along the bottom as if she's been sleepwalking through a wet prairie.

"Our Bible passage tonight is Luke, chapter 12." The Reverend closes his eyes and recites: "Jesus said to them, 'Watch out! Be on your guard against all kinds of greed; life does not consist in an abundance of possessions.' And he told them this parable: 'The ground of a certain rich man yielded an abundant harvest. He thought to himself, *What shall I do? I have no place to store my crops.* Then he said, *This is what I'll do. I will tear down my barns and build bigger ones, and there I will store my surplus grain. And I'll say to myself, You have plenty of grain laid up for many years. Take life easy; eat, drink and be merry.* But God said to him, *You fool! This very night your life will be demanded from you. Then who will get what you have prepared for yourself?* This is how it will be with whoever stores up things for themselves but is not rich toward God.'"

The Reverend has memorized this, word for word. Eva follows along on the pamphlet, glancing at Josh. He sits with his hands folded. He looks tired; his eyes strain to stay open, to show respect for his father who tells his flock to consider the ravens, the wild flowers, and to put your trust in God that he has a plan.

Tina's head turns ever so slightly in her direction. But Tina's eyes don't land on Eva; they land on the man named Steven, sitting beside her. Tina breathes deep and returns her gaze to her folded hands. Then Eva Steven's head rises a few inches, and she catches his eyes turning to Tina. She must be a good fifteen years older than him, and yet Eva can see in his facial muscles the look of longing.

"Provide purses for yourselves that will not wear out, a treasure in heaven that will never fail, where no thief comes near and no moth destroys. For where your treasure is, there your heart will be also." The Reverend stops, leans back in the small chair as if his large frame can't get comfortable. He takes a deep breath and wipes sweat off his forehead.

Linda Stone raises her hand. The Reverend nods to her. "The first part reminds me of the sheriff's department," she says. "How Henderson does whatever gets him votes in the next election instead of doing his job. He says his department can't afford to spend more resources on my son's case. How is that possible? It's his *job*. It's why we pay taxes."

"The sheriff is afraid," the Reverend says. "He's been re-elected so many times that he thinks he's Caesar. Now his department's sins have come to light, and people are seeing for the first time just how incompetent he is."

"It reminds me of how the banks take our money first," says the man with the dark gray beard. "All I get after harvest is a check that says *Void* because I owe so much."

"Debt makes slaves of us all," the Reverend says.

"It makes me think of Wilson's Dairy," says a bald man with heavy, sunburnt cheeks. "You know, how they overbuilt without asking permission first? They knew they had the county over a barrel—pardon my language. They knew the county wouldn't make them tear down their buildings, even though everything was too big."

"We depend on Wilson's Dairy," the Reverend says. "And they exploit us." He turns to Steven and smiles gruffly. "Apologies, Steven. I know they're your employer."

The ugly man just shrugs. "I don't work there because I want to."

The woman to Eva's left raises her hand. The Reverend nods to her. "The last part reminds me of the Walton family. They got so much money they don't even know what to do with all of it. I don't even make enough to cover my husband's insulin. And he could give me a raise. I know he could."

"Woe to he who cherishes a dollar over a life," says the Reverend.

Eva's mind creates something on the spot and she decides to improvise her script: "It reminds me of a bond trader I knew who would bet on risky loans. He'd sell them to gullible people and get these big commissions. Then the loans would go bad and people would lose their houses."

People nod their heads. The Reverend looks at her but doesn't say anything.

"I've been without a smartphone my entire life," says one of the men sitting near the Reverend. He's younger, almost Eva's age. "I don't think any of us need one. It's a waste of money."

The Reverend nods. "We're taught to consume. We're encouraged to spend."

Eva feels an irrational ping of annoyance. That guy clearly wasn't listening to the Gospel passage—he missed the point entirely. Eva's story had been better, yet she'd received no affirmation from the Reverend.

You hate him, she mentally reminds herself. *There's no need to pine for his acceptance.*

"We are blessed to have such a wonderful community here," says the Reverend, unbuttoning his sport coat. As always, the left sleeve has been removed and deftly sewn shut. "But we are under siege. Our way of life is under attack. The university in Fayette uses our tax dollars to spread its Marxist propaganda. Wilson's Dairy shuts down our family farms and poisons our water wells. Wal-Mart turned Main Street into a ghost town, leaving only bars that prey on *regulars*. I hate that word. Regulars! Those are our husbands and wives and cousins and children in thrall to the bottle. Those are *people with souls*."

Nods of assent. Eva sits still, hands playing with her empty cup of cider, twisting it into a shiv. She wonders what would happen if she killed the Reverend right now. What would happen if she got up to get a refill of cider, but instead stepped behind the Reverend and stabbed his throat? Would they disperse, or would someone new rise up and replace the Reverend, fulfilling the authoritarian void? Do these people *need* him?

"Go through the Bible and you'll never find God impressed with rich men," the Reverend continues. "The rich are too full of sin to curry favor. My father worked in the lead mine, like so many people in Carthage. And when my father got sick, did the mine's owner help him? Shelter him? Clothe him? Pay his medical bills? No. My father was fired because he couldn't work a full ten-hour shift."

He looks around slowly, meeting eyes with each of the Stones and sharing a silent moment of empathy with them that could have won him an Oscar.

No one speaks. No one even breathes. Eva can feel the hot air suddenly still.

"We know what's in our hearts," the Reverend says, meeting each person's eyes one by one. When he reaches Eva, he continues: "We know we're good people, and that can be frightening when we're under assault from every direction. We're told to be truthful, but must also police our language. We're told not to kill but we allow mothers to murder the unborn. We're told to trust the law, but our own police officers cavort with whores when they're supposed to be protecting our *children*."

Mrs. Stone stifles a sob. Eva watches Mr. Stone's hands grip his jeans.

Suddenly, the Reverend's body jerks. Eva feels her heart begin to race. What's happening? Some kind of stroke? A heart attack?

"Should we—"

"Hold him!" orders Tina, grabbing the Reverend's right hand. Josh grabs his father's left shoulder. The Reverend's eyes roll up. His mouth hangs open in a wide O. He begins to seize violently. What's happening? Eva feels nervous energy course through her legs, pins and needles. Her head feels light. Is he dying? Is he epileptic?

The seizing slows but Tina and Josh continue clutching the Reverend.

Then the prayers come.

"My sister, please help her, God. Her diabetes is so bad!"

"Witness," the Reverend whispers.

"My farm. I just need a couple days of dry weather to plant the corn. I can't go in the red another season."

"Witness," his voice cracks.

"My leg … just heal it. Heal it already or give my doctor the good grace to cut it off. I can't take the pain anymore and I don't want no more painkillers."

"Witness."

"My boy," says Mr. Stone. "He's not like his parents. He's like us." He pounds his chest with his fist. "He's good like *us!*"

"Please, God, he's a Christian," says Mrs. Stone. "He gave away all his toys this summer because he wants to serve you and only you. Please, please oh please bring him back!"

"Witness!"

Eva watches them barrage him with prayers. And in their prayers, they reveal their most intimate fears, their most desperate pleas. She feels her skin crawl. With these secrets safely in his heart, he can prey on them forever. He can bleed them dry like slaughtered hogs.

Finally, he slumps in his chair, exhaling a long breath that fills the circle with the scent of sweet apple cider. He looks around, blinking. His eyes are glassy and bloodshot. "How long?"

"Five minutes," says Steven. "We all got in a prayer."

"Praise God," says the Reverend. He looks to Eva. "Did you get a chance to say something, Sofia?"

"No," Eva stumbles. "I wasn't sure … what was happening." She wants to add that he's a fucking piece of shit, the worst type of scam artist who preys on the most gullible, desperate people and he should fry in Hell.

And maybe there's something in her facial expression that says just that, because the Reverend's smile dims ever so slightly.

A phone goes off, breaking the spell. Eva is surprised to see Josh pull an old flip phone from his pocket. He answers, murmurs an "OK," then closes it. "A couple cows are out," he mumbles, lowering his head.

The Reverend's face reddens. Tina draws in a deep breath and holds it. Eva sees that Josh has done something horrible. He's interrupted this holy event.

She has to help him. Even though Sofia wouldn't be socially aware enough to realize the dangerous change in the suffocating, hot room. Even though Sofia's character hasn't yet undergone any sort of change that would make her empathetic, the way she used to be before her job transformed her into a selfish, greedy monster. "I can drive you back," she offers, then turns to the Reverend. "If that's OK."

His chin dips into a subtle nod. His eyes are no longer warm. They're suspicious.

10

Frogs

EVA LEADS THE BOY outside. Cicadas buzz. Crickets chirp. Nature is alive and celebrating a temporary reprieve from the rain. Find a partner while the mating is good. Eva unlocks her car. When Josh sits in the passenger seat, she can smell him. He's wearing some of that body spray shit that teenagers should be forbidden from using.

Exploit his feelings.

"You smell a helluva lot better than my car normally does," she says with a smile.

"Thanks," he says in a low voice. His voice sounds deep and husky. Comically unnatural.

Eva turns on the car's headlamps and does a Y-turn on the road. The tires rolling on wet pavement makes a soothing hissing sound. She pretends not to know how to get back to the Jenkins farm, letting Josh lead her to a back road that winds around a towering sandstone bluff. The road runs up against a stream. The water is high, partially flooding the edge of an empty field of weeds. The water looks dark, like molasses.

"You like taking care of cows?" she asks.

"It's all right."

"I had a friend from college who grew up on a farm," Eva lies, thinking back to her own childhood. "Her dad used to let her sit with him in the tractor while he spread manure. She said it was always a ton of fun."

He looks out the window. "It's scary sometimes. But I guess tractors can be fun. My grandma drove a tractor to school once."

"No kidding! Why?"

"Car broke down, I guess. She used to take her horse into town all the time, too. Just tied it to a lamp post in downtown Carthage."

Eva laughs. She's pretty sure she heard her dad mention once that he saw a woman doing that when he was growing up. "Could you imagine bringing a horse into town now? The kinds of looks people would give you?"

She can see, in the darkness, a little smile creep up his face.

"I'm holding out hope we get hovercrafts in our lifetime," she says. "I'd love to fly over Wisconsin and look at all the pretty farms."

"Yeah, I guess. Might get a little boring after a while."

"Oh no," Eva says. "Wisconsin's got so much hidden beauty. There are whole areas that were under ice during the last Ice Age. Big glaciers moving around millions of tons of dirt and rocks!"

"Really?"

"Totally."

Josh gives her directions to turn right at the next road. Eva slows and turns, the headlights cutting across a rolling field with rows of sprouting corn leaves. They pass a dead possum on the side of the road. "Poor critter," Eva murmurs.

"Possums are gross."

"Possums eat ticks," Eva says. "What's grosser? Possums or ticks?"

"Ticks, I guess." He's grinning now. "You said you did finance stuff, right?"

Eva's heart goes cold. What kind of question is that? Is he *testing* her? Did the Reverend order him to test her? No, no. That would be insane. But *shit*. She very casually says, "Yes, but I'm more of an investor than anything else."

"I was thinking of buying a new skid steer."

"Oh. And that's … what, exactly?"

"Like a little bulldozer. It has a detachable bucket. Mostly you can use it to scoop manure and grab bales of hay."

"Sounds super useful."

"It is!" He nods vigorously. His entire demeanor has changed. Less shy, all of a sudden. "But I don't understand how to do it. I keep reading about assets and liabilities. I don't understand how leasing something works."

"It's a little complicated," Eva tries, "I think you'd be better off owning your own equipment."

"But then the value goes down every year, right?"

This fucking kid. "Yeah, but a lease has its drawbacks, too."

"Farm equipment is expensive no matter what."

Eva knows. Growing up, she always looked at her family's bank statements. She was obsessed with the columns of red and black numbers. Once, she snuck a peek at her uncle's Excel spreadsheet and was frozen in terror at the half-a-million-dollar cost of a combine. Loan terminology pops up in her mind, just words that she heard over and over at family dinners. "You don't want too many liabilities, Josh."

"So I should have assets, right? Does that sound right?"

"Assets add value to your farm operation," Eva says, bullshitting to the Nth degree. "You're a smart dude!"

Josh grunts. "First time I've heard that."

"I still think you could get a lower monthly payment so long as your credit is good."

He doesn't say anything. At first, Eva's glad. But there's

something strange about his silence, so sudden. "*Is* your credit good?"

"No."

"How bad?"

"My dad took out a credit card in my name. After my grandma's stroke we had a bunch of medical bills. We couldn't pay off the card on time and had to make a bunch of late payments."

We. As if Josh had any say in the matter. That piece of shit Reverend.

"I'm sure that was hard," she manages in an even tone.

"She used to like me. She taught me everything about dairy cows. She always said you can't go wrong with growing cows." He licks his lips. "She hates me now. You saw …" He stops. He's getting choked up.

"Strokes can change a person."

"What do you mean?"

"They just … aren't the same anymore. The stroke damages the brain. It starts to work differently." Eva fights the urge to ask the question at the tip of her tongue: *why does your grandma think you killed someone?* "She's seeing something else. The image her eyes take in gets scrambled, like bad TV reception."

"It's hard to deal with her. My ma's got patience. My sister always had lots of patience."

Eva feels her heart thump against her chest. She's so unprepared for this moment that she can only utter an "Ah?"

"Miriam used to babysit all the kids in our congregation. That was her job."

"Sounds like a huge handful."

"It was," he says with a vigorous nod. "Especially when Elliot was a little kid. He seemed really messed up."

They're silent for a few beats. Eva listens to the sound of the tires humming over wet pavement, fighting the urge to pull over and grab him by the collar of his shirt and demand he tell her what happened to his sister.

"You should be more careful around the Reverend."

Eva's heart nearly leaps out of her chest. She swallows hard, suppressing her anxiety. "What do you mean?"

"Don't talk without permission," Josh says. "The Reverend doesn't like it when girls do that. And you should only drink water. Sugar is bad for women."

"Oh." She wills her hands to loosen their grip on the steering wheel before the skin around her knuckles cracks open.

"And you should nod more. He likes it when people agree with him."

She's surprised to feel a pain of guilt, unable to be as open with him as he is with her. "Do you normally give random people such helpful advice?"

He shrinks in his seat. Not an easy thing to do, given his size. "I just wanna be helpful. You're nice and I don't want him to kick you out."

Jesus Christ, did she fuck up that badly? Was it that obvious? She takes a shaky breath, willing herself to calm down. Sofia wouldn't care as much as Eva. Sofia doesn't understand how dangerous the Reverend truly is. "I appreciate the advice, Josh."

"We're up here on the right."

Eva turns onto the Jenkins' driveway. The headlamps illuminate tracks in the concrete where heavy wheels have worn it down, letting water gather. With the windows down, she can hear frogs bellowing. The ones on the driveway hop madly out of the way as Eva's car approaches them. Hundreds of frogs, splashing in the puddles, the only creatures in Kane County actually enjoying this historically wet weather.

As they get closer to the house, Eva can see the escaped cows standing near the loafing shed. They glance in the direction of the car but stay put.

"You want some help getting those cows in?"

"Nah," says Josh. He opens the car door. "I hope you stick around, though."

"Maybe I will."

He shuts the door. Eva turns in the driveway and heads west on Swamp Angel Road. When she can't hold it in anymore, she screams at the top of her lungs.

She messed up.

11

Ramirez

INSTEAD OF FOLLOWING Highway O into Carthage, Mason finds himself driving down Swamp Angel Road for the umpteenth time this week. Mason turns off the windshield wipers and turns on the brights. Dull light reflects off water tracks on the old road. He passes the Jenkins property, then the Cranston family farmhouse and their muddy cropland that runs down a soft hill, terminating at the edge of the forest that Professor Bernie Leftwich had identified as a place to search.

Mason slows just beyond the forest, pulling over beside the soggy, overgrown lawn of Edgar Ramirez's property. There's a sign standing awkwardly like an old gravestone, advertising fresh eggs for $3. The Ramirez home is nice: two stories, yellow siding with white trim and a white metal roof. There's also an old, free-standing garage and a homemade chicken coop attached to it. Chickens are free-ranging on the grass between the garage and the house, keeping away from the puddles. Mason has no idea what they're pecking at. Lightning bugs? Ticks?

Edgar's truck is parked in the driveway. There's a sign affixed to the driver's side door:

Eddie's Edging – Painting – Roofing – Gutters

Edgar comes out to greet Mason before he gets to the front door. Mason's head runs through his file automatically. Edgar Ramirez. Graduated from Woodrow Wilson High. Divorced. Three kids. Girlfriend works at Lowe's. Two drunk driving arrests in the last four years. Home alone the night Elliot Stone went missing (kids were with ex-wife, girlfriend was out bowling with friends).

Edgar's what the Carthage police would call "Legal." Mason's former partner in Milwaukee sometimes threatened to call ICE when they worked the Lincoln Village neighborhood. His partner hated Mexicans. Had a hierarchy of Latin lineages; whatever bullshit metrics he used, Mexicans were the worst. Ecuadorians were the best—"They're pretty OK, most of the time"—and from what Mason could piece together, that judgment stemmed entirely from a single experience his partner had had with an Ecuadorian Uber driver.

"You finally done with the night shift?" Edgar asks. He's friendly, but not overly so. If he killed Elliot Stone, he kept a good poker face throughout the initial questioning with Sheriff Henderson. Maybe it's just the yellowish glow of the patio light, but Edgar looks drunk.

"Going in now," Mason says, using his nose to breathe so he can gauge Edgar's sobriety.

"Don't work yourself to death, deputy." Definitely been drinking.

"I'm actually here about the eggs."

It takes a moment for Edgar's mind to register the connection. "Ah-ha! Come this way, good sir."

He leads Mason around the squishiest parts of the front lawn, to the old garage. A pair of lights illuminate the wet driveway. The chickens follow, heading back toward the safety of the coop—a good idea with coyotes in the area. Mason pretends to admire the property, looking for any evidence of anything else out of place. Elliot Stone was on his bike—a five-speed blue Trek. It's a long shot to think the bike might be discarded somewhere in plain sight, but murderers aren't always rational.

There's a field just northeast of Edgar's property. An old fence with a string of electric wiring keeps in a group of black steers picking at weeds in an unplanted field. Beyond the shadows: a gambrel roof barn. Rotten wood siding catches on the wind, slamming loudly in the evening air. A bundle of green bale twine sits on top of a pile of rotten wood and fallen branches.

That land used to belong to David Bauer.

"You out of the motel finally?" Edgar asks.

"Not yet."

Edgar slides up the garage door. A light blinks on, revealing a very orderly setup. Tool bench. White fridge. Old boxes of beer stacked next to a green garbage bin. Punching bag hanging down from the ceiling. "You got a frying pan and hot plate?"

"Yeah. It's a small one but it works fine."

"That motel is a pile of shit," Edgar says. "Sheriff should have just paid the deposit on an apartment. Least he could do for you."

Mason imagines Edgar returning from happy hour on the night of Elliot's disappearance, passing the forest between his property and the Cranston fields, not bothering to turn on his headlamps even though the trees are casting long afternoon shadows over the road. He imagines Edgar's truck swerving—maybe he was fiddling with his phone or maybe one of the headlamps wasn't working—and the truck's fat grill collides with the boy's head, and the tires crunch over the bike.

"At least there aren't any cockroaches," Mason says with a forced smile.

"That you know of. You know that's the motel all those pigs were using, right?"

"I've heard."

Edgar snickers. He takes Mason to the refrigerator. Mason looks around, makes a note of the shovel resting in the corner, its metal spade covered in dried mud.

"Your boss give you the whole story?"

"I pieced it together."

"They weren't pretty. The strippers, I mean. Not pretty enough to risk your job over. Or your marriage. I mean that from experience. I cheated on my first wife. Never was worth it, not once. The sex was always shitty. Biggest regret of my life." He hands Mason a carton of eggs. "Those strippers? Even uglier than the ladies I fucked."

Mason fishes in his wallet for a fiver. "Was it an open secret?"

Edgar shakes his head. "Nah. Carthage has a little more sensibility than that. Problem is social media nowadays. All it took was a couple slaps and one of the stripper whores was on Facebook complaining about her cop sugar daddy. Whole thing blew up after that."

Robin Wells' first article was about a part-time UW-Fayette student—moonlighting as an exotic dancer to earn extra money—who revealed on Facebook that police officers in Carthage and a couple Kane County sheriff's deputies were sleeping with strippers at the Sapphire Lounge. More articles followed as women came forward. The backlash was widespread. There was anger at the officers involved. Anger at the strippers for participating. Anger at Robin for not outing any Fayette officers. The comments section on each article revealed something simmering underneath it all. Resentment from Carthage residents who felt Fayette's police department must be involved, too. A couple nasty threats to Robin, who was accused of trying to ruin good officers' lives based on the unsubstantiated account of a *prostitute*. Plenty of people casting the dancers as dirty and shameful and deserving of the abuse.

"You think the sheriff put you up in that hotel on purpose?" Edgar asks. "Like, to test you and shit?"

"The thought's crossed my mind."

Robin's follow-up stories were like a flood. It looked bad. Real bad. Heads needed to roll.

Three sheriff's deputies. Four of the six Carthage police officers.

And that massive influx of job openings gave Mason, himself a disgraced former police officer, a chance to start over.

"No money's necessary," Edgar says with a wave.

Mason puts the five-dollar bill in Edgar's hand. "I'd like to avoid giving the sheriff any reason to fire me."

Edgar laughs and pockets the money. "That was a test. Congratulations! You're the first cop to actually pay for my eggs."

"You mind if I wash my hands quick?"

Edgar leads him inside without hesitation. Mason takes off his boots at the entryway. The house has a very 1970's style to it, with wood-paneled walls and old, beige carpeting that's accumulated some wicked stains. Kids' toys dominate an entire corner of the living room, colorful and plastic. The flat screen TV is on and tuned to Telemundo.

Mason washes his hands in the kitchen sink and looks around, noting the dirty dishes, the corn flour on the countertop, the Batman cookie jar. He grabs a blue dishtowel hanging from the oven handle. He carefully hangs it back just as it was, scrutinizing the kitchen one more time. Nothing out of place.

"Thanks," he tells Edgar, who's taken a seat in the recliner and seemingly forgotten about the officer of the law in his house. "I'll be back in a week for more eggs."

"I'll tell the chickens."

Mason goes outside, shutting the door behind him. No suspicion from Edgar. No nervousness. No distrust. No shadowing Mason to the kitchen.

Outside now, is his real intent. The only way he could get the right angle without appearing suspicious was to go inside the house, then come back out. Because from here, as he steps off the patio, he can very casually follow the gravel path to the driveway. He can see the front of Edgar's work truck.

And from this angle, with help from the patio light, he can see it.

A dent in the front bumper.

And something else, too: in the corner of the windshield, a green parking sticker for the Kane County Parks.

WEDNESDAY

12

True Devotion

EVA ARRIVES at the Grant Boyd Wilderness Preserve at 10:08 a.m., a few minutes late, parking behind a sheriff's SUV on the gravel drive leading into the prairie. It's hot and humid from the sweat of corn lingering in the air. Ragweed worries at Eva's eyes, as if the very sight of it is offensive.

She remembers this as a child. The land stretches between the Anderson farm to the south and Cedar Rock Road to the north, protecting a dozen Native American effigy mounds shaped liked bears, each one twenty feet across. There are famous pictures of the wilderness preserve taken from the sky, where the bears look like they're queued in line to climb over a tall bluff to the west. There are two hiking trails; one leads east, the other leads northwest, weaving around the effigy mounds. The western bluff stands tall, revealing layers of gray rock pockmarked with holes and a few shallow caves. Eva's father always insisted on getting out here in the summer to do bird watching.

The rest of the preserve is prairie. Tall grass interspersed with pretty blue flowers and no trees. Before human settlers, the prairies in the Driftless Area burned almost every year, killing any tree saplings. The DNR keeps this tradition alive with controlled burns. Eva remembers seeing the fires as a child and being so angry, unwilling to accept her father's patient explanations.

She walks to the end of the gravel drive, where the sheriff is standing with the Reverend, Tina, and close to a dozen others. Eva remembers Sheriff Henderson as something of a blowhard who occasionally stopped by Carthage High to talk about the dangers of meth; luckily, she never crossed paths with him. Some of the others she recognizes from the church service, but there are a couple strangers dressed in long pants and rain jackets. Some wear baseball caps. Most—excepting Eva—were smart enough to wear boots.

She waves to the Reverend. He and Tina meet her at the little gate.

"So glad to see you, Sofia," says Tina. She has a warm, pretty smile. She's wearing a dress cinched up a few inches with a safety pin, revealing a pair of black rubber boots.

"I got tired of sitting in my motel room," Eva says. Sofia wouldn't *admit* to wanting to help, but Eva makes sure her desire comes through a little bit in the nonchalant way she speaks. "I didn't expect the grass to be so high. Do you think I need bug spray?"

Tina looks at her husband. He gives a nod. "Stay right here," she says, hurrying back to their car.

The Reverend glances over his shoulder as Sheriff Henderson starts announcing the search party's plan. They're going to form three groups, and he has a printed list of the do's and don'ts when it comes to searching for a missing person. The sheriff doesn't say "body," he says "person." The advice basically amounts to *Don't touch possible evidence.* They might get lucky because the next storm isn't scheduled to hit Kane County until about 6:00

p.m. but everyone should expect a drizzle in the meantime and there's no quitting halfway through.

"We're going north to south," Henderson announces, "then south to north. Then east to west, then west to east." He glances at the Stones. "It'd be better if the Stones didn't participate, Reverend."

"It would be better if we had a police force to assist," the Reverend responds coolly. Eva's shocked at the fluid retort, as if it was prepared.

Sheriff Henderson glances at Eva. "Well, you're welcome to go to Kane County voters and ask them to increase my budget."

"Today's search is a volunteer search, and the Stones are volunteering."

Henderson's fingers tap his laminated map. Debating whether to accept this fight, Eva thinks. Finally, he turns back to a few others who have just arrived to go through the plan again.

"Good turnout," Eva says.

The Reverend grunts. "People from Fayette. I have no idea how they heard about today's search." He's upset by this. His eyes glare at the sheriff, his right hand absently picking at the loose seam where his left sleeve should be. It's an old, worn button-down shirt.

Tina returns with a can of bug spray. It's heavy-duty stuff, the kind that can ward off ticks and smells like cancer. Eva sprays it on her shoes, her jeans, and the back of her neck, pulling up her hair. Then, just to be safe, she gets the shoulders of her blouse, too.

"We're going to stay with our congregation," says the Reverend. "The Stones need our support."

"Spread out in a line," Sheriff Henderson announces. "Take pictures of anything suspicious, mark them on the map grid, and put a red flag nearby. Make sure the designated map holder marks off every grid once it's been searched."

Eva has been nominated as the map holder for her group.

She's immediately glad she used a liberal amount of the bug spray. The moment they enter the preserve, she can hear the hum of gnats and mosquitoes. Tall grass forces everyone to walk slow. The congregation is spread out, looking down as they walk while Eva stays behind them and uses the count of her footsteps to mark off squares on the map grid. She expects them to break out into song at any moment, but they're all eerily quiet. Henry and Linda Stone flank one end, Tina and the Reverend on the other.

The other two search groups slowly diverge. Someone calls out a beer can and Eva dutifully makes a note. She swats away mosquitoes buzzing near her ears. She's doing her best to avoid the muddiest areas but she can feel wetness sponging through her tennis shoes. Ahead, the Reverend is muttering something to his wife about the sheriff, how Carthage was founded by religious families who kept order in their congregations without law enforcement butting in.

They reach one of the bear-shaped Indian mounds and debate whether to continue over it or give it a respectful berth. The Reverend at least has the decency to point out its spiritual significance, but Henry Stone desperately pleas for someone to check the top, where the wildflowers and grass stand tall and thick. He looks like he's ready to cry, but it doesn't quite reach that point, and he's clearly embarrassed that people can see him this way.

The Reverend patiently suggests they go around out of respect for the mound.

"Elliot always liked to explore," Henry explains with a shaky voice. "That was the Ho-Chunk in him. He couldn't be outside often enough. But you could work him hard and then in the evening, he was always so normal. He'd just curl up with us on the couch and we could forget about his problems for a few hours."

It's all horrible improvisation coming from a man who obviously doesn't understand how to deal with his own feelings.

And it's clearly not moving enough for the Reverend. But before he can say anything, his wife stands on her tip-toes, pulling him close, her hand gently rubbing his chest as she whispers something into his ear. She steps back.

The Reverend places his fist on his hip and sighs. "Meet me on the other side," he says. He climbs to the top of the hill, walking slowly from one side to the other. "Nothing," he announces.

It's another hour before the congregation gets to the southeast end of the prairie. Red-winged blackbirds perch on impossibly thin reeds, chirping at the trespassers. A drizzle has soaked everyone's hair and the warm weather has caused everyone's face to flush. Ahead is a large forest that—according to Eva's map—butts up against three other farms in the area. One is the Anderson farm, which the sheriff made clear no one was to trespass on.

Mr. Stone comes across a couple bullet casings from a hunting rifle. He stabs a red flag into the wet soil and Eva marks the location on her map. As they draw closer to the forest, they come across a pair of sandhill cranes who fly away when they realize the trespassing humans aren't going to deviate from their course. Sweat and bug spray intermingle and gather in the corners of Eva's eyes, causing a painful, stinging sensation that no amount of tears will alleviate. This is a waste of time. She's getting no information, and there's no opportunity to bond with the Reverend as long as she's stuck following behind them.

Twenty feet away from the first trees, they stop. The forest is thick with maples and oaks and pine trees. A few fallen moss-covered logs lay near the edge, but there are enough open clearings to walk through.

"This was an old dumping ground," says Linda Stone. "My grandfather's tractor is here, somewhere."

Another congregant says his father left a steel plow here after it got damaged by a boulder hidden under the soil. The Andersons always let local farmers use their backroad to dump things in the forest. Eva senses an unspoken truth: previous generations of the Anderson family were *better*. She remembers Ryan and Tracy Anderson, remembers their son who was only a toddler when Eva moved to California. She remembers seeing them at the McDonald's next to the Piggly Wiggly sometimes, sharing a big box of nuggets.

"We've still got good weather," says the Reverend. He looks around. "I think we should try and comb this entire forest before doubling back."

"The sheriff—" one of the congregants begins, but the Reverend cuts him off.

"I don't trust him any more than I trust the rest of his people. Who do you think will do a better job searching this area? Us, with the Stones," he motions to Mr. and Mrs. Stone, "or the sheriff, who's probably thinking about *other things* while he works? Or maybe should we leave it to the volunteers from Fayette, who don't know this area at all?"

Eva studies the Stones. Linda's face looks ashen and pale, her sunken eyes staring off into some memory hiding deep in the forest. Mr. Stone's face is glistening with sweat. He's nearly as big as the Reverend, only rounder in the stomach and with a heavy neck that folds underneath his whiskered chin. He's wearing the same shirt that he wore to the Bible study the night before. Both of them wear fat, silver wedding rings that squeeze the flesh of their fingers.

Everyone approaches the forest in an almost choreographed pace. Eva can feel a sense of dread forming in the congregation, as if it's a foregone conclusion that Elliot has been discarded here with the rest of the dead farming equipment. The thought is eating away at Mrs. Stone's soul, and she's dealing with it by very slowly shutting down, slowing her walk so that the row of congregants bends like a wet stick ready to snap. Henry Stone doesn't know what to do with his feelings so he's channeling it into a quiet rage. His hands tell his story, clenching and un-clenching; he wants to go into the forest but he's afraid of what he'll find.

They stop at the edge. The leaves of maples and oaks rustle gently, beckoning. But no one steps forward. Eva feels a nervous energy run down her arms. She needs more time with the Reverend. Josh's warning runs through her head over and over—her mistakes, and now she's second-guessing every choice she's made with the part of Sofia. The way she second-guessed every audition that didn't land her a role.

Failure.

She needs to redeem herself in the Reverend's eyes so he trusts her.

She needs to find his daughter.

Eva steps closer to the Reverend. She remembers Josh's warning about acting too assertive. "What does God say, Reverend?"

The Reverend takes a deep breath. "Tina, go with the Stones and the Mueller family along the west end. Sofia, you have the map so the two of us will walk due south. Everyone else take the east end. Spread out as wide as you can and call to Sofia and me if you find anything."

Everyone splits up, trudging into the forest and plowing bravely through areas where the undergrowth is penetrable. Eva thanks God for throwing a little luck her way, following the Reverend between maple trees to their first discovery: an old, white Cadillac with long tailfins. A white ash tree has sprouted from where the front seat once was, leaning out through the broken driver's-side window. Eva pushes away a branch of green compound leaves, marveling at the vehicle. Rust runs up the front of the hood. The paint has peeled in the pattern of the negative space between tree branches, where sunlight above beat down for decades at familiar times of the day.

"Cars," the Reverend says, "are the worst investment. They depreciate the moment you put the first mile on. I'm surprised your co-workers didn't pressure you into buying a nicer one."

Eva's ready for this. She knew she'd have to explain her sensible, average vehicle. "I had a Beamer for a while, but I got sideswiped by a truck and my insurance wouldn't pay the full cost of repair. I had to dump it."

"In a forest?" he asks with a smile. His eyes trace a pattern on the forest floor, where heavy shadows loom underneath the arthritic limbs of tall oaks whose leaves contain the youthful light-green pigment that only exists in late spring. Here, Eva and the Reverend are shaded and cool and sheltered from the drizzle. Eva's shoes squish damp leaves into the soft ground, leaves that fell last fall and are the sharp brown of the wooden floors of the Jenkins household.

Birds chirp overhead. Eva looks up, watching a robin take flight from the branch of a maple as they pass underneath. The other congregants are so far away now, hidden by trees and brush, that it seems as if she's all alone here with the Reverend. He steps over a fallen oak branch without giving it a second glance. Eva passes it and thinks she could grab it and hold it across the Reverend's neck, kicking the back of his knee and using his weight to hold him in place while she violently chokes him until he gives up the truth about Miriam.

And if he didn't … maybe she could bring herself to kill him.

"These vehicles," says the Reverend, "are a reminder that wealth can decay. This graveyard was a last resort. It was a place for desperate farmers to throw away worthless machines cheaply, quietly, and quickly."

They walk deeper into the forest. Sunlight penetrates the canopy in dozens of radiant beams, shining down on an old tractor just ahead. Rust has eaten away at the red paint and vines crawl over it like a creature trying to pull it down into the earth. A single vine leaf rests over the top of the tailpipe.

"That was nice, what you did at the Indian Mound," Eva says, hoping to flush the Reverend out of his own thoughts. "I read somewhere that those are very, very sacred sites."

"Henry Stone is a very stubborn man. He should never have let his son go off and work for that farmer. He should have come to me, like the other parents in our congregation. I know how to keep young people busy and out of trouble. I know who around here can be trusted."

"He's taking it hard."

"His soul is conflicted," the Reverend says. "His wife laments the loss of a son, but Henry laments the monthly check. Did you know the government will pay you to foster a child?"

"I've heard that before."

"Elliot always had behavior issues. Too much energy pent up, like a livewire. He needed structure and discipline, but that was an impossible task, given the boy's mental faculties. Sometimes I wish ..."

He doesn't finish. Eva senses this is important. She waits in silence, imagining herself a woman in his cult waiting to be spoken to.

"My daughter used to be good with Elliot. If Miriam had been watching Elliot, he would never have gone missing. She would have seen him home."

They walk around a rotten log. The Reverend kicks it with his shoe, flipping it and revealing a congregation of grubs and beetles. "Henry Stone has always been ... *cautious* about accepting God's path for him. The disappearance of his son is testing his faith. I empathize. It wasn't until I returned to Carthage that I found my true calling."

"You left?" Eva asks, surprised. She can only always imagine him here.

"When I was twenty years old. Back then, you either farmed or you worked in the lead mine. My family didn't own a farm so I was destined for the mine. But the mine scared me. All the men who worked there were mean and they drank a lot and wasted their money on fancy automobiles just like that Cadillac back there. I wanted something better. So I left."

"Where'd you go?"

"Southwest," the Reverend says with a chuckle. "My friends and I were doing religious work in Dallas when we came across an ad for a warehouse for rent. It was a bad neighborhood, but dirt cheap. We had this idea to found a new church, one where people could worship on their own time and study theology. We wanted a place of learning, like an academy. To us, the Bible was this vast frontier just waiting to be explored."

This seems entirely out of character. Eva, intrigued, asks, "Were you all Methodists?"

The Reverend shakes his head. "But we worshipped Christ, raised by TV preachers. We'd been indoctrinated into the gospel of prosperity, so we all believed eventually, God would reward us for our hard work. We toiled in our warehouse and took turns preaching. People began showing up, and pretty soon we had a few dumpster divers who kept the fridge full and a few street musicians who covered the monthly rent. The rest of us could dedicate our time to our scholarly work."

They walk slowly around the tractor.

"I put up drywall around a little living space for me," the Reverend continues. "My friend just put up curtains. His neighbor reclaimed a little white picket fence about knee-high. We were carving out our own niches, decorating the warehouse with whatever we could find, until it resembled this beautiful little city. Everyone contributed in their own way. This nice lady—I never learned her real name—cut all our hair but she never cut hers. Let it grow down to her waist."

"Wasn't the warehouse owner upset about all this?" Eva asks, following him under a few pines where the undergrowth is bare. Brown needles carpet the forest floor.

"The owners were slum lords. As long as we paid rent we were the best tenants they'd ever had. We were fixing the place up, too. The only staircase in the warehouse was nearly falling apart when we moved in. I spent over a month getting it in good condition again—not *great* condition, but good enough that you didn't need to worry about falling through a rotten step."

He takes her closer to the silver maple trees ahead. They've consumed an old bulldozer, sprouting from rusted holes, pushing at the steel, growing *around* its metal arm attached to the bucket, as if the steel has been absorbed into the bark.

"Then one day I was walking home," he says, stopping in front of the bulldozer, "and I saw this giant wooden statue sitting in the parking lot of an accounting firm. I went inside and asked about it. The accountant told me it was for a celebration in the desert, but family business had waylaid him. I told him I would take it off his hands for a hundred bucks. He offered two hundred if I could get rid of it before they opened up the next day.

"So I called up everyone in our congregation. We dismantled the whole thing and brought all the wood to the warehouse. We had enough to panel all the hideous concrete pillars and enough left over for a nice wood floor on the second story where we held our church services." He smiles, running a hand across the bulldozer's exterior. "Someone said the way we'd built all these little stalls, and all the wood we'd used to pretty it up, it looked like an Ark. The name stuck."

The muscles around the Reverend's thin lips tighten. His hand absently pets the bulldozer, as if it's an anxious beast. Eva feels adrenaline flood her body. Has the forest grown darker?

"And more people started coming to our service. We were saving up enough to buy the warehouse. We told ourselves God was providing. We treated Christianity like a toy that we could manipulate however we wanted. I tattooed crosses on my left arm, doing all the work myself. I liked the pain. I slept with a woman who'd travelled from California and we did drugs to enhance our experience with God." He laughs at that. Eva is too mystified to feign a response.

He walks closer to her, passing under the shadow of an ancient oak tree whose limbs are so heavy that they bend downward like a clawed hand. Eva backs up, afraid now. What does he know? Can he see through her? Is that why he's telling this story?

The Reverend walks past her, around a red pine. Fallen branches sit around the trunk, rotting.

"Every worship service was packed," he continues. "People wanted to hear about a forgiving, loving God. They wanted to read Bible passages and form their own understanding and craft a personal relationship with their creator. Don't like this passage? Ignore it. Think this other passage means something different? Good for you." His tone has become mocking, condescending. He shakes his head. "We believed our prosperity was a message. We tallied up God's blessings in the bank accounts and our amenities."

Eva walks with him. He has his head down, panning left and right. He's still looking for clues as he talks.

"Then, one afternoon, I woke in my stall to the smell of smoke and screaming." He stops, doesn't turn around. "It was coming from upstairs. I don't know what happened or how it started, only that when I ran to the staircase, I saw flames through the open doorway leading to the second floor. There were hundreds of worshippers upstairs, screaming for help. Some of them tried jumping through the flames, tumbling down the stairs. More flung themselves from the second-story windows. It got so hot that I could see the ceiling turning orange and I could feel it on my skin."

A warm breeze picks up, howling low between the trees. Water falls from the leaves. Eva feels drops run down the back of her neck.

"I had to do *something*," the Reverend says. "I thought maybe I could break through the ceiling on the north end of the warehouse, where there was water damage. I used an axe and got through the ceiling but part of a rotten beam collapsed and pinned me." He indicates his missing arm. "When I came to,

I was outside. Firefighters had rescued me, but my arm was beyond saving. Along with twenty Christian souls."

They stop beside an ancient Ford pickup truck resting against a massive ash tree that has slowly pressed against the metal exterior, bending one corner of the front hood as if the truck had collided in slow motion. The ash tree is dead, a casualty of the emerald ash borer. The Ford's grill is cracked, a gaping mouth full of sharp teeth.

"God took my tattooed arm," the Reverend says, running his hand across the hood of the Ford, "and God took my flock. He destroyed the Ark. He destroyed everything we had. That was when I knew who I really was."

Eva composes herself, swallowing dry saliva. "How did you know what God wanted, though?"

The Reverend smiles. "He told me. He said, Anthony, you've lost your way. So I reread the Bible and I realized *this is the Word of God*. Prosperity isn't a reward. It's simply greed."

"Reverend!" shouts Rodney, emerging from a thick patch of ferns to their left. He reaches them, panting heavily, mouth hanging open. "We found something. We found *bones*!"

Eva feels her heart race. The Stone boy. Did they find him? Would the sheriff ask for statements from everyone? Would he interview Eva and force her to tell the truth?

She has plenty of time to panic while the Reverend gathers up the rest of the search party.

"Sofia," he says, startling her. "*Sofia*. You've got the map. Come."

Eva walks nervously behind the rest of the congregation. Mr. and Mrs. Stone walk with her, each of their steps intentional and forced. Henry has his arm around his wife and she's already crying, blowing her nose into a wet tissue. They make their way around a dense cropping of red pines with narrow trunks trailed by dead branches, to the eastern edge of the forest where there's a twenty-foot buffer strip of grass between the trees and ankle-high winter wheat so starved of nutrients that it's turned a yellowy green.

And there, scattered atop soggy green grass, are a few bones. Not bleached-white bones. Bones picked of the best meat by wandering coyotes. Bones that are yellow and fresh. Bones that resemble a femur or a humerus, and one curved rib.

Above, pitch-black vultures circle, a mobile of death over a child's crib.

The Reverend's wife and the congregants stand around the bones and pray. Linda Stone sobs, unable to hold anyone's hand because she keeps blowing her nose again and again into the wet tissue that's flaking apart. Henry just stares at the bones as if sheer willpower could knit them back together. Eva can feel so many emotions stirring in the air that she can almost hear them, humming and buzzing like gnats taking flight. She feels dizzy.

Thunder rolls across the sky.

"My great-great grandfather kept a skull in his home," the Reverend says quietly. Eva starts; he's stepped beside her, the pupils of his eyes black like corridors into a great unknown. "My grandmother asked him once who it was and he said long ago, when he moved here, he went to war with the Indians. Blackhawk and his tribe. And he killed many of them and brought this skull home. And my grandmother asked why the skull was small, like hers. He had no answer. And he never spoke of it again, and my grandmother never saw that skull again."

The sheriff arrives with the rest of the search group. He orders everyone back and lets a middle-aged man—a professor from UW-Fayette—get close to the bones with a pair of vinyl gloves. The man moves each bone delicately, lifts each one up. Eva watches, wiping rainwater from her face, her entire body shaking even though the damp air is hot and thick. She breathes through her mouth but can still smell a hint of the lingering stench of rancid meat.

"Fear of God kept our ancestors' greed and bloodthirst in

check," the Reverend whispers. "Manifest Destiny gave them the excuse to be who they truly were."

The congregation's prayers die down and all that's left are the calls of sparrows from the edge of the forest.

They wait for an eternity. A raven flies overhead, landing on the branch of a maple.

Finally, the professor stands up and rips off his gloves. "It's a calf."

Mrs. Stone begins sobbing even harder.

"Praise God," the Reverend whispers.

"Stop crying," Henry tells his wife. Eva watches his fists clench, then unclench, then clench. "Stop crying!"

"Hank," says the sheriff.

"Stop crying!" Henry screams, grabbing his wife and shaking her. Eva feels adrenaline course through her body. She steps back, letting the sheriff brush past her. Henry's face is scrunched up, red, taut and strained. Not a single tear escapes from his glassy eyes but sweat is squeezing out of every pore. He looks like he's ready to explode.

"Stop crying!" he screams louder, shaking his wife so violently that she collapses on wobbly legs. The professor and the sheriff both try to grab him. Henry brushes off the sheriff and punches the professor in the face, causing blood to spurt out of his nose. The professor collapses next to the calf bones and Henry follows, landing hard and punching the professor's face again and again; blood rises in three thin ropes as he lifts his fist, whipping at Eva's jeans.

The sheriff shocks him with a stun gun and pulls him off the professor. The professor is crying, gently touching his red face. Henry Stone's entire body is quivering, his bloody right fist clenched tightly, his eyes staring up at the ceiling of gray clouds so low that they might collapse the world. Eva looks down at Henry and knows even now, he doesn't understand what to do with all the emotions trapped inside. He's a man who's spent his entire life strangling these alien feelings, permitting only the most violent emotional reactions, and now his body is shutting down so entirely that even his breaths are forced and labored.

Eva turns to the Reverend. He looks at Eva, then nods to Mr. Stone as if to say *Here. Here is a man whose ears are finally open the word of God.*

13

The Gravity

MASON PARKS his white Chevy in the gravel parking lot at the foot of Russel Shot Tower. There are other vehicles parked here, and their windshields each bear the Kane County Parks sticker.

Robin gets out first, melodramatically inhaling the muggy warm air.

"I have yet to meet a man who knows how to use the proper amount of fabric softener," she mutters.

Mason glances at the two hampers of clothes in the back-seat. "It's the laundromat's washing machines. They always smell funny."

Robin looks around. "Christ, this is a helluva longshot."

"We're killing two birds today." He leads her across the parking lot. Their shoes crunch on wet gravel. Ahead is a towering dolomite and sandstone cliff, its exposed rock layered like waves near the top and more pockmarked near the bottom. Tenacious white pines cling to the cliff in a few precious places where there's some soil. A wooden tower runs down the side of the cliff, bottoming out at an old structure with an A-frame.

Around the tower, green grass has been freshly cut, the lawn-mower leaving muddy tracks in a criss-cross pattern. About a hundred yards in every direction of the shot tower is dry-mesic forest, full of oaks and hickories with sprawling canopies and low undergrowth good for hiking.

"Why the runaround?" Robin asks. "Why not just come clean to the sheriff and question Edgar Ramirez about the dent on his truck?"

"Because Ramirez sits on the board at the Carthage Chamber of Commerce."

"Ah." Robin flashes him a shit-eating grin. "Old Henderson still thinks he can win their endorsement, even after the strip club scandal? The self-confidence of men never ceases to amaze me."

"It would be wonderful if I knew someone who could very quietly ask around and see if he's tried to get the dent fixed."

Robin groans. "Carthage car mechanics don't like me. It's an ex-boyfriend thing."

They take the path up the hill. It curls around the cliff, inclining sharply every ten or so feet with a wooden step. Mason relishes the feeling in his legs. It's been too long since he's exercised regularly. He'd gotten in such good shape after the incident in Milwaukee. His therapist had told him exercise was good for depression.

"This is horrible," Robin says behind him. The clouds are low and heavy, moving like a dark sea in a squall. "It smells like Pin-Sol and rotten leaves out here."

"It smells like my motel."

"I can't imagine how you haven't gone insane living in that dump."

"I play board games."

Robin gives him a funny look, but doesn't say anything.

"I collect board games," he explains, embarrassed. "For fun."

"Even when you play them alone?"

"I used to get grounded a lot as a kid." He has no idea why he's confessing this to her. "So I made up rules to play board games alone. I'd pretend to be different players with their own personalities. It got pretty easy."

"It *sounds* like an intense, complicated form of masturbation."

Mason says nothing. Why the hell did he open is mouth in the first place?

"Well, if you want to move, pick any road around here," Robin says, waving her arm at the valley to their right. It's possible to peer between the white pines and see more than a mile of forest, right up to a bluff where the land is farmed in squiggly contours along a rolling hill. Three neat plateaus of well-drained winter wheat, dark and green. Mason loves that color.

"Maybe something a *little* less remote."

"You're thinking Carthage."

The thought has crossed his mind. It has a good small-town feel. There are lots of houses for sale. A café, a grocery store, a sub shop, a Wal-Mart. And Fayette's nearby, if he needs to catch his breath in a larger town.

"Mase, take my advice: rethink that plan. Carthage is dying. You buy a house there, it'll be worth half in ten years. Also? The pizza place in town is absolute garbage. Rubber cheese. And the owner is literally a white supremacist. He goes to city council meetings and complains about Mexicans. He goes on record to talk about how important it is to keep Carthage racially *pure*."

"If that's his goal, then he should give his pizza parlor to the Sioux."

Robin's face lights up. "Look at you, Mr. Woke Policeman! How did *that* little nugget of truth slip into your brain?"

A Youtube documentary. But he sure as hell isn't telling her that. "I read up on the area before I was hired by Sheriff Henderson."

"Well *you* can go ahead and share your fascinating Wisconsin history at the next Carthage City Council meeting," she mutters. "The white supremacist is less likely to murder a *man*."

"Why is Fayette doing so well?" he asks, genuinely interested. "Is it the university?"

"It's a lot of things," Robin answers, looking out at the forest. "University money is good, obviously. But farmers around Fayette embraced organic farming, too. Helped them weather the tough times. Immigrants are always willing to work the organic farms."

"Why?"

Robin sighs. "Short answer? Because the organic farmers treat them better. America has gotten a little polarized, in case you haven't noticed."

Mason runs his fingers along the wet dolomite rock, across the holes shaped like Swiss cheese. When Elliot Stone hasn't monopolized his thoughts, he's been thinking about Kane County's *unofficial* missing person. So far, though, her sheltered life has been near-absolute. "You ever hear about Miriam Jenkins taking another job, besides working for David Bauer?"

"No," Robin says absently. She's trying desperately to choose the best steps to keep her sneakers clean. "Someplace specific you want me to check out?"

"I was thinking the Sapphire Lounge."

Robin laughs, hopping up one of the path's waterlogged steps. "That's pretty crazy. Then again, if Miriam's got too much of her ma's blood in her ..."

"What do you mean?"

"Tina Jenkins was wild before she married the Reverend. Rode with a local gang of bikers. 'Gang' is a strong word, I guess. More like filthy assholes on Harleys. They closed a different bar every night. Probably dealt a little meth on the side, if I had to guess."

"What the hell happened to Tina?"

"Road rash," Robin says. "They were speeding through

downtown Carthage. Tina's boyfriend had a spill and she went rolling on the pavement. Came to a stop right at the doors of the the Reverend's church. Serendipity."

"And her boyfriend?"

Robin cuts a finger across her throat. "Always wear a helmet."

They reach the top, where there's a neat little clearing with a few picnic tables. A family is eating lunch together. The father swats a fly and complains about the wet benches. He looks up when Mason walks by and stops talking, recognizing the deputy even though he's not in uniform.

"Don't you just love the power that uniform gives you?" Robin asks. She tightens her hand into a fist. "Authority just radiates outward and cows the local villagers into submission!"

"I can't tell if you're being funny right now."

She opens the door to the shot tower, giving him a coy shrug.

Inside, Mason breathes a sigh of relief. The room is small, most of its wall space taken up with pictures and little placards explaining the process of smelting lead and pouring it down the tower shaft. But the shaft itself is cordoned off by an impressive chain-link fence, painted a glossy white. Slabs of stone form a platform, and the fence has been screwed into the rock, running all the way up to the wooden rafters of the ceiling. There's no way to throw anything larger than a quarter into the shaft.

A young man wearing a green Kane County Parks t-shirt is standing next to a stone niche, where a cast-iron smelting pot sits. He's got a dark tan and his hair is combed to one side. He looks like the kind of kid who actually enjoys working at a historic landmark.

"You're Deputy Taylor?" he asks.

Mason nods and holds out a hand. "Teddy Cox, right?"

"Yeah."

Robin's head snaps in Mason's direction. Now she gets what he meant by "killing two birds": the Cox family has a big farm—lots of acres that jut up against the Jenkins property on the south side of Swamp Angel Road. Sheriff Henderson only interviewed Teddy's parents regarding the night of Elliot's disappearance.

"I'm not on duty today, but I was hoping you'd let me ask a few questions."

"No problem." At least he's not nervous. Mason hates it when people act nervous for no reason. It just makes questioning them more difficult.

He looks around. "I've gotta ask, even though I'm pretty sure of the answer. There's no way to get that fence open, is there?"

Teddy shakes his head. His fingers wrap around the chain links and give them a pull. "No gate or anything. It's just screwed into the rock."

"How long's it been there?"

"A few years now, I think."

"What about down at the bottom? That little building at the base of the tower is where they used to collect the lead bullets, right?"

Teddy nods, effusively jumping into a scripted history. "See, they used a sieve up here and then as the drops fell they became perfect spheres …"

Robin walks behind Teddy and gives Mason an amused expression.

"Can people explore the bottom of the tower?" Mason interrupts after a few minutes of polite listening.

Teddy shakes his head. "I've *never* seen it open to the public."

"Could someone break in?"

Teddy offers a teenager's trademark shrug. "We could check, if you want. I think I've got the key."

"Let's do it."

Teddy leads them outside, back down the winding path. Now Mason can feel it in his knees. He needs to get back to exercising. "You were home the night Elliot Stone went missing, right?"

"Yup."

"Did you see any strange cars on your road that week? Ones you didn't recognize?"

"I don't think so. But I work here full-time when I don't have classes."

Mason tries a different tack, hoping he's not being too leading. "You remember seeing a white truck parked here at all recently? Would have had a big yellow logo across the side."

"What, you mean the remodeler's truck? Ramirez or something?"

"Yeah."

"Not lately. But he's brought his kids here sometimes."

"What about the night Elliot Stone went missing?"

"No. But *someone* definitely drove by our house."

Robin and Mason look at each other.

"We were watching TV in the living room, so we didn't have a good view of the road," Teddy explains. "But through the kitchen window, you can see the headlights of cars as they pass on Swamp Angel. I went to make some popcorn at, like, 7:30. I remember seeing headlights."

"Who's out in the early evening?" Robin asks. "This time of year."

Teddy exhales, puffing out his cheeks. The kid's impressing Mason with his thoughtfulness. "Too wet to plant. I guess maybe David Bauer could have done some manure spreading."

Mason gives Robin a thankful smile.

Teddy leads them to the old wooden structure at the base of the hill, directly underneath the shot tower. He fiddles with the lock; flakes of rust fall away. Teddy pulls open the door, unable to resist going back into tour-guide mode and explaining how the lead balls were collected. Less than half were usable. The ones that didn't form right were taken back to the top of the tower, melted down again and dropped.

"The guy who owned this tower was a real ball-breaker," Teddy says. Robin chuckles and he gives her a strange look; he doesn't seem to realize the incredible pun he just made. "He was pretty serious about only selling the perfect shot. It all went to the Union army during the Civil War. I did some Googling of Winston Russel on my phone and he really hated the South. He thought General Robert E. Lee should have been hung."

"Sounds like a stand-up guy," Robin says brightly. She and Mason follow Teddy into the little building.

"This thing's been closed for *years*," Teddy says, fumbling for a light switch on the wall. A single bulb turns on, revealing an empty room. Old, dusty placards hang on the wall, next to squares of clean wall that no doubt used to hold framed pictures. Ahead, there's a beautiful wooden door in the farmhouse style, chipped and weathered at the edges, held in place with a heavy iron latch.

Footprints in the dirt lead to it, back and forth.

Teddy tries the lock, but the key that fits the tumblers doesn't turn—the old lock is rusted shut. Mason steps back and kicks the door. Screws snap off the rusted latch. Mason pulls on the lock, tearing the latch out of the old wood.

"Cool," Teddy says. He pulls out his phone and turns on the flashlight function. Robin does the same, illuminating the dolomite cave beyond. Mason walks behind Teddy while the boy points out the interesting features of the rock: all the little dimples and holes were probably lead or zinc deposits. Some decayed naturally, forming the telltale Swiss cheese-like gaps. But some of the bigger pieces were probably mined when they built the shot tower.

"Say, Teddy," Robin says, interrupting his spiel. "You see Miriam Jenkins around lately?"

Teddy clicks his tongue. "I don't think I've seen her in a while, now that I think of it."

"Your parents mention anything about her?"

"They mentioned how she looked bad, once."

"What do you mean?" Robin asks, not quite hiding her annoyance at the vague answer.

Teddy shrugs. "They just said she wasn't looking good. That's all I remember. It was, like, half a year ago. My parents are real gossipers."

Mason shines his light ahead. They're coming up on the tower shaft. There, sitting in the center, is a circular pool made of mortared, cream-colored bricks about waist-high. Mason walks around it, shining his flashlight on the ground and along the walls. He shines his light into the pool. There's no lead shot, no water, and no body. He's about to turn back when he remembers the footprints in the dirt. Professor Leftwich had mentioned caves carved by streams. He again walks slowly around the massive pool, panning his flashlight across the porous rock walls. Halfway around, his beam stops on a hole, low and angular, its insides glistening.

"That cave go anywhere?" Robin asks Teddy.

"I dunno," the boy says. "I don't know anyone who's even been in here."

Mason gets on his knees so he can shine the light deeper inside. Like a blood vessel, he thinks. The morbid side of his mind imagines someone crawling through here, maybe backwards, dragging the body of a small boy. He crawls inside.

"Jesus Christ," he hears Robin mutter, her voice echoing farther down. "Careful, Mase!"

The flashlight bounces as he crawls, but he can see where the cave curves. He can see patches of soft limestone in the walls now. This must have been an old stream, its slightly acidic water eating away at the limestone over thousands of years. It came through here and exited at the base of the cliff. Miners dug out the lead and zinc, leaving an unnatural cavern, perfect for Winston Russel's shot tower.

Mason follows the curve, where the cave opens a little wider. The ground is wet and cold, soaking through Mason's pants. His knees ache. He can hear the sound of bubbling water. His flashlight shines on something on the walls, near the ceiling. Mason turns awkwardly onto his back to get a better look.

A painting. It's old and faded but Mason's imagination can fill in the gaps in the red paint. A thunderbird, its wings spread wide. And: a deer with exposed ribs. He turns around and continues crawling, following the bend to the left.

He can see something up ahead. He moves closer. The rank smell of mold reaches him.

He gets closer. The cave opens up wider; a gentle stream emerges from a hole in the smooth limestone, runs past Mason, and disappears through another hole. Mason can almost stand up here; he crouches, walking to an object next to the wall. Not big enough to be a body, it looks almost like a dead animal of some kind, black and thick. He reaches into his pocket for a pen and carefully moves it. It unfolds, peeling away in layers. Underneath, protected from the moisture, the fabric has retained its color.

Clothes. *Children's* clothes.

14

Method Acting

EVA PACES in her motel room, biting her nails, thinking over her encounters thus far. Dinner. Bible Study. The search party.

The mistakes.

It wasn't just the things she said, the way she acted … it was her whole demeanor. Slipping in and out of character. Letting her real feelings show through on her face. Not inhabiting her character between "takes."

She'd been so careful planning everything. Even her costumes were carefully picked: button-down floral blouses and oxford shirts with neutral colors, jeans and colorful socks. Clothes that serve Sofia's character. Clothes Eva hates so much that she's just wearing a white undershirt around the motel.

"God damn it," she whispers.

The shitty motel wi-fi finally pulls up the search results for "Religious Ark" on the *Dallas Morning News* website. Eva walks over to it, scanning the links until she finds a promising headline.

20 DEAD, 18 INJURED IN WAREHOUSE FIRE

Eva clicks the link and starts pacing again while the web page loads. She should have better memorized Sofia's backstory. She should have never quit her Hollywood improv troupe. She's rusty. She's stressed. She's not thinking straight. She was a fool to think memorizing a few stories would be enough.

Actors must reflect the world around us.

Another thought nags at her: the Reverend's story of the Ark. It was a *monologue*. It was practiced and memorized and clean. He's used it before.

The news article pops up on the screen. Eva's eyes scan the text, parsing every paragraph, her mind processing the words and comparing the news account to the Reverend's story, filling in the gaps.

Black mold growing in the basement …

Electricity stolen from an auto repair shop next to the warehouse …

A spark from an old refrigerator, catching on bundles of paper money left in a pile on the floor …

The only stairwell rotting and falling apart, repaired so inadequately that it collapsed as people fled the fire …

Smoke so thick and black that congregants had to crawl on the floor, searching for a window …

Flames so hot that survivors remember feeling their skin beginning to melt …

"Jesus," Eva whispers. How can she reconcile this with Sofia's character? How can Eva meet the Reverend again and hide her disgust? She knows too much about him. She knows too much about how he operates. She's studied people like him to prepare for this.

Authoritarians are self-righteous. They believe they're better than everyone else. Authoritarians are hypocrites. Authoritarians employ highly compartmentalized thinking. Authoritarians are ethnocentric and aggressive.

The Reverend is all of these things. Eva is aware of what he's doing, which is why Sofia isn't fitting in.

She stops pacing and looks out the rain-spattered window. The strip club across the street has turned on its neon light to beckon potential customers. Her stomach aches. She's so sick of energy bars and apples and chips that she's been craving another of Tina's horrible home-cooked meals. After returning from the prairie, she lay in bed with a growling stomach, playing her interactions with the Reverend over and over and over, trying to remember all the crucial things she said.

All the crucial things *Sofia* said.

She goes to her suitcase and picks up her diary. The source of her energy, Sofia's character, motivation, feelings, everything. It's the diary of Eva's worst year in Hollywood, recording in excruciating detail the part of "Jennifer's Friend," the biggest role she'd ever taken on. The stressful callback. The screen test. The phone call saying she'd won a part that could bankroll her acting career for an entire year. Eva was supposed to just be the comic relief for the serious actress in the lead role who was making a career comeback after a few years in mostly B-movie garbage.

But Eva had nailed her lines. Improvised the funny scenes. She'd poured it all into that role and had the director and crew in stitches. She'd built an entire life for "Jennifer's Friend," right down to favorite ice cream flavor for break-ups (Chocolate Fudge Brownie). Things that would never appear onscreen but would nevertheless affect the way Eva approached every take. Her part expanded during an on-set rewrite and pretty soon, she was being added to *more* scenes.

Then production just … fell apart. The budget ballooned after filming a beach scene at an exotic resort ended up costing more than expected. A new director was brought in to clean up the mess.

And Eva's entire role was left on the cutting-room floor.

Her diary chronicling the fallout now sits in her suitcase, highlighted and pored over again and again to relive that horrendous pain. That feeling of absolute failure. The terror that her entire acting career was a waste of time because of this one incident. She'd kept the diary because, like any aspiring actress, she thought she would someday be able to tap into those dark feelings for another character.

Failure.

She thought hard work would turn her into a star. She thought her acting skills would be enough, that she would be different from the thousands of other talented thespians who have the exact same cliched thought. And after ten years, what has it gotten her? One major role discarded on the cutting room floor and a nationwide shampoo commercial.

This isn't just about finding Miriam. It was never *just* about finding Miriam.

Eva closes her laptop and smashes it against the corner of the dresser. She throws her dirty clothes everywhere because Sofia is a slob and isn't used to cleaning up after herself. She goes into the bathroom, fills up the sink with soapy water, and tosses a used pair of panties and socks in there, as if Sofia has just decided that doing laundry any other way is a waste of time.

She puts on the only outfit in her suitcase that she actually likes: a gray blouse and suit pant combo that she can wear over a simple black undershirt. It's the outfit she wore for the role of Assistant to the Board Director for a TV show on Netflix—mostly background work with a few lines in each episode. But this particular outfit was so comfortable and looked so good that Eva had to steal it. She matches it to a pair of black flats, her only spare shoes, then walks back into the bathroom.

She lays out her makeup case. Her hands are shaking a

little bit so she takes a deep breath, clutching the edge of the faux-marble vanity top. She looks into the mirror. The woman staring back isn't the same girl who left Carthage all those years ago. There's no more zits. The hair is no longer short and frizzy and streaked with whatever wild colors were on sale that month at Walgreen's. Here, in front of the mirror, is the only place where Eva prays. "Please God don't let me forget my lines," she says out of habit. Normally, she's sitting. Normally, there's a person on-staff to help with makeup. But Eva has been around enough sets to pick up more than a few tricks. Contouring the cheekbone, finding the line with a gentle smile. Mascara heavy around the eyes so that when she cries, it looks more dramatic. Powder caked on with haphazard taps of the brush so that in a few hours, it will begin to flake.

She thought it would be easy. She thought the Reverend would give up his secrets after a few scenes. But he's more dangerous than she ever thought.

So how far are you really willing to go?

"To the end," she whispers to her reflection. And if this is the last role she ever takes, then so be it.

15

Stakeout

MASON SITS at one of the tables away from the bar, next to a row of video slot machines. Nina Larsen sees him and brings over a Coke, then immediately jumps into a tirade about how the Milwaukee Brewers need to trade for a pitcher to get back to the playoffs. Mason is only half-listening, still thinking about the clothes he found inside the cavern this morning. One look and Mason knew it was all too faded and old to belong to Elliot Stone. Too random, too, as if the clothes—underwear, shorts, shirts—had been collected over time.

He turns his phone over so Nina doesn't see the photos he'd taken at the scene.

Robin walks in and takes a seat. She's changed into a flashy blue blazer and a tight skirt that reveals a pair of runner's legs. "Nina, do me a huge favor and bring me an iced tea." After the waitress leaves, she says to Mason, "This your secret hideout, detective?"

"It gets the job done." The Buccaneer Pub sits at the far end of Carthage's little commercial strip with a Wal-Mart, a Starbucks, a Lowe's, and a couple fast food joints. It's where the entire town of Carthage shops and gets a snack. The Buccaneer is for people who want greasy bar food. Mostly people coming to and from Kewaunee Lake.

"Owen Murphy," she says.

Mason's head immediately cycles through Owen Murphy's file. 43 years old. Convicted of child pornography charges. Released on parole, works construction part-time. Lives in the trailer park a few miles from Swamp Angel Road. "What about him?" he asks.

Robin pulls out her phone and turns it on, then slides it across the table. Mason picks it up, reading the text twice before it fully sinks in. "He worked for the Kane County Parks system? This is a pay stub. How the hell did you get this?"

Robin gives him a sassy look. Her cool emerald eyes betray a sharp intelligence. "Look at the date."

Less than a year before Murphy went to jail on child porn charges. "Holy shit, Robin. He would have had access to the shot tower. He would have had a key."

Nina returns with an iced tea. Immediately, the waitress launches back into conversation, complaining about the Indian casino while Robin listens with wry amusement. The blackjack is getting more expensive. She loves playing cards. If the Indians just hired a better chef they'd have her hooked for a lot longer. But she can't eat the shitty food they serve in the cafeteria.

"It can't be too much worse than this," Robin says, nodding to the nachos on Mason's plate. Grease and cheese have soaked them into mush.

The waitress laughs. "You'd be amazed at how badly someone can mess up spaghetti." She returns to the bar, underneath a hanging light designed to resemble an old-fashioned lantern.

Robin raises an eyebrow. "I might have to bring that one over to my side. I bet she hears all sorts of juicy gossip in a place like this."

Mason struck up a conversation with Nina when he first arrived in town. He'd almost written off the thirty-something waitress with the sad face, but he'd been so lonely and desperate for company that he'd made the mistake of asking her about local supper clubs. Then she'd sermonized for an hour, rattling off a dozen and ranking them by the quality of their fish fry and potato pancakes. He'd enjoyed every minute. She was like the friend-of-a-friend, a person you meet out for drinks who knows your world but only on the periphery.

It had helped him cope with the loneliness.

Suddenly, everyone's phones blare with an emergency warning. Mason looks around the bar. Some of the people in here are afternoon regulars. Lots of the same people who were here the evening the Amber Alert went off. It hit every cell phone in the pub, rising like a crescendo, each phone's musical role determined by carrier: Verizon first, then AT&T, then Sprint and T-Mobile. People looked at their phones, saw Elliot Stone's name, and went back to their food.

Now, they all glance at their phones to see a severe thunderstorm warning.

Mason pulls a twenty out of his wallet. "I need to take this pay stub to the sheriff. Between this and the kids' clothes, we could put the squeeze on Owen Murphy ..."

"Take me with you," Robin says.

"Not this time. I'll text you later."

She flashes him a mischievous smile. "I want something in return for all this free work."

He puts his wallet away. Immediately, his sleep-deprived brain thinks *sex*. If it wasn't so unethical, he'd probably say yes. She's an attractive woman and he's tired of sleeping alone.

"I want you to bring me a board game."

"Oh. Uh."

"Uh. Uh." She mocks him with a goofy face. "You think I forgot about your little confession at Russel Shot Tower? *Me*?"

"I mean, I could bring something if you're serious …"

"Make the first game easy. But fun. And magical—I like magic." She rattles off each demand on a red fingernail.

"Fine. You have my word."

She picks another nacho, grinning up at him. "Godspeed, detective."

Mason returns to his car and heads back to the government building in Carthage. Inside, he gives Patricia a wave and immediately makes a beeline for the coffee maker, refilling his travel mug even though the last thing he needs is caffeine. His head is rushing like it just received a hit of cocaine.

He interrupts the sheriff while he's eating a PB+J. It's the only meal he's seen Henderson eat for the past two weeks. "I hope you're not here to spring more surprises on me. I've already got a ream of paperwork to fax over to Milwaukee so we can test those clothes you found."

"Owen Murphy used to work for the Kane County Parks."

"No shit," Henderson says through a mouthful of bread. Jelly sticks to his teeth.

"Let me stake out his place for the afternoon," Mason begs. "If I can catch him violating his parole in *any* way, we can use it as leverage. Give me *one* afternoon, boss."

Henderson debates it while chewing, then waves him on.

Mason hurries to the locker room, grabbing the keys for the unmarked car that are hanging from the corkboard near the doors. His hands are shaking a little bit. This could be a break. This could be something.

The Toyota Corolla is a donation from an impound lot. It's old, not too reliable but Deputy Dave Williams' grease monkey of a brother has kept the engine running. Locals recognize it, which kind of defeats the point of an "unmarked car," but Owen Murphy's spent enough years behind bars that he probably doesn't know it exists.

It has Bluetooth, too. The philosophy podcast Mason has been listening to automatically turns on. He shuts it off.

He takes Highway G north to Swamp Angel Road, turning left, heading away from the Jenkins farm, the Cox farm, the Anderson farm, the Ramirez property, the Bauer farm. He stops at the intersection of Little Valley Road. The Stone property is tucked snugly in front of a sandstone bluff shaped like a crescent moon. Five miles away is the trailer park, nestled in a copse of pine trees just off Highway 15. The speed limit drops to 25. There have apparently been more than a couple nasty accidents involving cars and farming vehicles at the blind intersection.

Mason turns right at Highway 15, which cuts through a sandstone hill, exposing light brown waves of sedimentary rock stained dark by rainwater. He turns left on Pine Drive. There's a hundred Pine Drives in this fucking state and half of them lead to little trailer parks.

At the corner is an old bar called The Last Stop. Mason drives past it, past the driveway that leads up a little hill to the trailer park, and sees Murphy's green Honda parked outside his trailer. Just beyond the trees is a big farm with solar panels running along the road. Mason does a Y-turn and heads back to The Last Stop, parking behind the building. From this vantage, he can see into the trailer park while keeping the Toyota partially hidden.

Mason allows himself to get into a daze, half-watching. He did stake-outs sometimes when he worked for the MPD. The trick is to get in a zone, a fugue state where you're watching enough to catch the important stuff, but not so alert that your bored mind starts cannibalizing itself. It's easier if you have a partner who's not awful, a perk Mason never enjoyed. All his partner did was complain about how the entire world was against him, and the last thing he wanted was any blunt honesty. He just wanted a sounding board, someone to tell him he's right and everyone else is wrong. "Maybe skip the bar and spend some time with your family" was never the appropriate response to his problems.

Toby Williams. That had been Mason's partner. Constantly opinionating about everything, like he needed to apply captions to the entire world. Granny Smiths are the best apples. Fords are shit. Tom Brady is the best quarterback. Starbucks makes the best mochas. Asians are the smartest race. Being stuck in a car with Williams was like being forced to read the worst accounts on Twitter. But he'd covered for Mason the night of the incident. He'd lied for Mason because that was the brotherhood.

And then Mason had gone and fucked him over. Fucked over the police union, which had publicly defended him. Fucked over his chief, who'd gone out of his way to shield Mason from the press.

Mason stares at Owen Murphy's trailer, refusing to blink, frozen in the memory of the night of the incident. His eyes are so dry they hurt. But he refuses to blink. He can feel his heart pounding against his chest.

He should have been punished. Imprisoned. *Something.*

Mason knew what kind of man Toby Williams was, as well as he knew any of the other officers in his squad. He'd heard about other incidents, rumors of police abuse that never made news headlines. He still went out for beers with his *brothers.* He still partied with them on weekends. He befriended their families and attended their fucking weddings.

Mason grips the steering wheel. God damn him. Not just for the incident—for everything. For turning into someone so horrible. For trying so desperately to fit in. For calling them brothers.

And worst of all: for begging the forgiveness of a family he destroyed. For making a promise to them that he can never keep.

Across the road, Murphy walks out of his trailer carrying a trash bag. He puts it in the trunk of his green Honda and looks down Pine Road.

"Shit!" Mason ducks down. He knows immediately what's happening and knows exactly what he needs to do. He runs into the bar, pulling his badge from his pocket. The bartender is standing behind a dingy bar whose mirror is lined with old photos of the lead mine. Miners drinking at the bar. Miners playing a baseball game at Carthage Park with City Hall in the background. Liquor bottles are arranged in rows like a church choir.

"I'm taking your trash," he tells the bartender. "Don't tell anyone I was here."

"Can't imagine how it would pop up in conversation," says the man, pulling the white trash bag from a container behind the bar. He ties it off and tosses it to Mason.

Mason runs back outside, throwing the bag in the trunk. He starts the car and peels out of the parking lot. Murphy's already gone but Mason knows where he's going: the landfill up on White Hollow Road.

The philosophy podcast he's been listening to automatically turns on.

"When you surround yourself with people like you," says the host, "you become stuck in an echo chamber. You start to think all your beliefs are normal, no matter how wild. See, we think our brains are designed to find truth, but that's not true. Our brains evolved to keep us alive. Part of that is fitting into social groups. That's why cults can seem really looney to those of us outside that social group. But inside the group, especially if it's insulated from the scary outside world, strange beliefs and actions seem perfectly normal."

Mason's foot presses down on the gas pedal. He's going seventy down Pine Road, slowing just enough to take the winding turns as the road snakes around a rolling hill with contoured corn crops in neat little rows, curving like a crescent moon. The car's wheels hydroplane on the wet grooves in the road where heavy truck tires have worn down the asphalt.

"This can permeate any in-group," the professor continues.

Mason feels a little stab of ice in his chest. "New recruits enter the police force. To fit in, they adjust their beliefs to whatever the other officers believe. Maybe the other officers treat certain neighborhoods as a jungle. Some people with certain skin aren't trustworthy. They're dangerous. So to fit in, the recruit believes those things, too. And once you convince yourself that people of color are less than human, you start to *treat* them as less than human."

Mason punches the stereo to turn it off. He speeds over the next hill, then slams on the brakes. A stop sign. A horrible fucking stop sign that he nearly blew right through. His heart beating so fast that it *hurts*. He can see Murphy's car a mile ahead, crossing train tracks that lead south to the old lead mine.

Along the right side of the road, the limbs of oaks have been carefully groomed underneath electrical lines, forking up to the sky. Wind blows across the branches; leaves usher the old Corolla toward his target. His foot feels like lead on the gas pedal. He's a wild deer and his past is a hungry predator and if he just goes a little faster, he can leave behind forever his last night on the MPD.

"You're getting too close," he whispers.

He forces his foot off the gas and flips on the cruise control to maintain the space. He can smell the methane from the landfill. Murphy's car disappears around a forested bend in the road. Pines and oaks climb up a sprawling, unnatural hill. Around the bend now and Mason can see the flashy sign for the waste management company right in front of the turn-off. Murphy's car is winding its way up the curving road leading to the top of the landfill.

Mason's keychain clinks against the steering wheel around each turn up the landfill. His mouth is dry. At the top of the landfill, he can see how it stretches out flat, about twice the size of a football field. A parked bulldozer sits next to a white trailer with the company logo emblazoned across the side.

Murphy's green Honda is parked near the trailer. He hasn't gotten out yet. Mason gives him lots of space, driving to the other end of the parking lot. He parks, then reaches in his backseat for a Milwaukee Brewers baseball cap, then steals a side-glance.

The man is out of his car now, pulling the heavy white garbage bag out of the trunk. Mason gets out, glancing up at the black crows circling against a backdrop of gray clouds. He slowly opens his trunk, grabs the garbage bag. He walks a good fifty feet along the edge of the concrete parking lot with his back to Murphy. It smells like spoiled meat and the stench tickles his nostrils. Crows hop on garbage bags, ripping them open with their beaks. Beads of rainwater gather on plastic containers. A turkey vulture has taken a twisted pink doll's head in its talons.

Mason tosses the bag, scattering the crows. He walks slowly back to his car with his hands in his pockets. Murphy is already back in his car, pulling out of the lot.

Mason grabs a pair of vinyl gloves from the glove compartment, putting them on with shaky hands. Alone now on the top of the landfill, he runs to the place where Murphy was parked and searches the mounds of trash where the man had been standing. Rats and mice scurry. There's a white garbage bag, the only garbage bag not soiled and soaked by rainwater, the only one not already ripped open by vermin.

Mason pulls it to the edge of the lot and rips it open. This is it. He can feel it. There's a break in the heavy clouds; the sun beats down on the back of his neck and casts a shadow over the bag's contents. Take-out containers. A ketchup bottle. Plastic wrap. Rancid meat and rotten bananas whose smell turns Mason's stomach. Disappointment washes over him so hard that he feels his vision tunnel.

He sifts desperately through the garbage, flinging aside spoiled food and packaging for a shaving kit and cans of Mountain Dew and Burger King wrappers. There has to be something. He has to solve this case. He has to make things right. He has to square himself up with the universe and whatever God is watching.

Paper instructions for a DVD player. A package of gum. Used tissues.

"Fuck!" he screams, ripping the bag further, spilling mustard-stained paper plates and battery packages and an old, crusty towel. There has to be something. He needs this. He needs to bring peace to Elliot Stone's soul.

With tears in his eyes, Mason spreads out everything that's left. It's nothing. It's garbage. Plain old garbage.

No.

Wait.

In his fit of desperation, Mason had tossed the towel, partially unfolding it in the process. He feels a chill run down his spine, unwrapping the towel. He has to look at what he's found for a few panicked breaths, until his brain can fully register what his eyes are seeing.

A wet, wrinkled pair of boys' underwear.

16

Goodbye, Eva

EVA MISSES the sunset in Kane County. California's sunsets have nothing on the Driftless Area, where the sun can ignite fields of soy and corn with brilliant oranges as it dips behind sandstone bluffs, leaving long shadows that crawl over cropland. Even now, with most of the fields wet and empty, she can find beauty in the orange reflecting off standing water—little pools of glowing gold. She takes her car down familiar back-country roads that have become part of a new bike trail that starts in Fayette. It's another irony of the symbiosis between the two towns: these roads were initially paved for milk tankers. Now the dairies are gone and a white line has cordoned off part of the road for bikes.

She turns onto Badger Road.

It was UW-Fayette's agriculture department that went out and trained a new generation of farmers on proper cultivation methods. It was UW-Fayette that saved this region from its own greed and ignorance. A sign standing in mud advertises a new university initiative to re-forest the most flood-prone areas and preserve the remaining soil. Too little, too late, she thinks.

She parks at the gates of Trengrouse Cemetery just as a gentle rain picks up. Immediately, she sees the cemetery has changed: on the hill near her mother's grave, the dead oak's roots could no longer hold back the torrent of earth. Part of the steep hill to the east has been eroded, causing a mudslide that's buried some headstones and drowned others so the stone crosses look like claws reaching up out of the brown earth. Dead ash trees lay like the grief-stricken, prostrating at the foot of the hill. Gone are the Andersons, the Stones, the Heisners. Only the tombstone of Eva's mother stands untouched.

And across the path: the graves of the Jenkins patriarchs.

Beyond, there's more damage. The uneven ground has opened up like the jaws of a massive beast, swallowing a dozen graves. A few wooden caskets sit half-submerged in black mud. A corpse, nothing more than a skeleton wearing a tattered black suit, hangs out of one casket, an arm reaching for the edge of the sinkhole. Rainwater trickles over the edge, slowly eating away at the earth. These graves should have never been buried here. Now, the earth is reclaiming it all.

Except the Jenkins graves. And it's so unfair, Eva thinks.

She turns back the way she's come, awash in memories of a younger self in the cemetery practicing Goneril's lines for the Shakespeare in the Park production of *King Lear*. Those memories are bittersweet now; if she tries real hard, she can still feel the optimism that coursed through her after every nightly ovation. The impatience to leave this place and make her mark in an industry that chews people up and spits them out faster than Wilson's Dairy goes through heifers.

Eva understands why this cemetery is falling apart: Carthage is dying. And she knows why some people, in their desperation, turn to authoritarians like the Reverend. She understands why Sofia would, too, and what it would take for her to truly open her ears to the Reverend's God. All this time, she'd been treating him like a predator. Like a hungry wolf lurking in the shadows, eyeing up the weakest prey. But that's not what the Reverend is at all.

The Reverend is a *scavenger*.

She gets back in the car and grabs her phone to speed-dial her father's cell. Before she does what's going to come next, she needs to hear his voice.

"Sweetie?" he answers.

Eva smiles. "Hey, pops."

"How's the weather?"

"72 and sunny. You?"

"More rain coming. The good news is I'm the proud owner of a brand-new lake."

Eva laughs and pulls out of the cemetery parking lot, heading west. "Try to sell it as a tourist destination. Less pollution than Kewaunee Lake."

"It'd be nice for fishing." She hears the pain behind the humor in his voice. He can't hide that from her. He never could. She's so close to him and he doesn't even realize it. She wants to go to him, to bury her face in his chest, to smell his musky deodorant, to cry onto his old t-shirt and apologize. She'd promised to be a movie star. She'd promised him she would win awards. All she's ever wanted was to show him that all his love and support were *worth* it.

"Listen, did you ever hear anything more from that private detective?" she asks.

He pauses a beat. "No."

"Did he ever—"

"How's acting? Got any new gigs lined up?"

Failure.

Eva slows at the next stop sign and turns south. She never told him about her role as "Jennifer's Friend," about the pain and humiliation she'd gone through when it was cut. It would break his heart. He wouldn't understand. And there are only so many ways to explain to your supportive parent that you aren't good enough, that the world doesn't think you're as special as Mom and Dad thought. "Well, I didn't get a part in a TV show because they thought I looked too old to play a college student."

"They're idiots. All I do is watch TV and ask where all the good actors are. Your high school had a dozen better than all of them. Why is it so hard for these people to see real talent?"

Eva smiles. He would walk into a movie studio and say that to anyone's face if she just asked. "I do have a gig right now. A big one."

"Good. Tell me about it."

"I play a woman fed up with her job. A real down-and-out loser."

"You want me to fly out so you can practice with an audience?"

Eva laughs. When she was fifteen years old, she made him watch her favorite films. Wizard of Oz. While You Were Sleeping. Gosford Park. Fargo. He let her pause the movies over and over and over, acting out the lines of different characters while he pretended to be the director and demanded new takes. He always encouraged her.

It breaks her heart to hear the pain in his voice. The way he's trying so hard to hide it.

"My character hits rock-bottom at a casino," Eva says, composing herself before she can burst into tears. "She takes everything left in her bank account to the poker tables and loses it all when she hits a bad beat. They have to drag her out of the casino kicking and screaming."

"Sounds great. Make sure you beg for your money back. People always think that works but the casinos don't care."

"I will."

He chuckles into the phone. "I just re-watched the movie where you're the aid worker. I really liked it. You were the only actor trying in that movie."

It was nothing. Five lines in a single scene where she delivers some bad news about criminal activities on the U.S.-Mexico border, where asylum seekers had been denied entry into the U.S. She was typecast as a Mexican Red Cross volunteer, but damn it she made those five lines count. She wanted the audience to feel what it was like to risk everything for a new home. For a new life.

She takes a deep breath. "I'll … drop you a text when I'm done. I'll come and visit. Love you, Dad."

"Love you, too."

Eva hangs up, taking the next turn, squinting at the harsh light of the massive electronic marquee welcoming her to Kewaunee Casino and advertising special drink deals. This is it. No going back now. She parks and walks inside. Her nose picks up the scent of cigarette smoke and air freshener. The musical sound of ringing slot machines attacks her eardrums.

I'm going to find Miriam Jenkins.

And to do it, Eva will lose herself completely in the role. No matter the risks. Because the truth is Eva and Miriam's lives are intertwined now.

Even if Miriam doesn't realize it.

17

Warrant

MASON SITS with Sheriff Henderson and Deputy Tim Clark in the sheriff's office. They've got a plate of donuts someone bought from the bakery up the street earlier in the day. Henderson looks tired and frazzled—he hasn't left his office since the afternoon. Clark looks excited to be doing anything other than patrols.

It's nearly 10:00 p.m.

"Helluva day," Henderson mutters. He's mowing through a pair of jelly-filled donuts, the bakery's specialty. Stress-eating. "When will the underwear and clothes come back from the Milwaukee crime lab?"

"At least another day, maybe longer. Murder scenes take precedent."

"Fucking hell," Clark mutters. He's got a cream-filled donut, its powder gracing his upper lip. "We should get priority over gang-bangers, man."

Mason, ever the outsider, has chosen a chocolate cake donut. He takes a bite so he doesn't have to respond to Clark.

Henderson looks up at Mason. Jelly accumulates at the corners of his mouth. "You got a good feeling about this?"

"I did," Mason says. "When I found the underwear this afternoon." He sets his empty plate on the edge of the sheriff's desk, next to his table lamp. "But it was obviously washed. I can't say for sure the lab will find anything."

"Come on," says Clark. "We got a secret cave full of kids' clothes. We know Murphy worked for the Parks. And now we caught him throwing away a pair of boys underwear at the landfill. That can't all be coincidence."

"Is this normal pedophile behavior?" Henderson asks. "Keeping little trophies?"

Mason shrugs. Henderson grabs a third donut. He'll only eat half of this one. Mason has seen half-eaten donuts discarded in the sheriff's waste basket near the door. The man has some willpower, enough to sometimes beat back temptation. Probably why his name was never connected to the strip club scandal.

"When does that bastard work tomorrow?" Henderson asks Clark.

Clark pulls out a little notepad from his pocket. "He's doing construction on a house in the new subdivision going up in Fayette. That's a seven-to-seven job, for sure."

"If we wait for the lab report," Mason says, "and they don't find any DNA, will that make getting a search warrant more difficult?"

Henderson nods, mulling the options while he chews. Mason knows he's doing calculations in his head. Budget calculations if the search turns up nothing. Budget calculations if the search turns up something. How all of this will play out in November's election. He tosses the uneaten half of the donut into the trash can. "Boy, Will's gonna be pissed to hear from me."

"He should thank you," says Clark. "This might be his chance to put that pedophile behind bars forever."

"Yeah, yeah." Henderson grabs his phone. He uses his pencil's half-chewed eraser to dial the county district attorney's home phone number. "Hey, Will. I'm fine. You sleeping already? Oh. Is it any good? I don't have Netflix. Can I rent it at Piggly Wiggly?"

Clark nudges Mason's arm, flashing a smile. This is probably the most excitement Clark has seen in years. A chance to bag a murdering pedophile. It doesn't get much better than that.

"Listen, one of my guys found a pair of underwear," Henderson begins. He rolls his eyes. "Now hold on, let me at least give you all the details before you get mad."

Mason listens to the sheriff explain it all. Henderson's precise and ethical. No embellishments. If it doesn't fly, it doesn't fly. But the DA is OK with it, and pretty soon the two of them are back to discussing some movie before Henderson finally hangs up.

"Warrant will be faxed here at seven tomorrow morning," the sheriff announces. "Wait till eight o'clock and take the SUV. I don't wanna kick up any dust on this 'cause we don't have much without that lab report, and the last thing I need is Robin Wells at the *Courier* sniffing out another department fuck-up. Don't go trashing his trailer."

Clark grins. "You think Murphy would actually invite that bitch to sniff around?"

"I think if he's innocent, he'll be more than happy to give us one more headache. So be thorough and clean. Got it?"

Mason nods. He goes to the locker room and grabs his wallet and keys so he can go home and finally get a good night's sleep.

But when he gets back to the motel, he lays in bed, staring at the ceiling and wondering why the hell he has such a bad feeling in the pit of his stomach.

THURSDAY

18

Broken

SOFIA LAYS SOBBING at the entrance to the casino, hands pressed down on the hard concrete. It's 1:45 a.m. The Native American security guard is checking his phone and trying for the umpteenth time to smooth out his black blazer. Sofia had been clutching it for dear life when he dragged her outside. She'd screamed into his ear, shouting profanities first and then, as the entrance grew closer and closer, whispered promises of money just as soon as she gets back onto her feet. The incorruptible guard simply offered her a choice: leave or we call the police.

But Sofia couldn't leave. She'd misplaced her car keys.

A white truck pulls up to the entrance. Through wet eyes, she recognizes the hulking figure of the Reverend in the passenger's seat. His son Josh stays in the car, watching through the window.

Sofia runs to the Reverend and embraces him, squeezing hard. His one arm wraps tightly around her body. Sofia can't stop sobbing. She feels so safe now. Protected. Everything will be all right now. The Reverend will fix everything.

"It's all right," he soothes. "What happened?"

"I lost it all," she sobs. "They won't give any of it back. They won't give anything back!"

The Reverend gently guides her to the truck, helping her into the backseat. As he shuts the door, she catches her reflection in the window; black eyeshadow runs down her cheeks like malar stripes. She looks longingly at the casino. She could sell her car, maybe. Cash out part of her Roth IRA. Just enough to win back what she's lost.

The Reverend speaks with the Native American guard for a moment, then shakes his hand and returns to the car. "Well," he says, "the good news is you're banned from the casino. So at least *that* temptation is over."

"I threw it all away," Sofia sobs. "My entire savings on a FUCKING JACK-HIGH FLUSH!"

Her raised voice makes Josh so uncomfortable that the boy accidentally depresses the gas pedal while the car is still in park. He changes gears and pulls out of the parking lot. On the drive down Highway O, Sofia recounts what happened while the Reverend patiently listens. She was bored, so she took some money to the poker table. She started doing badly and withdrew more money, then she got caught in a big hand and she hit the card she needed for a flush. But it hit her opponent, too, and he had a higher flush. He went all-in. Sofia thought he was bluffing so she called his bet.

"And now it's all gone," the Reverend says softly.

"It's all gone," Sofia says. "There's nothing left."

"You were on the wrong path," says the Reverend. "And God put a boulder in your way to try and save you. Now, you have to make a choice. Do you follow the sound of God's voice, or do you walk around the boulder?"

"I follow the sound," Sofia sobs. "I follow it."

"Pull in here," the Reverend tells Josh, pointing to the Sunshine Motel up ahead.

Josh pulls into the narrow motel parking lot. The headlamps illuminate gentle drizzle pelting the pale stucco exterior.

"Grab your stuff," the Reverend tells Sofia. His tone has hardened. "Do it now while your head is clear and your ears are open."

Sofia gets out of the car and walks to room 5. She uses her keycard to unlock the door. She turns on the light, revealing the mess of a motel room, the world of a degenerate with no moral compass and no hope. She leaves the smashed laptop and grabs all her clothes, stuffing them into her suitcase.

There's a knock on the door. She turns, expecting the Reverend. But it's not him. It's the young man staying two doors down. Mason is wearing a pair of old shorts and a white t-shirt. "Everything OK?"

Sofia wipes her eyes. "I'm fine." Go away, she thinks. Go away, go away, go away.

"Leaving?"

Sofia gathers the mess of stuff laid out on the dresser. "Please. Just …"

Her ID falls to the floor. Mason picks it up and is about to hand it to her when he sees the name. He looks at her, wide-eyed.

"Oh my God."

"My name," she says, grabbing the card, "is Sofia Lopez."

Mason doesn't let go. They hold it together. Their eyes lock in silent communication, two telepaths hashing out an intense argument in complete silence. The air conditioner clicks on with an emphysemic whir.

"Everything all right?"

Mason rips the ID from Sofia's grip and turns. She breathes a sigh of relief as he deftly slips it under the waistband on his boxers.

"Deputy Mason Taylor, is that right?" the Reverend says. "Enjoying the Crossroads?"

Mason turns back to Sofia. "Are you *sure* you're all right?"

My name is Sofia Lopez.

"I know what I'm doing." She hefts her suitcase to the truck. Josh helps her get it into the backseat, pulling up his loose-fitting polka-dot pajama bottoms.

"Go to bed, deputy," the Reverend says. "Or have a night-cap at the Lounge with the rest of your law enforcement friends."

Sofia lets the Reverend's son toss the suitcase into the spare seat. She gets inside, feeling a chill pass through her body as soon as the truck's gears are shifted into Reverse and the locks automatically turn. As they pull out, the headlamps illuminate the young deputy's concerned face.

No going back now.

They drive back to the farm. Worms litter the road, retreating from the soggy soil, squirming in the harsh glare of the headlamps. Josh parks next to the house and gets out, hefting the suitcase from the trunk. Frogs songs ring in Sofia's eardrums. An owl calls out from somewhere in the dark. This valley is the end of the world, sitting on the precipice of infinite darkness.

"Joshy," the Reverend says, "We'll put her in the spare room."

Josh takes the suitcase inside, leading Sofia down the dark hall off from the living room.

He opens the door to the spare room. Pewter cats sit on the floating shelf next to the window. Pink sheets are pulled tight over a twin bed. Floral wallpaper covers the walls. Dolls sit on a bookshelf beneath a row of homeschooling textbooks. This was once a *girl's* room; it must have belonged to their daughter, Miriam. Sofia clutches a wet tissue in her right hand. Her puffy eyes hurt and her caked makeup feels dry on her skin. She can feel Josh's eyes on her, hot and confused and lustful.

She stumbles to the bed, collapsing and burying her face in Miriam's old pillow. She begins gently sobbing. Josh's heavy weight presses down on the bed. His hand rests on her back. "My sister cried sometimes," he says gently. "I never knew what to say so I just did this."

He keeps his hand on her back, gently, until she stops sobbing. Then he gets up, turns out the light and shuts the door.

Sofia holds her breath, listening in the darkness. The Reverend's voice carries down the hall: "She needs to work. Let her sleep in, then have her help you with chores. Wear her out so she doesn't have to think about all the bad things in her life."

"Is she OK?" Josh asks.

No answer. A shake of the head, maybe?

"Why'd she spend so much money at the casino?"

The Reverend sighs. "Because money poisons our souls."

"That's why you burn it?" Josh asks.

Sofia hears the Reverend's voice lower an octave in his answer: "That's why I would burn all of it if I could."

19

Brotherhood

DEPUTY CLARK PULLS onto the driveway leading up the hill to the little trailer park where Owen Murphy lives. The branches of tall pine trees loom over the handful of trailers, isolating them in every direction, their own little community. No families—otherwise, Owen Murphy wouldn't have been allowed to live here. What secrets do his neighbors carry?

8:13 a.m. Judging from the empty parking lot, Murphy is definitely gone.

Mason shifts in the passenger's seat. He pulls the ID from his pocket. The California driver's license belonging to the girl from the motel. The *imposter*. He stares at Sofia Lopez's real name, plays out their first conversation in his head. She said she was looking for someone. Miriam Jenkins?

Deputy Clark pulls off his sunglasses. "I'm using the battering ram."

"You'll piss off the sheriff."

"I'll take the blame. It's fine. Seriously, I'll even tell him you told me not to."

Mason wonders if Clark has something on Sheriff Henderson. Given what Robin told him about her investigation of the strip club scandal, it seems pretty likely that Henderson learned the whole story. It would have been the only way for him to limit the fallout. Mason suspects that the sheriff chose a few fall guys, probably urging them to protect their fraternal brothers by falling on the sword to keep the scandal from embroiling the entire department.

They get out and walk up to the front door of Murphy's trailer. Mason pulls out his notepad, checking the address one last time. Raindrops plunk onto the paper, absorbing quickly and smearing the ink.

"All right," he says, and steps back as Clark slams the steel battering ram into the door. Only he puts too much of his weight into it—the damn thing is just a flimsy trailer door, after all—and he goes stumbling inside, landing hard on the floor. Mason helps him up and hands off a pair of vinyl gloves.

The trailer is immaculate. The sink is clean. The carpet has fresh vacuum lines. The furniture—a sofa, a coffee table, a TV stand, and a recliner squeezed into one corner—is all mismatched, but in OK condition. A blanket covers the sofa. Mason pulls it away and checks the dirty cushions. They smell pretty bad, hence the blanket cover that's clearly been doused with lemon-scented air freshener.

"Huh," says Clark, opening the handful of plywood cabinets under and above the sink. "I was expecting a mess. Maybe a few squirrels in cages and shit."

"Squirrels?" Mason asks, running his hands underneath the TV stand.

"Creepy killers always keep squirrels."

Mason walks into the bedroom, tearing off the bed covers, going through every drawer of Murphy's IKEA dresser. It wobbles a bit every time a drawer is pulled open. He takes his time here, looking for anything that doesn't fit Murphy's XL size. He pulls out each drawer, checking the back and inside. He checks under the bottom.

Nothing.

They search the carpeting for loose spots, reach above the window blinds, lift the mattress and the sofa and the recliner. A black grease stain on the carpet under the recliner. Mouse turds under the sofa, along with a few spare coins. Mobile homes have tons of hiding places; Mason got up early this morning to research it so he was prepared.

He checks inside the spring bar for the toilet paper roll.

He checks the bag inside an old, upright vacuum.

He checks the spaces between the cabinets.

He removes the toe-kicks.

He checks behind the framed family pictures on the faux wood-paneled wall.

Mason feels a burning anxiety in his chest, tight and sharp. It's the same feeling he had at the landfill when he hadn't yet found the pair of underwear. Only now it's getting worse with every minute that passes and they find nothing. Doubt sets in. He was wrong. He was so obsessed with finding the killer that he let his own biases get the best of him. Murphy's a child porn addict who did his time. Doesn't make him a killer.

He checks the couch again, unzipping the old cushion covers and reaching his hand in.

Nothing.

"Here we go," Clark says.

Mason turns excitedly, then his heart sinks.

There, sitting on the coffee table, is a little baggie of heroin. Clark, kneeling on the floor, waves his hand like a magician.

"You found that? In the coffee table?" Mason asks.

"In the drawer."

"I checked the drawer."

"So I looked again," he says, exasperated.

"We're looking for evidence of Elliot Stone. That's what the search warrant says."

He points to the baggie. "We can seize everything he owns with this. *Everything.*"

The white refrigerator hums in the silence. Mason feels a chill run down his spine.

"There won't be prints on there." He doesn't know how Clark might react to a full-on confrontation. Appeal to reason first. Try to convince him to change his mind. Again, the brotherhood thing. This obsession with protecting Clark even though what he's doing is dirty.

"Murphy can't win with a jury around here," Clark says confidently. "He'll fess up if he killed the Stone boy."

Tell him he's dirty.

"What if he didn't kill the Stone boy?"

"Then it's one less pedophile fuck in our neighborhood for ten years."

"His lawyer will bring up the strip club scandal. They'll attack your credibility."

Clark taps his chest and smiles. "I've already made peace with my wife, man. I can't get in more trouble with her no matter what gets out. Hell, the fact that I would lay it all on the line to put a creep like Murphy behind bars might actually get me off the couch."

"They'll bring up *my* history," Mason says. "Murphy won't even need a high-priced lawyer to get off. He'll be able to represent himself and still get acquitted."

In Clark's eyes now grows something dark and unbending. "I'm not just thinking about the Stone boy. I'm thinking about my own two kids, man. We put this guy away and we're heroes to every parent in the county."

"I won't lie," Mason says. He's proud to hear conviction in his voice, even if he's terrified of how Clark might react.

"Fine, don't lie. Keep your goddamned mouth shut and let me do the talking."

"I'll tell the truth."

"Fuck you!" Clark shouts. He grabs the baggie and throws it at Mason. Mason tries to duck but the baggie hits him in the shoulder. Powder lands on the carpet, on his uniform, on the corner of the coffee table, coating it like chalk.

Mason holds his breath while it settles in the air. He can feel his heart thump against his rib meat.

"You're a fucking *killer*, Mason." Clark bares his teeth. His face has gone red as a beet. "And you have the nerve to make *me* out to be the bad guy here? Putting away a pedophile should be a no-brainer!"

Mason's mind races a mile a minute. He wants to wipe the heroin off his uniform, but if he makes any sudden movements, he thinks it's a 50-50 shot Clark will take a swing at him. He can imagine them struggling on the floor, dispersing the heroin everywhere, sticking to their sweaty skin.

"This is your fault," Clark says, pointing to the white powder laying atop the carpet. Mason imagines they're same words he spoke to the exotic dancer he abused, setting off the chain reaction that ended with Mason's emergency hire.

"Call it in," Clark says. "That's all you gotta do. I'll handle the rest."

Mason takes a hesitant breath. "I'm not calling it in."

"Fine. Good luck explaining all this." Clark grabs the battering ram and gets up, kicking the broken door as he leaves. Mason, shocked, listens to the SUV start up, the tires grinding on wet gravel.

His shoulder radio crackles to life. "Dispatch, I've got a bad case of food poisoning. Mason needs a pick-up at the suspect's place of residence."

"This is Sheriff Henderson. I'm on my way, Mason. Hold tight."

Mason doesn't respond. Head swimming, he walks quickly to

the little closet just off from the kitchen. It's full of junk, already rifled through. Mason grabs the little red vacuum and plugs it in, using the lift-away function to carefully vacuum his uniform and hair and neck. He runs it slowly across the old coffee table. Then he reattaches the roller and goes over the carpeting, following Murphy's pattern, thorough but quick.

His heart races. Clark has fucked him royally here. He's a hypocrite through and through, just like every other officer who uses the bonds of "brotherhood" to manipulate. Maybe that's how Clark survived the stripper scandal. Maybe he gave the sheriff a sacrificial lamb.

Mason detaches the dust bag, then puts the vacuum back. He takes the bag outside and walks around back, where the trailer park butts up against a forest. He walks fast under the tallest pine trees, listening to birds chirping above. Wind rustles raindrops from the needles. He goes a good two hundred yards, swatting mosquitoes the whole way, and finds a decent-sized rock. He lifts it up, digs into the soft soil with his fingers, then deposits the dust bag in the hole.

He pulls the ID from his pocket. He looks at Eva's photograph, how different she looks from Sofia Lopez. He knows why he let her go with the Reverend. He's not yet sure if there's a connection between the Reverend's daughter and Elliot Stone, but he knows for a fact Eva will have an easier time finding answers than him.

"Good luck, Eva."

He tosses the ID in the hole. He kicks soft dirt over it, then returns the rock to its place.

Instead of going back the way he came, Mason heads south to the road. The sheriff's SUV pulls up beside him. "Where were you wandering off to?" Henderson asks after Mason gets in.

"Blowing off steam."

"So nothing?"

"Not a goddamned thing. You talk to Murphy?"

"Yeah. I told him I had some deputies searching his place. Told him about the underwear we found."

"He seem surprised or no?"

Henderson shrugged. "Not especially. Said he bought 'em from Target. Spur of the moment thing."

That's pretty specific, Mason thinks. Which means it's either the truth, or it's scripted. "He sound embarrassed?"

"God damn it, I dunno. I've never asked a grown man about boys' undies before." Henderson stops at the intersection to Highway O, then turns east toward Carthage. "I told him about the cave with the clothes. Told him we know he worked for Kane County Parks before he went away on child porn charges. He just shrugged."

Mason's cellphone buzzes. He pulls it from his pocket, looking hard at the text message, reading it twice to be sure. "Test came back. Underwear's clean. No DNA on the clothes from Shot Tower Park."

"Damn!" The sheriff pounds the steering wheel. "This felt like our break, didn't it?"

"Sorry, boss."

"Not your fault. So you didn't find anything at all? Nothing out of place?"

"Nothing. Listen, I know you don't want me hassling Edgar Ramirez ..."

"Damn right I don't."

"But I think we need to eliminate him from the list of suspects. There's a dent in the front bumper of his truck ..."

"Mason, let it go."

Mason turns to him in alarm. "What do you mean?"

"I mean you're working yourself to death. Coming to work like a zombie on no sleep. Investigating off the clock."

"Elliot Stone *can't* have disappeared without a trace."

"You know how much this investigation put us in the red? Two fucking weeks and we've used up all the overtime I budgeted for the entire year. You know how hard it is to convince people around here to *voluntarily* raise their taxes so my department can have just a little more money?" Henderson sighs. "I promise I'll keep coordinating volunteer search parties."

"At least let me ask Edgar about his truck—"

"God damn it, leave Ramirez alone!"

"You just want his support in November!"

"You're God damn right I do! I love this job and I'm sure as shit not gonna lose it just because some Indian boy decided to run away!"

"You're going to lose it because your officers were fucking strippers!"

The sheriff pulls over onto the side of the road. He turns to Mason and reaches out.

Mason flinches. Henderson sees something on his neck. The heroin. Mason missed something. He hasn't had a haircut in over a month—a few flecks of white powder probably stuck to his neck hair. Henderson pulls his fingers back. He's clutching something small and black between his thumb and pointer finger.

A dog tick, its little legs squirming.

Henderson squeezes it until the juices sluice out of the body. He fixes Mason with a hard glare. "Be careful out here. It's more dangerous than you think."

20

Fresh Start

SOFIA WAKES to the sound of knocking at the door. She sits up, discombobulated, unable to shake the feeling that she's still in her condo in Milwaukee. But no—last night wasn't a bad dream. She's lost the last of her savings. Not only that ... did she really have a total meltdown and get kicked out of an Indian casino? Holy shit.

"Come in," she mumbles, keeping the pink bed sheets up near her shoulders. Her head hurts; she always gets such bad stress headaches after playing poker.

Josh pokes his head in. "Hey."

"Good morning," she says, embarrassed to be here, in this alien bed. Embarrassed he saw her crying last night.

"It's noon."

"Oh." Sofia's impulse is to check the clock on her phone, but she's left it in her suitcase, turned off, and she's only wearing panties and her black t-shirt. It was so hot last night, even with the window open. The soft pat-pat of raindrops on the storm screen and the chirping of crickets lulled her to sleep. She dreamed of poker chips shuffled between fingers.

"The Reverend has chores for us to do. I mean, you don't *have* to help, but then he probably won't let you stay here. Idle hands are the Devil's workshop, he says."

"I'd rather help than lay in bed feeling sorry for myself. What are we doing?"

"I have to feed the calves." He clears his throat and looks away from the bed. "You got jeans?"

"Yes."

"Better wear 'em."

"OK. I'll be right out." She waits for him to shut the door, then crawls out of Miriam's bed. She grabs a pair of jeans from her suitcase and slips them on, then puts on a white t-shirt and her sneakers. She takes a moment to search Miriam's dresser drawers for a hairbrush. The young woman's clothes are very neatly folded, but the dressers aren't very full. Just enough missing to pack a suitcase. But where is she? Sofia wonders.

She lets her hands slip between the clothes, setting aside a flowery dress, moving pairs of white, cotton panties. No make-up box. No style magazines. No *dildo*. Her fingers brush over a piece of paper, folded tight, hidden inside a pair of panties. Sofia unfolds it, curious, and reads it:

How can you promise you'll protect me? Where will you take me? How will you hide me? I won't live inside my whole life with the shades drawn, living in constant fear. I won't give up the sun. You showed me so much, and I'm both grateful and angry. I'm grateful to have seen it and experienced it. I'm angry because it's a world in which I can never live.

Sofia folds it and puts it back. The melodramatic letter was obviously written to an admirer. Not her business, and now that she's read it, she feels guilty. She's always been a little bit of a snoop—her mother's influence. Her mother always gossiped with friends every Sunday after Mass, much to the priest's chagrin.

Still. This is a strange room for a woman in her late-twenties. The wooden chest at the end of the bed, decorated in an assortment of My Little Pony stickers, opens to reveal old toys awash in pinks and purples. It's as if Miriam had decided one day that all the artifacts of her childhood were no longer valid, sweeping them into the box. Frilly, hand-crafted pillows with Gospel passages elaborately stitched across the surface sit on a crafting table underneath the windows overlooking the soggy backyard. A long, framed picture of a giraffe hangs on one wall. A bookcase made of old wood rests against one wall. A cabinet with two doors sits on the bottom, and inside are cloth dolls. Some of the dolls look new, others look a decade old or more.

Enough snooping.

Sofia goes to her suitcase and grabs a twisty tie to put her hair back in a ponytail. That will have to do for the day.

Josh is waiting for her in the kitchen with a cup of coffee.

"I thought you might need it," he says. "Even though it's lunchtime."

"Thank you so much," Sofia says. "I don't normally sleep so late, just so you know."

"Good afternoon, Sofia!" Tina calls from the dining room.

Sofia peeks her head in. Tina and her mother are sitting at the dining table. Spread across the surface are hundreds of family photos, most in grainy black and white. "Hi Tina and Wilma."

"Well, how about this?" Wilma says with a smile. "It's … it's so good for you awake."

"Look, Ma," Tina says, sliding a picture in front of her mother. "This is you and your brother on a horse-drawn wagon."

"Into town," Wilma says with a laugh. "It's … the horse. We brought corn meal to the badgers."

"That's great. Stay here, Mommy." Tina gets up and walks

into the kitchen. Her bright smile warms Sofia's heart. "Sweetie, have a seat. Let me make you a little breakfast."

"Oh. Uh, that's not necessary. You've already done so much …"

"Nonsense. If you're going to help Joshy all day, you'll need your strength."

Sofia adds cream to her coffee and drinks it fast so it burns her throat like a red-hot poker. She likes her caffeine to hit her like a bullet in the brain. Poor innocent Josh, a bit flabbergasted at the sight, puts the empty mug in the sink. They wait while Tina fries up a pair of eggs and microwaves a few strips of bacon while she hums to herself. It's the happiest Sofia has seen her. Tina brings the plate of food into the living room; Sofia follows while Josh stands like an awkward teenager in the kitchen.

Tina watches Sofia eat for a few minutes. Then Wilma begins shifting in her seat, groaning as if in discomfort.

"Here, mommy," says Tina, sliding a picture across the table to Wilma. It looks like a black-and-white photo of Miriam, sitting on a swing next to a pig the size of a small car.

"Is that *you*?" Sofia asks Tina incredulously.

Tina nods. "And my pet pig. That was before I ran away to Baraboo."

Sofia frowns, glancing at Wilma. "She ran away?"

"Joined the circus!" Wilma exclaims with a laugh. "Wild, her. I always tried."

Tina rests a hand on her mother's, rubbing gently along the bubbling blue veins. "You did wonderful, Ma."

Sofia eats her meal, looking at the photos, feeling the headache ease. When she's finished eating, Josh leads her down into the basement. There are clothes hanging on hooks next to a little cubby with towels and soap. The clothes smell like shit. The basement is cluttered with furniture, boxes of tools, an old sink, shelves of canned sauces, a hundred old vases and lunchboxes and jars and enough Christmas ornaments to fill out a market stall.

On the workbench are two boxes full of money. Cash. A pair of brass collection plates sits on top of them. Just the sight of it—probably close to ten thousand dollars in large bills—is enough for Sofia to conjure delusions of grandeur. If she just had an hour at the poker tables with this money …

Josh goes to the little cubby to grab a pair of manure-stained rubber boots. While his back is turned, Sofia grabs a stack of the cash and stuffs it in the back pocket of her jeans.

Josh points to an old wooden door on the other end, next to a white washer and dryer set with rusting edges. "That door leads out back. I'll meet you in a second."

Sofia goes through the door, up concrete steps and out the back door. Outside, it's warm and muggy. It rained again during the night; the pool of standing water in the backyard is so deep that only the very tips of the blades of grass are breaching the surface. Frogs and toads croak madly. A hungry crow sits perched on a low branch of the oak tree. Beyond the farm, beyond the valley, rain pulls down black clouds like the roots of a diseased oak.

Sofia gently rubs her puffy eyes. She looks at the barns behind the house, wondering how many cows there are, wondering how she's going to get her life back on track. This is crazy, being here. And yet the thought of going back to Milwaukee and her horrible life is so terrifying that she can't even consider it.

Josh joins her wearing his work clothes, shutting the door behind him. "This way."

They walk toward the barns. The stench of wet manure hangs thick in the air. To their left is a big building with a massive white garage door. "What's in there?" Sofia asks.

"Used to be for big farm equipment. Now the Reverend just parks a few old cars in there. He buys them at estate sales sometimes. That's where we get all our stuff."

"Ah! That explains all the mismatched furniture."

Josh gives her a curious look. "Is it ugly?"

Sofia shakes her head emphatically. "Nah. Your dad and mom have good taste."

They reach the driveway. It's wet and slathered with brown shit and straw. To the right is a sort of half-barn. The roof is held up by old wooden creosote posts. The heifers are held in by sheets of corrugated blue metal with rusted holes. Some of the sheets are bent and hanging at awkward angles so that a few of the ladies can poke their heads through and nibble at stray weeds.

Josh calls the building a loafing shed.

Behind a row of cobbled together gates stand dozens of big cows, watching. They have brown fur; some have white spots. They moo when they see the humans.

"What kinds of cows are these?" Sofia asks.

"Jerseys and Guernseys," Josh says. "You can tell the Jerseys because they usually have black noses and black eyeshadow. Guernseys usually have pink noses."

Sofia holds out a hand. A Guernsey with big ears ambles over and sniffs with her pink snout.

Across the driveway is a long, brick building. There are round, metal fans built into the exterior along the top. Josh opens the door and leads Sofia inside. There's an open space in the center of the building, and four stalls on either side divided by wire fencing attached to metal posts. Feed panels run along both sides.

No. Sofia wouldn't know what they're called.

Metal headlocks run along both sides. Twelve adorable calves congregate in each stall, some already standing near the headlocks on knobby legs, others relaxing on fresh straw toward the back.

"Oh my God, they're ridiculously cute," Sofia says. "Please tell me we're going to feed them."

Josh's expression brightens. "Yup."

They walk around a pair of pallets stacked with milk substitute packaged in heavy bags. At the other end of the open space in the center of the building is a hot water heater. To the right of the heater is a white sink. Sitting on a shelf above the sink are a dozen red pails. To the left of the water heater is a workbench with a notepad and tubing and antibiotics in little white bottles and a small, green cabinet full of strange-looking tools.

Josh turns on the hot water and grabs the hose attachment. He uses it to fill a large, white bucket sitting next to the pallets. He points to an open bag of milk substitute. "Eight cups of powder, and hot water to the black line. Mix with a whisk until all the powder is dissolved."

"Got it, boss." Sofia gets to work, scooping powder into the bucket of water. When she's counted off eight, she grabs the whisk sitting next to the open bag and starts swirling the powder around in the water. Lingering chunks dissolve quick, turning the water an opaque white. It smells sweet, like a protein shake.

"Oh!" Josh says, slapping his head. "Always add water first, by the way."

"So the powder doesn't stick to the bottom?"

He grins and nods. He gets the twelve red pails down from above the sink and lines them up in front of the first stall's headlocks. Twelve pails. Twelve headlocks. Twelve calves per stall. "An even amount in each pail," he says. "Calves stick their heads through the feed panels, then you lock them."

Sofia hefts the bucket over, grabbing it from the bottom and carefully pouring an equal amount of the milky liquid into each pail. Josh sets them under each feed panel—not "headlock," as Sofia had thought of them. The calves frantically position themselves for the milk—all but one, a shrimpy Jersey who can't seem to find the last empty spot and instead tries to squeeze between two Guernseys who are already greedily sucking from their pails like little pigs.

"Watch this," Josh says. He holds out a hand. The rogue calf's mouth closes around his fingers, sucking wildly. Josh leads her around the others, to the last empty headlock. Once she sees the pail, she immediately lets go of his fingers. "My grandma taught me that."

"Gross, but awesome." Sofia watches him lock the panels. "Another round?"

He nods. Sofia brings the bucket back to the pallet and uses the hose to refill it. She starts counting out the scoops of milk substitute, trying a little on her finger when Josh's back is turned. It doesn't taste like sugary milk. It tastes *salty*.

"Do you like baking stuff?" he asks.

"My ma was a good baker," Sofia says. "She used to make this porridge bread that was so thick and dense and flavorful, you didn't even need butter."

"Women are always good cooks." Josh pulls the pails sitting underneath the second group's feed panels. Half are filled with grain pellets, half are filled with water. He dumps all the water into another bucket and takes it outside, spilling it onto the driveway. Then he refills the pails with fresh water. "My ma cooks for us every night. Sometimes, she cooks for other families in the congregation, too. I want a wife someday who cooks."

The first stall is done with its milk treat, but that hasn't stopped the calves from lapping at the bottom of the pails with their tongues. Josh removes the pails while the calves strain their necks to get one last lick. Sofia fills the pails with more milk substitute. Josh puts the pails underneath the second group's headlocks.

The sound of wet slurps fills the burn.

"I like your mother's food," Sofia says. "That dinner the other night was great. Not too salty. I'm really used to restaurant food, and it's always too salty."

"My sister always said my mom's food needed *more* salt."

"I guess, if that's your taste. But trust me: it gets old. Sometimes, it's all you can taste on the food. Even in the soda."

Josh's eyes widen. Sofia realizes he thinks she's serious. "Sorry! That was a joke."

"Oh." His face reddens a bit. He forces a laugh and takes another bucket of old water outside. "I've never been out to eat at a restaurant. The guys on the football team always thought that was weird, but the Reverend says it's a waste of money."

"You ain't missing much," Sofia says. She laughs at the calves as they desperately slurp at the last few drops along the bottom of the pails, then toss the pails with their snouts. One, after giving up, begins sucking on the ear of her neighbor. The one whose ear is being sucked just stares up at Sofia with a look of humorous resignation.

"That's a Guernsey," Josh says. "You can tell from her pink nose, see? They're super dumb. If I was a cow, I'd probably be a Guernsey."

"Josh!" Sofia gives him a look of indignation. "You're running this entire operation single-handed! No dumb person could do that."

The boy smiles shyly and returns to collecting the old water from the pails. Sofia fills another bucket of milk substitute, inhaling the sweet smell through her nose, watching Josh toss the water out the front entrance. She thinks he could probably skip dumping the old water, not spend so much time liming the runny shit in the stalls and a dozen other little things, but Josh cares about their comfort. Every group gets slightly different treatment. Every group gets Josh's attention.

"They're so freaking cute. Did your sister ever help you feed them?"

"No. She had to babysit all the kids in my dad's congregation. That was her job."

"Oh. Well, babysitting is fun, sometimes."

Josh chuckles. "Not with those kids. They're all really retarded."

Sofia frowns, but lets the comment go. "She must have baby-sat Elliot Stone, then."

Josh uses his foot to sweep away grain pellets that have fallen under the pails. "Yeah, she was pretty good with him."

"Does Miriam ever come visit?"

Josh grabs the pails for the next group. "No. You can prep another bucket of milk replacer."

Sofia gets back to work on another bucket, scooping more of the sweet-smelling powder. She hopes she hasn't upset him. She's being too curious, maybe. Digging into a family situation that she doesn't understand and making Josh uncomfortable. The Lopez family habit of snooping.

She decides to change the subject. "My ma made good pies."

"What kind?" he asks, immediately interested.

"Apple. Peach." She brings over the bucket for the third group, pouring into the empty pails. "Sometimes cherry. Only after Mass, though. It was like a present for getting through church."

"Why's yours called *Mass*?"

"Different versions of Christianity have different names for stuff, that's all."

"But isn't that weird? There's only one God."

Sofia steps back, watching the older calves naturally form a row, each selecting a panel without any assistance. She doesn't really have an answer for Josh because she was never all that religious growing up. Especially after her mother passed away.

"Why do you lock their headlock thingies?" she asks.

"Helps them get comfortable and familiar with the panels," Josh explains. "When they're older, they need to be calm while the cow fucker—I mean!" He slams both hands over his mouth, his face turning a crimson shade of red.

Sofia bursts into laughter, doubling over. "Cow fucker? *Cow fucker*? Who the hell is the cow fucker and why is he not in prison?"

"Please don't tell my dad. Please, please don't."

Sofia shakes her head. "Absolutely not. Josh, you have no idea how much I needed that." She laughs again. "Please tell me that's just a nickname or something!"

"It's the breeder," Josh explains with a sheepish grin. "His name's Steven. He's actually a really nice guy. It was my sister's joke, I swear it."

"I believe you, don't worry. Just be glad you're not Catholic."

"Why?"

She preps another bucket of formula. "Well, because Catholics believe in confessing their sins. You sit in a little closet and you tell a priest all your sins and then he has the power to forgive you. Can't keep secrets or you'll go to Hell."

"Do *you* believe that?"

Sofia thinks about the question as she whisks the powder into the water, creating a whirlpool. The last few chunks of formula dissolve as they swirl downward. "I used to."

They finish feeding the rest of the calves. Sofia notices the group in stall five has horns budding, but none of the others do. They're the oldest and the friendliest, letting Sofia scratch behind their ears and play with the little tufts of hair on their heads. One is bug-eyed and reminds her of Lisa Simpson, the cartoon character.

Josh leads her back outside. Puddles gather where the concrete has been pulverized by the wheels of heavy farm machinery. Chunks of broken concrete have been tossed next to the calf building.

"Another storm coming," Sofia murmurs. "God, I hate this rain."

"Farmers are gonna be mad," Josh says.

"How much can crops handle?"

Josh shrugs. "Depends on how well the land drains. It's already pretty bad in some places. Let's go take a look."

She walks with him along the north group feed panels, to the vehicle shed just beyond. Josh makes a note on the whiteboard about one of the calves—"1832 lethargick, 1878 thrush," he writes. Then he grabs a pair of binoculars from a shelf full of tools that includes a case for a revolver.

Sofia wouldn't recognize what's in that case.

She turns away from the vehicle shed and gives Josh a wry smile as he fiddles with the binoculars. "Spying on your neighbors? I totally approve."

Josh blushes. "I like to watch the hawks." They walk around the south group, to a large hill of wet dirt. They climb to the top, where they can see miles and miles of land stretching out across the valley. "Look at that!" he exclaims, giving her the binoculars.

Sofia looks through. An entire field of winter wheat is drowning in standing water. It runs right up to a white house, engulfing the picket fence and part of the yard. "Wow, that can't be good. What can they do about it?"

"Wait for it to dry out and drain. Nothing else to do."

Sofia glances down at the two smaller dirt mounds to her right. One looks fresh; the other looks older, more settled and covered with knee-high grass. "What are those?"

"Composting mounds. We should get back to work or the Reverend will get mad."

He teaches her how the skid steer works. Sofia watches him dump dry silage along the north group feed panels; cows walk over and find a place to stick their heads through. Josh shows her where *not* to take the skid steer: the moat of manure around the silo. He tells her he once fell in and got soaked from head to toe. Sofia's getting used to the sweet, pungent smell of the wet manure that's been tracked everywhere by the skid steer's wheels; it's smellier near the moat, though.

"Can you drain the moat?" she asks.

Josh shakes his head. "There's too many chores that need to get done. My grandma just kinda let the farm go to heck before her stroke. I think she wanted to be done with it."

"It's probably hard to watch your family farm go under," Sofia says gently.

"Go under?"

"You know … like, *die.*"

Josh takes a deep breath and looks down. He doesn't like talking about his grandma. Sofia makes a mental note of it as she walks ahead of him with a broom, pushing silage as close to the feed panels—and the hungry cow snouts—as possible. Josh follows behind her, locking the panels after the cows poke their heads through. The steel stanchions squeak.

By the time they're finished locking the north group's panels into place, the cow fucker arrives. His stereo is blaring classic rock. "Hey, Josh," he says with a friendly smile.

Sofia raises an eyebrow at Josh. He blushes and grins at their secret. "Hey, Steven. This is Sofia. She's helping with the chores."

Steven turns to Sofia, grins, and clasps his hands together. "Oh, right! I think I saw you at the Bible study on Tuesday."

"Sure," she says, pretending not to remember his ugly face.

"Glad you're helping out Josh. This is too much work for one person." He slips on a pair of long, plastic gloves, then grabs a white tank from the back of the truck. "How are Wilma and Tina doing today?"

"Good as can be," Josh says.

"Wilma and I used to shoot the breeze every day," Steven tells Sofia, setting the tank of bull semen next to the gate. A mosquito lands on his forehead and he swats it absently, leaving a smear of blood on his acne scars. "Wilma had a great sense of humor. She used to take her horse around the county and stitch up clothes in exchange for eggs and meat. Told me the quality of her sewing work depended entirely on what the farmer was willing to trade."

"That's wild," Sofia says with a grin. She likes hearing stories like that. Suburban families don't cultivate those kinds of stories.

"I'm gonna get a bunch of fencing repaired while Steven

helps spread manure," Josh says, taking Sofia back around the other side of the silo. "Maybe the two of us can shore up all the weak spots in the west group's pen. If you don't leave, I guess."

"I'd be happy to help," Sofia says. The prospect of making long-terms plans feels good.

They walk around the last remaining silo, giving the manure moat a wide berth. The south group watches them approach. There's a feed bunk blocking an old vehicle entrance, locked in place with a heavy chain. Off to the side is a pile of manure sitting next to an old ditch choked with prairie grass and wildflowers. A big cube of hay sits next to the feed bunk. Together, Josh and Sofia break up the hay, which peels apart in thick pads. The hay is packed tightly together, Josh explains, and the cows will have trouble digesting it like that; Sofia uses her hands to rip it apart. It reminds her of tearing apart shredded wheat cereal with her fork.

It isn't until they're done that she sees the old pitchfork resting on the ground, half-buried underneath a wet pile of hay. Sofia decides not to say anything in case the oversight would embarrass Josh.

"Four buckets of grain," he says. "Two in the bunk, and two inside."

Sofia goes to the stainless steel grain dispenser outside the calf barn. She fills two buckets and carries them back to the south group, maneuvering around the manure-stained puddles. Not that her sneakers aren't already soaked with shit, she thinks. They're not great shoes anyway.

She dumps the grain pellets over the hay, then goes to get two more. She's begun sweating. The buckets' broken handles dig into the soft skin of her fingers. Their weight strains her shoulders.

Josh opens the gate for her. She sidles past a couple curious Guernseys, walking underneath the shelter of the loafing shed where a floating feed bunk sits, half-full of hay. Here, under the shelter, she can smell the acrid stench of urine and shit. She has to walk very carefully, because the manure is piled up and mixed with straw for bedding. She could very easily lose a shoe.

The moment she pours the grain over the hay, the rest of the cows gently swarm her. She laughs, nearly slipping on the manure as she gets out of the way.

"Were you serious about the whole confession thing?" Josh asks when she comes out. "Is it really that easy? You confess, and then you're forgiven?"

"Yup."

His lower lip trembles. He blinks a few times, then looks up at the encroaching dark clouds. "We got one more thing to do before it rains."

Sofia follows him back to the vehicle shed. Sitting on one of the hay bales in the back, he's got a tray of milk and little milk bottles laid out. Carefully, he removes a square pad of hay. There, sitting inside a little niche, are two adorable raccoon cubs.

Sofia feels her heart melt. "Josh, where the hell did you get them? They are literally the cutest things I've ever seen!"

"Sometimes baby raccoons hitch a ride in the hay," Josh says. "I try to save them when they're separated from their mom. It … it never works, though."

"I'm going to help," Sofia states, gently petting one of them on the top of the head. They're adorable beyond words, right down to the black shadows around their beady little eyes. "It's funny how a cute, helpless animal can change your mood like a switch, isn't it?"

Josh smiles and gives her a voracious nod. He preps a bottle and gives it to her. She feeds the coons one at a time, laughing as their little hands reach out and clutch the bottle with a human-oid intensity. They're hungry and anxious to play. Sofia and Josh tease them with straw, poking their furry bellies.

When the coons finally get tired, Josh very gently puts them back in the niche and puts the square of hay back in place. They can get out if they really want, but they're safer out of sight for now. "My grandma used to pay a guy to come here and set raccoon traps on the farm," he explains. "Once they were caught, the guy would just shoot 'em. The gunshots would wake me up in the morning sometimes."

"They're too cute to kill," Sofia says. "When they're older, I'll help you find somewhere we can release them. Someplace safe."

She walks back down the row of north group feed panels with Josh, angling her hips because the stack of stolen cash tucked under her waistband is pressing uncomfortably into her stomach. Steven has finished, marking the inseminated cows with a pink symbol on each haunch. Josh unlocks each of the panels as they walk back down the driveway and the cows quickly pull back from him. Again and again, they all react the same way, all down the row.

They fear him. They're afraid of this sweet, shy boy.
But why?

21

Magic

ROBIN LOOKS SUSPICIOUSLY at her cards. Behind her, The Buccaneer's hanging pirate skeleton watches over her shoulder. They're sitting in the corner booth near the front window. A neon Miller Lite sign hangs above them. Stuffed parrots—real at one time—line a shelf in dignified repose, serving as an audience for the battle taking place on the table.

"Take your time," Mason says. "Read carefully what each card does."

"And I have to tap these cards," she says, pointing to three land cards laid out on the table next to their half-finished plate of fajitas, "in order to cast a spell."

"Yeah, that's the idea. The lands contain magic called *mana*. Do you have any land cards left in your hand?"

Robin raises an eyebrow. "Should I really reveal that to you?"

"Well. We don't have to get super competitive yet."

They're playing *Magic: The Gathering*. He thought it would be better to start here before he brought in any of his more complicated board games. Plus, *Magic* games go quick; they can play a few hands before he has to start his shift tonight. So far, he's used his available cards to cast two creature spells. Robin killed one of them with a fireball spell, and she took great pleasure in its destruction.

"I'm done with my turn," she says cryptically, giving him a cute, mysterious look.

Mason draws a card from their shared deck. Usually, players each have their own deck of cards filled with magical spells, but this simplifies everything for the first go-round.

He sips his Roy Rogers. The grenadine is overly sweet and perfect for a warm, humid evening. Enough sugar to keep him awake through the night shift without any extra coffee. "This is good. Wasn't looking forward to stopping at Starbucks tonight."

"I thought you always get a cup of iced coffee before your night shift."

He's surprised, as always, by how much she knows. "I do. It's just …"

"They know about what you did?"

Mason looks up from his cards. Robin's got a good poker face. A pretty poker face. There's something so very *Wisconsin* about the way a blue neon beer light illuminates a pretty woman's features. "I don't know for sure. Maybe I'm paranoid."

"You *are* paranoid. But not wrong. Some people have heard about it."

He'd bet anything it was Deputy Clark who spread the word. "I'm surprised I'm not fired yet. I'm done with my turn."

"Mase, half of Carthage probably likes you *more* for it. Henderson's probably keeping you around because it makes him *more* electable." She draws a card and lays down another land. She turns all her land cards sideways to draw magic from them and casts a creature spell. A wyvern.

Mason draws another card. It's an enchantment that will grant his creature extra armor. He casts it on his goblin. Robin watches him with studious concentration, eyes narrowed. Scheming how to kill him. "I'm done with my turn," he says.

Led Zeppelin comes on through the digital jukebox.

Robin shifts her body, examining him with her cards fanned in front of her face. "OK, so can I ask you a tough question? For my story."

"I can't stop you."

"Why'd you do it?"

"We got a call to investigate a suspicious person in one of the parks in downtown Milwaukee. It was late at night. I approached him cautiously. It looked like he was pulling something from his pants. I assumed it was a gun."

"No, but really, *why* did you do it?"

Mason takes a deep, shaky breath. "Because I worked with some bad people who saw the world in a very black-and-white way. I wanted to fit in. I had to. Guys who didn't fit in got pushed out fast. It's like, you had to assume this war mentality. Like, the ghetto is a jungle and you can't let your guard down. If you don't think that way, you're putting your fraternal brothers at risk." He shuffles the cards in his hand, pretending to look them over so he doesn't have to meet her eyes. He can still remember that night, the way he felt. He'd been sure the man had been pulling a dangerous weapon. But when he lay on the ground, bleeding to death, Mason could see clearly that it had just been a bottle the man had dug out of the trash can. He was collecting bottles for recycling money.

"That's how I rationalized it, anyway." Mason curses himself for confessing such deep thoughts. It'll all end up in a news article, he's sure.

"I'm attacking you."

"It's fine." He sips his Roy Rogers through the little straw. God damn it, what was he expecting? That this was a date or something?

"No, I mean I'm attacking you. With my worm thing."

"Oh! OK, I'm going to block with my goblin. He's got stronger armor than your wyvern's attack, so …"

Robin lays down a thunderbolt spell. "I'm dealing two extra damage to your goblin."

Mason forces a smile. "You killed him. Congratulations."

"Your turn."

He draws a card. "So what about you?"

Robin eyes him cutely. "What *about* me?"

Mason summons another creature. A little orc that can do one unit of damage. "Come on. You could have gotten a better job by now. You're a damned good journalist. What drove you to stick around here for so long?"

She grunts, crossing her legs as she draws a card. "Small-town newspapers are dying. It's bad, Mase. Without local news, all these people," she waves her cards around the pub, "lose their community. Pretty soon, they're getting all their news from Facebook."

"So what?"

Her eyes pierce him, serious and sharp. "Now you're starting to sound like a journalist. Are you sure you never heard what happened to me?"

"I swear it," Mason says.

Robin sighs and sets down her cards. "A friend of mine was raped my senior year in high school."

Mason looks at her. He doesn't let a single muscle in his face change. His friends in the MPD had no problem being racists, but when it came to a woman's "purity," at least a white woman's purity, they always took it seriously. They taught Mason how to show respect and compassion. At the time, he'd deluded himself into thinking deep down, this was proof they were good people. Honorable. Now he looks back and sees something far more twisted.

Robin smiles. "You look like you're holding in a shit, Mase. I'm done."

"Sorry." He draws another card, thankful for the opportunity to scan his hand. Nothing to do. No spells to cast. "I'm done. Did the police know who did it?"

"Oh, that was easy. It was the tight end for the high school football team. Problem is, no one believed her."

"But a rape kit—"

"No one *believed* her, Mason." She draws a card, lays down another land, then turns her land cards sideways and summons a demon. "Town newspaper wouldn't even write a fucking story about it. Like it never happened. So guess what bright-eyed little Robin Wells did?"

"She wrote a story." He lays another land card. "I'm done."

"You're damned right she wrote a story. Front page for the high school newspaper. No permission from teachers. Did it in the dead of night so no one could stop me. Distributed it in the lunchroom like a fucking newsie. I'm attacking you with my demon."

Mason nods and takes the damage. "So what happened?"

"I got expelled from school. Had to get my GED during the summer with all the dipshit drop-outs. Rapist graduated with honors. The girl he raped? My *friend*? Killed herself a few months later."

"I'm so sorry, Robin."

"That's OK." She wipes a tear from her left eye, looking out the window overlooking the parking lot. Rain pours in streams from the eaves. "Not like it fucked me up or anything. Just kidding of course it did. Not like I think about her every day. Just kidding of course I do."

Mason casts another creature spell. This time, it's a rock giant. "His name was Tramon Perry."

"Who?"

"The young man I killed." Mason wipes tears from his eyes. "My union tried to cover for me. They put out this press release—I'll never forget it—that listed Tramon Perry's arrest record, as if that somehow justified my fuck-up. My partner lied for me and said he saw a weapon, too. I couldn't take it. It all felt so fucking wrong."

"So you publicly apologized." Robin grins. "I have to admit, when I read about all the backtracking the department and the union had to make after you did that … it was pretty impressive."

"I'm done."

Robin draws a card. "Ever say that to yourself? When you're alone?"

"Every day for an entire year after the shooting. I was staying with my parents, sitting alone in my childhood bedroom, just thinking about it." Getting out his old board games, using the old rules he'd devised to play them alone, just like he'd done as a lonely child.

"What's the point in doing all this?" she asks, waving her fanned cards around. "Knowing no amount of good you do will actually change anything in the long run?"

Mason thinks about the Stone family. About Tramon Perry's family. "It changes things for some people."

She laughs bitterly. "I tell myself I go after these dark stories because I want to expose the truth. But sometimes I think I'm just trying to force people to care."

"Go ahead and kill me already."

Robin attacks with her monsters. Mason can only defend against one with his rock giant. The demon gets through unblocked, dealing lethal damage.

"So that's it?" she asks.

Mason shrugs. "I used to think adulthood was a static thing. You are who you are. And after what happened in Milwaukee, I hated who I was. So I've been trying to change ever since."

Robin smiles. "I mean was that the end of the game?"

"Oh. Yeah." He chuckles. "Killed by a demon. What do you think?"

"I think my little brother played this game for, like, ten years."

She finishes her glass of ice water. "And I remember asking you to bring a *board* game. So you'll have to try again."

Mason can't suppress a smile. "Deal."

Robin's phone buzzes. Mason holds his breath as she checks the text.

"Edgar Ramirez just showed up at Sal's Pub," she announces. "Ordered a beer."

Mason pulls up directions to the pub on his phone. It's tucked on a back road off Highway CC. "I've never patrolled that section of highway on a weekday."

"If he sticks with beers, he'll be there till bar close."

"Perfect." He lays out a ten and a five on the table for the waitress. Good enough for the fajitas, soda and a tip. Robin's hand reaches out and grabs his.

"Mase. If you go after Edgar Ramirez, Sheriff Henderson will *definitely* lose the support of the Chamber of Commerce. Are you *sure* you want to do this?"

"We didn't find anything at Murphy's trailer. Ramirez is the only lead we have left."

"Maybe it really was a random abduction," she says. "Or maybe we're wrong and Elliot really did just run away. You could let this go."

"I *can't* let this go."

"I won't write the exposé about you," she says, her eyes pleading. "You don't have to put your job at risk. Look, I can tell you're a decent cop—"

"It's not about my job." He gets up. "It was never about my job."

22

Fire

THE EVENING FEEDING starts at 10:30 p.m. The calves have eaten well all day, so Sofia orders Josh to go back to the farm and get a good night's sleep for a change. He puts up a little fight, but she demands it, promising to feed the raccoons before she comes back in.

Once the calves are fed and everything is cleaned up, Sofia steps outside into the cool night. The moon is a sharp scythe, harvesting chafe. Cows in the north group are already huddled in the loafing shed, laying on bedding of manure and fresh straw. She walks behind the demolished silos. The heifers in the south group are young—after the calves are a certain age, they're moved from the calf barn to the south group. Josh sets up gates to lead the confused and frightened calves out of the barn without any possibility of escaping down the old, overgrown ditch. He promised to show her one day.

"It must still be hard," she'd said earlier tonight, "when something goes wrong. Without any help."

"My mom helps sometimes," he'd responded. He doesn't like

to complain. He doesn't know how. The Reverend has taught him that toiling is good for the soul.

"I hope your sister comes back soon," she'd said innocently. But Josh had only nodded and continued dumping out dirty water from the feed pails. He was distracted all afternoon, and Sofia started to wonder if maybe he misses his sister, wherever she is.

Now she's reached the end of the row of dismantled silos. Here, on the west end of the farm, is a pole barn to her left, piled high with bales of hay and a pile of sweet-smelling silage. Just in front of her is the west group, and off to the right of that is a much smaller pen full of pregnant cows ready to be transported to Wilson's Dairy. Between them are two composting mounds, monuments to Josh's failures. This isn't precisely true, Sofia thinks, but it's obviously what *he* thinks.

Sofia walks around the sludgy manure gathering at the end of the west group's headlocks, a massive pile waiting to be spread as fertilizer onto neighboring fields once the winter wheat is dry enough to harvest. She enters the vehicle shed and grabs the nursing supplies. She mixes water with formula powder into the smallest bottle. She twists on the second-smallest rubber nipple, then gently removes the layer of hay that Josh has set in place.

The racoon kits are safe. Covered in their own shit, but safe.

"Here," she says, gently pulling them to the front of the bale so she can set them on the green shop towel.

Sofia wouldn't know how to clean them.

She gently wipes their fur with the towel. "Gross," she tells them. "So gross. You're lucky you're cute."

She bottle-feeds them, lets them play around on the top of the hay for a while, then tosses them back into their little niche. She replaces the square of hay and walks across the open area to the feed shelter. Beyond the towering stacks of hay bales is an acre of CRP land, all natural prairie and chirping crickets. Past that is a sprawling, unnatural lake drowning feeble rows of corn seedlings. This valley is beautiful. A few towers of rock jut up from the earth like chimneys, off to the northeast. The seclusion offered by the sandstone bluffs makes Sofia feel safe. It helps her forget about the rest of the world.

She walks back down the gravel path between the south group and the silo foundations. It's obvious that someone had attempted to dismantle the foundations with some kind of jack-hammer, but gave up after hitting an intimidating cement-and-stone mixture. A possum skitters past her just ten feet ahead, disappearing into the tall grass. She walks past the calf barn, examining the old gas pumps sitting at the end of the driveway where it forms a cul-de-sac. There's a worn path over here, lead-ing through tall grass on the north end of the calf barn. Sofia, enjoying the night, decides to take the path.

It takes her past the burn pile, which she and Josh had set ablaze in the afternoon using a few gallons of diesel fuel. There's nothing left but some melted bale twine and the coiling metal skeleton of an old mattress, a few coals still releasing thin curls of gray smoke. Farther east is a fallow field belonging to the Cox family. Fireflies blink off and on, a million stars in a sea of ink.

Sofia follows the path back toward the Jenkins house. The grass is high back here, along with weeds and tree saplings taller than Sofia. Nature has reclaimed an old milk parlor, now noth-ing more than a crumbling concrete foundation and old stalls made of rotting, waterlogged wood. Sofia recognizes it from the black-and-white photos Tina had laid out for her mother on the kitchen table. A single sheet of aluminum siding is still connected in one spot and Sofia has an epiphany: this building was taken down and repurposed for the other shelters. Wood reinforced rotting joists in the vehicle shed. Aluminum sid-ing patched holes in the roofs of the loafing sheds. The way of empires that conquered empires.

The path takes Sofia around the rear of the shop garage.

Here, in the moonlight, she finds something interesting. Next to a door that looks as if it hasn't been used in ages, are *drawings*.

Sofia crouches low to examine them better with her phone light. The drawings were made with markers on a strip of white aluminum paneling. Spaceships and astronauts and a few monster aliens with green tentacles. The astronauts are flying in the spaceship in one picture and in another, they're shooting at a green alien with a laser pistol.

Sofia thinks at first maybe they're drawings made by Josh, but no—the astronauts are *women*.

Did Miriam want to be an astronaut?

The last drawing is of the spaceship safely landing back on Earth. There's something curious about the picture: the trees are all pines. Sofia remembers visiting family when she was young. She remembers travelling south and seeing different ecosystems: the urban landscape of big cities, the sprawling deserts of Texas, the tropical swamps of Florida. She remembers drawing these places so they looked like the places she'd visited.

When Miriam drew this, she knew about astronauts and space ships. But she didn't know about Cape Canaveral, where NASA is located. She didn't bother drawing palm trees, maybe because she assumed pines grew in abundance everywhere.

Maybe because Miriam has no family outside the Midwest.

Stay in character.

She stands up and continues down the exterior, noticing more drawings of varying styles, most cartoonish except for one that's exceptional in quality. In this one, a boy with brown skin and long, black hair is standing next to a grain silo, holding an axe. Sofia is sure this is Elliot Stone, which means he probably drew this at some point when Miriam was taking care of him. It looks newer than the other drawings, the marker colors not yet faded by the elements. At the bottom of the grain silo, orangish-brown grain is flowing out of a hole.

The silo Jon Anderson died in.

As she nears the corner of the building, she sees a warm, orange glow lighting up the fresh-cut grass. She walks tentatively closer, turning and realizing too late that there's a little fire next to the house. The Reverend is standing in front of it with a cardboard box by his feet. He sees her immediately.

"What are you doing?" he asks sharply.

Sofia points over her shoulder. "I got done feeding the calves, and I noticed a path around back. I saw the old milking parlor."

"Our dominion over nature is always only temporary."

His eyes are red-hot coals, beckoning her closer. He reaches into the box and pulls something out, holding it up for her. It's a brick of money. Fives and tens and ones, fanned out like a deck of cards.

"What's this for?" she asks.

He chuckles. "Kindling. Courtesy of Henry Stone, born again into God's light."

She looks at the money, then down at the cardboard box. It's one of the boxes of cash she'd seen in the basement. "You're going to burn all of it?"

The Reverend nods slowly. "I don't do it during the day. You never know who's watching and this is technically illegal."

"But why?" Sofia asks. "I don't understand. You could donate this. Or use it to help people with flood damage."

"Did you know that people survived before money was invented?" The Reverend smiles, tucking his right hand behind his back. He walks around the flame; it's caught a heavy pine branch, doubling in size quickly and crackling like popcorn as the needles catch fire in a flurry of golden sparks. "People bartered and exchanged goods and services and charity and favors. My grandmother used to pay for her doctor's visits with half a hog." He laughs at the memory and stops behind the fire, the lines in his orange face thick with shadow. "Now, you can't go to an emergency room without being charged a hundred dollars for two aspirin."

"But there must be thousands of dollars here," Sofia says. "Think of what you could do—"

"Does having this money mean I'm *good*, Sofia?"

"No," she says angrily.

The Reverend steps out from behind the flame. "But God *rewards* good people, right?"

"Some of us," she admits. Somewhere on the farm, the barn owl calls out over the crackling flame. It sends a shiver down her spine. She moves closer to the fire to be in its warm light. To ward off any raptors lurking in the darkness.

"So here's my money," the Reverend says, motioning to the cardboard box. "Here is the proof that I'm a good person. Or wait!" He smiles and snaps his fingers. "Maybe God told Henry Stone to give me his nest egg as a reward for all my hard work bringing him into God's light! Maybe this is simply God's *blessing* to me. Maybe this is just the will of God and who am I to question the will of God?"

"I don't know if you earned this or not," Sofia says.

"I didn't. These," he says, pointing to the pile of money, "are simply promissory notes that indebt us to the Devil. I am the terminus of the prosperity gospel."

He tosses the money into the fire. Individual bills catch, flittering up in the heat.

"Now it's your turn."

Sofia's heart skips a beat. He knows. Of course he knows. *You wanted this.*

She pulls the bills from her back pocket. She's conflicted. She spent five years in college learning how important these paper bills are to keeping society running. She used to move millions of these paper bills around with a few clicks of her mouse. She gained money and she lost money, but she never once saw any money *destroyed*. It feels wrong.

"I know why you took it." He lowers his head. Firelight dances in his glistening eyes. "You think it'll bring you salvation. Just one more turn at the poker tables. Just one more bet. But the outcome never changes, does it?"

Sofia looks down at the stack of money. "I …"

"Free yourself," the Reverend urges.

She tosses the money into the fire. Because she trusts him.

And as she watches the faces of the presidents blacken and burn away, she feels *good*.

The Reverend tosses more money in. The ink produces little flashes of green inside the orange flame. Sofia takes more from the box, crumpling up the bills and throwing them in the center of the fire. The smell of the flame changes, growing heavier and tangier. She feels a surge of excitement, laughing at the sight. It feels better and better the more money she burns.

When it's all gone, the Reverend takes a deep breath. He's standing so close to the fire that sweat is beading on his forehead. "The truth is, I don't know if God favors me. All I know is that God works through me, and I serve him, and I'll do anything to protect my congregation from making the same mistakes I've made."

Sofia watches the black ashes of a twenty-dollar bill flit apart and lift into the air. She's stunned by the conviction in the Reverend's voice. The assurance that courses through him. He *knows* what's right. He knows how to live his life.

"Go to bed," the Reverend says.

Sofia, suddenly cold, faithfully obliges.

FRIDAY

23

Stakeout

MASON PARKS in the gravel driveway of an old farm at 12:20 a.m. on Highway CC, far enough away from Sal's Pub to be inconspicuous, but close enough to clearly see the parking lot.

Then he waits.

He stares at the bar's neon Miller Lite sign, thinking about what the young woman who calls herself Sofia. What is she really trying to discover on the Jenkins farm? Part of winning *The Deadliest Night* is anticipating which suspects are willing to give up information. Mason can visualize the question cards in his mind, applying them to different members of the Jenkins clan. Wilma would be unreliable because of her stroke. The Reverend would never talk. Tina would submit to her husband's will. Mason has already tried questioning Josh, and it amounted to nothing.

But what about Miriam, their daughter? It seems unlikely that there's a connection to Elliot Stone, but …

Mason decides he'll give Eva the weekend to sneak around as this Sofia character. Then he'll pull her out. See what she's learned. If the Reverend believes her story, she'll get a helluva lot farther than Mason ever could with him.

Mason flips through the file on Owen Murphy for the umpteenth time. This is the guy who should be the most likely suspect.

And yet.

Inside the file is a copy of the Wal-Mart receipt that Murphy provided to the sheriff. Murphy's credit card. One pair of boys' underwear. Proof that what Mason found at the landfill had no probable connection to Elliot Stone. And no DNA evidence on the old clothes found under the shot tower.

The only lead left is the dent in Ramirez's bumper.

At 2:10 a.m., Edgar stumbles out the front door. Mason watches him walk to the familiar white truck. It starts up and backs out, pulling east onto Highway CC, toward Carthage. Mason waits a few nervous breaths, then pulls out and follows him.

"I'm not pulling you over without cause," he says aloud. He's already decided this. He needs real cause. No, he doesn't need it. He *wants* it. He wants to play this by the book.

At first, Ramirez drives perfectly well. But then the truck begins to list right. Two wheels get all the way to the crushed gravel embankment and for a moment, Mason worries the truck might end up right in the drainage ditch.

Last chance to call it off. Find another way that won't piss off the sheriff and ruin his political aspirations.

Mason flips on the lights. The truck pulls over, stops, then pulls over some more and stops again. Mason turns on the spotlight and gets out, walking to the driver's side window.

"Morning, Edgar. License?"

Ramirez hands it over. His eyes have the sunken dead look of a drunk, his pupils practically floating. Mason goes back to his car and radios it in.

"Ramirez?" comes Clark's voice. "Oh, I'm so on my way."

Mason relays his location for Clark, then walks back to the truck. "Been drinking, Edgar?"

"A little," he mumbles. "You need eggs? Ladies laid some more eggs yesterday."

"Maybe in a week. Can you step out of the car? I need you to do a field sobriety test."

Ramirez curses and pops open the driver's side door. He stumbles out and walks with Mason to the back of the truck. Mason points to the white line along the edge of the road. "One foot at a time, please. Arms out wide." He demonstrates, holding his arms out like the wings of an airplane.

Ramirez gets two steps, then stumbles. He tries again, tipping precariously to the left and right. His white tennis shoes don't even come close to staying on the line.

"You're going in," Mason says.

"Fuck you," Ramirez mutters. The "U" comes out "uuuuuuu." He reaches into his pocket. Mason, heart racing, puts a hand on his gun.

"Get your hand out of your pocket!"

"I just want a cigarette," Ramirez slurs, pulling his empty hand away. His glassy eyes squint in the SUV's spotlight. "How'd you even get another job after you murdered a guy?"

Mason doesn't answer. Come on, Clark. For maybe the first time ever, Mason actually wants the shitty deputy around.

"Should I be scared?" Ramirez asks. His face twists into a menacing look of defiance. "You kill black folks but what do you do to Mexicans? You call us *spics* behind our backs, like everyone else in the sheriff's department?"

"Grab a cigarette," Mason says, rubbing his eyes. "Before Clark gets here."

Ramirez pulls a pack from his pocket and lights a cigarette. At the very least, it shuts him up for a few moments. Mason feels a drizzle of raindrops land on his head. Ramirez takes a long drag, longer than anything Mason has ever seen before.

When he exhales, the smoke comes out thick and heavy like the vapor of an e-cigarette. "You know Clark's gonna rough me up."

"Then you shouldn't have …" Mason stops. The comment came out so naturally that it disgusts him.

"What?" Ramirez asks. "Gotten drunk? I can't *not* drink."

"You have a good remodeling business. You have kids."

"You don't know what it's like to not belong." He takes another long drag, nearly enough to cash the cigarette. He exhales. "I have a cousin who's illegal. Lived in Carthage for twenty fucking years. Ran that café on Main Street everyone loves. One day ICE came and took him away, just like that." Ramirez spits on the ground. "Everyone was upset for a week. Couldn't believe nice Mr. González was an illegal. Then, his business got picked up for cheap by some retired dentist motherfucker. Didn't even have the decency to change the menu. Just reopened the restaurant, like my cousin never existed."

"I'm sorry," Mason says.

"At least you got balls," he mutters, taking another long drag. "Sheriff thinks I got power because I'm with the Chamber. Truth is I *had* to join. Only way for a Mexican to be taken seriously around here. They don't actually give a shit about my opinion."

Mason says nothing.

"Take me in." Ramirez finishes his cigarette and tosses it in the ditch. "Don't let Clark do it. I'll be lucky if he even gives me a pillow tonight. Let me at least sleep it off in comfort."

"I'll check on you," Mason promises. Another pair of headlights illuminates them. Deputy Clark parks behind Mason's squad car. He walks over with a big grin on his face.

"Henderson's gonna lose his mind when he hears you did this."

Mason zip-ties Ramirez's hands behind his back and reads him his rights. "Mind taking him in?" he asks Clark. "I'm dying here. I need to get a coffee somewhere."

"BP station on 15," Clark says automatically. So he *is* good for something after all.

"Thanks." Mason goes back to his SUV. He waits until they're gone, then grabs the portable black light and field kit from the passenger's seat. It's begun to rain a little harder now; he hurries to the front of Edgar's truck. The dent is still there on the bumper. Up close, Mason can see that it was once deeper, but someone's tried to hammer the metal from the inside, creating crescent marks like fingernails on flesh.

Mason crouches and turns on the black light, shining it across the front of the truck in one long, sweeping arc.

Blood.

Remnants of it, at least.

Mason turns off the black light function and turns on the flashlight, holding it in his mouth while he rifles through the field kit for a tweezers and magnifying glass. Slowly, he pans the magnifying glass along the truck's grill. Up close, he can see some of the fins are damaged and slightly bent, but clean.

He has one more idea. He opens the driver's side door and unlocks the hood. He reaches inside, behind the grill, searching slowly with the magnifying glass. Having the flashlight in his mouth is activating his salivary glands something fierce. He needs to manage his drool so it doesn't land on the grill, just in case.

Just in case …

There, near the bottom. Stuck where the grill is mounted with a pair of screws: hair. Mason grabs it with the tweezers, his hands shaking. He carefully bags it and returns to the SUV.

The rain picks up on the drive back. Water flows over the road in places where the drainage ditches have eroded. The headlights illuminate the eyes of a possum scuttling near the shoulder. Tree limbs shudder in the wind, leaves dancing.

Mason pulls into the parking lot for the Kane County government building and parks near the rear door, unable to stifle the twinge of excitement. He takes the hair sample to the DNR lab on the second floor. Technician Greg Williams is sitting in his office, watching a TV show on his computer and eating a little bowl of red grapes. He glances up when Mason enters. "I want two cases of beer for this. I skipped trivia night, man."

"You ever win?" Mason asks, handing over the bag.

"That's not the point." Greg takes the bag and leads Mason into the lab, turning on the bright halogen lights. They sidle up to a high-powered microscope and put on vinyl gloves. "Moment of truth," he murmurs, setting the hair sample under the microscope.

Mason watches, his fingers nervously fiddling with his belt.

"Blood evident," Greg says. He gently moves the slide, then adjusts the scope. "Right, so this is definitely not human hair. It's fur."

Mason exhales. "Deer fur?"

"Probably." Greg rubs his eyes. "I hope this was worth it. Can I go to bed now?"

Mason walks back downstairs, unlocking the storage room door next to the stairwell. He grabs a pair of pillows and walks down to the drunk tank. Ramirez is laying on the cot, curled up. Mason unlocks the door and hands over the pillows. Ramirez mumbles something that sounds like "The forest."

Mason crouches down. "What?"

"Why you go after me," he mumbles. He drools a little onto the bench. "Go after the kids partying."

"You said the forest," Mason says. "Are you talking about the forest near your house?"

"They always party there," Ramirez says. "Making noise all summer."

"When?" Mason asks. "Edgar, think: did you hear someone in the forest the night Elliot Stone went missing?"

"Just their lights," Edgar murmurs as he fades. "I saw their lights."

24

Horns

SOFIA WAKES AT 7:40, twenty minutes before Josh. She knows there's breakfast food in the fridge. She knows how to scramble eggs. It was one of the dishes her mother made really, really well. Sofia remembers learning with her mother standing beside her at the gas range.

"The trick," Sofia tells Josh when he stumbles into the kitchen, "is slow heat. Good morning."

He looks down at the yellow mixture in the frying pan. "You got the eggs from the fridge?"

"No, there's a chicken out back."

His eyes widen. Sofia inwardly cringes; she forgot he doesn't catch on to jokes.

"Just kidding!"

"Oh." He chuckles. "That's pretty funny."

"Then you want to gently fold …" She tries to demonstrate, but the soft mixture breaks apart into chunks when she tries to fold it with her spatula. "Whoops. Well, normally I use a non-stick pan."

Josh brews them a pot of coffee. Sofia finishes the eggs with a dash of salt and pepper.

"Any problems with the calves last night?"

"Everyone was good," Sofia says. "I finished in time to catch a break in the clouds. The stars are so beautiful out here. You ever wonder what it would be like to see Earth from space?"

"Not really," he mumbles, staring at the coffee maker. He has a very cartoonish sleepy face. "My sister was the one who liked space stuff."

"She ever do space camp?"

Josh shakes his head. Then, offhandedly, he says, "My dad has some family in some city in Alabama where there's a lot of space stuff. We've never visited, though."

Sofia heaps the eggs onto two plates. They stand at the countertop, drinking coffee and eating. She can sense some serious negative energy emanating from the boy. Maybe it's just a moody teenager thing. She could commiserate with that. She made her dad's life hell for a couple years when she was trying to navigate puberty without a mother present.

But this seems like something more.

"You OK?" she asks.

Josh shrugs. "We have to disbud this morning."

"Disbud?"

"Like, cutting the horns off."

"Oh."

"I wish you didn't have to do this with me, but the Reverend says you should learn everything."

"I'm sure it'll be fine." In her mind, Sofia imagines some kind of device that cuts effortlessly through the calf's horn the way a saw cuts through a dry branch that fell from a tree.

But Eva knows, and feels dread welling up in the pit of her stomach.

Stop.

My name is Sofia. I grew up in a nice Chicago suburb and watched the Disney Channel on Saturday mornings.

Tina walks into the kitchen just as Sofia is finishing another batch of eggs. She keeps the salt and pepper off, putting the eggs on a plate and setting it on the counter. Tina has to tuck aside her flowing white nightgown as she takes a seat on a stool. "You didn't have to do this, Sofia."

"I learned an important lesson yesterday," Sofia says brightly. "If you're not going to sit in an office all day, you can't live on salads and iced tea."

"Good food makes strong kids," Josh says, getting a chuckle from his mother.

"You taking Grandma to the antique store today?" Josh asks.

"No," says his mother. "Maybe tomorrow. Your father wants me to make some meals for the Stones." She sighs, looking at Josh, then Sofia. The wrinkles around her eyes, the slightly sagging skin running down her neck, the crease between her plucked eyebrows, all works together to give her an honest beauty. Still, there's a frailty lurking under her skin. And it's not just the lack of meat on her bones, either. Tina wears her stress like a wet blanket.

But for a brief moment, as her bright eyes move from Sofia back to Josh, that weight seems to lift. "This is so nice," she says. Then, as if she's breaking a law on par with attempted robbery, she pours herself a little mug of coffee and sips it conspiratorially, getting a nervous chuckle from her son.

Josh and Sofia take turns changing in the basement. Sofia has decided that the shirt and jeans she wore yesterday will now, out of necessity and circumstance, be her "work clothes." She sits on the folding chair under the showerhead, putting on a fresh pair of socks, feeling the soles of her feet pick up dust granules as she walks to the other end of the basement. She puts on Tina's rubber boots—donated graciously by the Reverend's wife after she saw what became of Sofia's sneakers yesterday.

The Reverend has an air conditioner in his bedroom. Sofia could hear it last night, humming. The rest of the house was stuffy and warm. Sofia tossed and turned in the bed that wasn't hers, inhaling the strawberry scent of Miriam Jenkins' linens, listening through the open window to cows hollering at rolling thunder. She'd been afraid in the darkness. Afraid the Reverend might be waiting for her this morning to escort her off the property. Afraid to go home and face a life she no longer wants.

She walks out the back door. Josh is waiting for her outside. A drizzle has picked up but Josh has a very simple solution: garbage bags with holes poked through them.

"It's the best I can do," he says, and the regret in his voice nearly breaks Sofia's heart. He's been nothing but nice to her. He draws from a well of strength that she doesn't possess, and he pours all that energy into his grandmother's farm.

"I'm tougher than I look," Sofia says, snatching a bag. "I didn't always lose at poker, you know. I won some pretty big pots in Vegas."

"How big?" he asks. They walk together to the calf barn, their boots splashing in puddles.

"One time, I fired a three-barrel bluff on a ten thousand-dollar pot."

"What does that mean?"

"It means I bluffed three times. All I had was a pair of twos. If the guy had just called me, he would have beat me." Sofia narrows one eye and taps her head. "But I got into his mind."

"Cool."

"Yeah, but don't gamble. Seriously."

"OK." He says it with a straight face, as if he'd considered throwing all this away to become a traveling scoundrel.

They walk into the calf barn. All the cuties are ready and waiting for breakfast. A couple are resting together on the straw like a little pack of stuffed animals. Another one—Sofia's favorite

Guernsey—already has her head poking through the headlock, tracking Sofia with hilariously bulging eyes.

They do the feeding together. Sofia follows Josh's lead, cooing to the youngest group, using her fingers like teats to guide the dumbest ones to open panels, taking the time to gently pet each of them on the back.

When they're done feeding, Josh grabs a box of tools from the cabinet beside the hot water tank. Sofia scrubs each of the milk pails in the sink with sanitizing solution, watching out of the corner of her eye as Josh brings out a device that looks almost like a curling iron. He plugs it into an extension cord and brings it over to stall 5, where the calves' necks are still locked into the feed panels. Immediately, Sofia can smell it: overcooked meat with just a hint of the stench of ground teeth after the dentist has drilled out a cavity.

"You can just hold them still," he says softly. "I'll do the hard part."

Sofia feels her nerves fray a bit. Josh holds the hot iron like a torch, showing her how to keep the calf's head still. "She's going to flinch. You have to hold her tight or it'll hurt more."

Sofia wraps her arm around the neck of the Guernsey in headlock 12—the one with the goofy eyes. Her heart begins to race as Josh squats and points down the hot iron.

Jesus Christ, he's not going to use any local anesthetic. Holy shit holy shit holy shit …

Stop. Sofia wouldn't know this.

"Josh," she says.

Sofia wouldn't know. SHUT UP.

She covers her trembling mouth. She watches in horror as Josh presses the iron down over the budding horn, angling it, turning, and scooping the horn out. It all happens so fast, but not so fast that the cow doesn't cry out in pain, jerking her head and surprising Sofia. She feels the skin of her arm pinched in the metal but she draws on some hidden strength of her own to hold the calf's head steady. Josh gets the other horn quick, following the same smooth motion.

Smoke curls up from the wound. The smell of burnt hair and flesh fills Sofia's nostrils. What's left around the cauterized wound looks like a bloody, copper ring. Her body dry-heaves uncontrollably.

"It's best to go fast," Josh says, his voice cracking. His eyes are wet with tears.

Sofia grabs the neck of the calf in headlock 11. A cute Jersey with dark, intelligent eyes. "Josh," she gasps, "can't you give them something for the pain?"

He disbuds each of the Jersey's horns before shaking his head. "I'm sorry," he whispers. Sofia thinks he's talking to her, but he does it after they're finished with the calf in headlock 10, too. He's talking to them. He apologizes to each one. He talks gently and reassures them that the pain is only temporary and promises to look after them. But there's something else, too: a darkness in Josh's eyes, the way he grits his teeth, the certainty in his fluid motions. The violence pains him, but he does it anyway with a brutal efficiency.

Every neck Sofia squeezes, she feels culpable. Dust stanches her sweaty forehead. Blood stains her bare arms. Beads like rubies collect on the tips of her soft hairs. Nine more to go. The smell is overpowering. Six left now. Sofia's arm muscles strain, sore, fighting back against animals in blinding pain. Three left. Sofa can't watch anymore. She looks away. Hot blood soaks through her jeans.

By the end, they're both in tears and the stench of burnt fur hangs thick in the warm air. Sofia, sobbing, collapses next to the pallet of milk substitute. Josh sits with the cows, talking to them and running his hands gently across the soft fur of their snouts. He talks to each one. Comforts them. An abuser apologizing for striking his wife.

"They'll never trust me again," he says. "Not the way they did before. That's the hardest part."

"They were in pain," Sofia sobs. "Josh, they could feel *all* of it." She can't stop crying. She's so horrified by the violence of it, the matter-of-factness of Josh's attitude.

Josh sits beside her. He puts a big hand on her shoulder. "They're safe now. They'll never accidentally gore each other when they get older. It's good for them."

Sofia can't respond. She can't look at her favorite calf.

"We get money from Wilson's Dairy to buy painkillers," he says, wiping tears off his cheeks. "But my dad doesn't let me spend it."

Sofia studies his glassy eyes, the dark shadows across his face. He's depressed. She can't believe she didn't realize it sooner and she's kicking herself now because she can remember her mother's depression. It used to swallow her mother up for weeks on end, when she would just stand at the kitchen window and stare at the crops. It was always worse when it was corn. Corn grows so tall that it can feel like an imposing wall, cutting you off from the rest of the world. It always made Sofia's mother anxious and sad.

And her father's depression. That was different because he tried so hard to hide it from Sofia. He didn't mope. He didn't cry. He just did his work and forced these smiles that broke Sofia's heart. She couldn't cheer him up; when she tried, he would present her with fake happiness that cut her to the bone. When Sofia became a teenager, she tested her father's apathy by being as wild an unpredictable as possible.

Sadness is a stream eroding the valley floor.

"I wish my grandma still helped," he says quietly. "I wish she didn't hate me so much."

"Why does she hate you?" Sofia asks. It feels forced. She cares, she really does. It shouldn't sound so forced.

"She knows I did something bad."

"Oh." Sofia searches for the right words. "Do you want to talk …"

"I wanna confess," he says. "So I can, you know, be forgiven. Or do I need a priest? Maybe you could take me to the Catholic church in Fayette."

"You don't need a priest," Sofia says. "You can confess to anyone. It's … it's about getting everything out in the open." She's lying to him. Worse, she knows she can get away with it because he's not bright. She feels a pain of guilt.

Don't stop.

"How bad is it?" she asks gently.

"Bad."

"Confess to me," Sofia says, trying to maintain an even voice, even though she can barely contain herself. She needs to know what Josh did. She needs to know if it has something to do with Miriam's disappearance. She needs to know what's behind those dark eyes.

"My father made me …" he whispers, struggling with the words. He stops, sniffs in deeply. Sofia leans forward, waiting.

Josh gets up. He blows his nose on his shirt and walks over to the cabinets. He pulls out a deck of cards. They're *Magic: The Gathering* cards—Sofia recognizes them. Kids in her high school theatre club used to play this game all the time.

"I always sit with the calves after I disbud," he says softly. "I keep them company all day to make sure they're OK."

"Josh, what—"

"I only play the white cards," he continues, his wet eyes serious and thoughtful. "They're the good guys. Elliot used to play with me. I'd let him win sometimes 'cause it made him happy."

"And you wanted to help him."

Josh nods. "My mom got so sad after Miriam was gone. So one day Elliot invited her to come play with us. My dad was gone for the afternoon and my grandma was taking a nap and my mom was just sitting at the countertop, crying."

"Because she missed her daughter?"

A shrug. Eyes looking down at the floor encrusted with wet straw. "The three of us used to play all sorts of games right here in the calf barn. It was our little secret."

Try to get him back to the confession.

No. He's hurting. Help him.

"Let's play." Sofia crosses her legs on the floor. "The calves can be our audience."

Josh sits with her. He deals out the cards. They play one game, then two, then Josh checks on the calves. One has begun bleeding so he gets a cream and puts her in a headlock, keeping her from moving while he applies the cream. Her knobby little legs quiver. Josh gets a cloth and wets it, then goes back inside the stall. Sofia watches as he very gently wipes the blood off the calf's face, reassuring her the entire time.

They play a few more games. Sofia has forgotten what real fun feels like. All this time, she's been chasing highs. At her job. At the poker table. She doesn't want to go back to her old life. Is it possible to start over from scratch? The very idea of it gives Sofia a thrill she's never felt.

Suddenly, the door opens.

The Reverend appears.

And when he sees what they're doing, he belts out a howl of rage that could cut a slit in the world.

<h1 style="text-align:center">25</h1>

Search

MASON AND ROBIN take a seat on a fallen tree log, sharing a little bottle of bug spray. It's 7:00 p.m. They've spent the last two hours searching the forest between the Ramirez property and the Cranston farm, constantly losing their footing, scratching their faces on wayward branches, picking burrs off their shirts. Moving north to south, just as professor Leftwich had recommended. Searching for any sign of Elliot Stone and finding nothing.

"You're sure Ramirez wasn't just mumbling something in his sleep?" Robin asks.

"I'm sure."

"Because drunk people sometimes do that."

He looks at her and smiles. She's broken a sweat, and her normally perfect ponytail has a few escaped strands that have fallen over her face. "Are we talking about someone in particular?"

She gives him a push that sends him tumbling backward, falling off the log and landing on soggy ferns. They start walking again. The forest floor is mostly clear of undergrowth, the ground squishy except where fallen brown pine needles serve as a makeshift carpet under a few clusters of red pines. In the wettest spots, their boots make a slucking sound when they pull out of the mud.

"Thanks for coming today," he says. "I know it sounds a little morbid, but searching for a dead body is much more enjoyable when you're not alone."

"Eek, that did sound morbid." Robin smiles at him. "I'll have to put that in my article now, just so you know."

Mason chuckles at the thought of Sheriff Henderson coming across that quote in the *Kane County Courier*. "Only if I can see my boss's face when he reads it."

"I don't know why you're so down. A one-week paid suspension? *And* you crossed Edgar Ramirez off the list of suspects? The sheriff basically gave you a vacation for doing his job."

Mason considers how to explain it while his eyes pan slowly along the forest floor, his boots kicking gently at the fronds of green ferns to reveal what lies beneath. "There's a hierarchy in policing, like the military. Going over someone's head is bad, even if it's done for good reasons. You're not supposed to disrupt the chain of command."

"Sounds like the type of bullshit rules manly men come up with to hide their mistakes," Robin murmurs in a sing-song voice.

They reach a place in the forest where the land rises sharply. Slabs of dolomite rock poke through sporadically like bone spurs, some bare and some covered with furry green moss. Mason uses his flashlight to walk carefully around it. There are openings, between the slabs, where thousands of years of rain have washed away sediment and soft limestone. Mason shines his flashlight inside one of the larger openings.

His breath appears at the edge of the opening, cloudy and white. Mason reaches his left hand in and withdraws it in surprise. It's freezing cold.

"It's the Algific talus slope," Robin says. "Remember Professor Leftwich telling us about it? His little geologic gem?"

Mason waves his hand in front of the opening again, feeling the warm air turn cold. The hill seems to be breathing, seems to be *alive*. He shines his flashlight inside.

Nothing.

Robin holds his hand for leverage and they climb halfway up the hill, walk all the way around, then climb higher and repeat the process. Aconitum grows freely where the layers of dirt are thickest, their dark blue flowers rising from each stem, resembling the hood of a monk's habit.

"That's poison, just so you know," she says, pointing to the plant.

"I know. I worked at a botanical garden when I was a teenager."

"Then what are these, Deputy Green Thumb?" she asks, pointing to another plant growing in the crack of exposed stone.

"Those are Keanu Leaves."

"You lying sack of shit!"

They climb all the way to the top, using their flashlights to search any openings big enough to fit a child. No sign of Elliot. They make their way back through the western end of the forest. In their silence, the chirping of playful birds sounds overwhelming. The tree limbs shudder in the breeze, shedding droplets of water from the last storm. Every cold droplet on Mason's face annoys him.

"I don't get it," he says. "Ramirez mentioned lights out here. But we haven't come across a single beer can or campfire."

Ahead, dead maples and pines lean at violent angles, broken branches caught and hanging to reveal the light-brown, fleshy inner bark. Robin leads the way to the edge of a massive sinkhole, at least twenty feet deep and twice the circumference. Some of the trees unlucky enough to be caught near the edge are still bravely clinging to survival, but only half their limbs are producing any leaves. Down below, rainwater has mixed with mud and dead leaves to create a soupy mixture God only knows how deep.

Mason sighs and looks at Robin. "Well, good luck down there."

Before she can push him again, he hops playfully out of the way, only to learn a terrible truth about Driftless sinkholes: their edges aren't hard and solid like a rocky cliff. His boot slips and he feels his center of gravity move toward the center of the pit; he reaches out and grabs the branch of a maple, feeling the bark bite into his skin as he slips another foot.

Just out of Robin's reach. She gets on her knees, looking down at him with an amused expression. "Well, you're halfway down now. Might as well look around."

Mason digs the heels of his boots into the wet mud, unable to shake the feeling that the sinkhole might open up again and carry him down into an even deeper cavern, deep enough that his last moment on earth would be in complete darkness.

Robin seems to read his thoughts. "Don't worry!" she calls down with dramatic flair. "I wrote an article on sinkholes in the Driftless. They're usually pretty safe!"

Mason reaches the edge of the soupy basin. He pulls on a dry oak limb that's fallen from one of the trees. He uses it to test the depth of the basin. The stick goes in further than halfway.

"No point in dragging this out," he mutters, dipping into the water. It's warmer than he expected, coated with a film of sludge that seeks out his bare skin. He feels the weight of his soaked clothes guiding him toward the bottom, where he can touch while his head stays above water. He moves slowly, simultaneously hoping and dreading to find Elliot's body. But he knows it's pointless. Elliot would have risen to the surface by now. He's not here.

Something hard digs painfully into Mason's hip bone. His heart begins to race. He reaches deep into the water, anticipating the claw of a corpse. But instead, his fingers brush against something smooth and angular. He grabs it, runs its fingers across it, can't believe what it must be. It's stuck, won't move, so he dives down underwater, catching just a snippet of Robin's frightened cry before his ears fill with water. He follows the object to the bottom, visualizing exactly what he's touching, and pulls its wheels from the mud.

He comes up for breath, dragging the blue bike onto the edge of the sinkhole. Above, Robin has found a long branch. Mason grabs it, pulling himself up the edge, dragging the bike by the spokes of its front wheels, feeling them dig into the soft skin of his fingers.

They stare at the bike in silence. Above them on a single branch, three black crows sit like bishops.

"Are you sure it's Elliot's?" Robin asks.

Mason wipes mud off in one long, sluicing motion. A five-speed Trek with a Power Rangers sticker on the handlebar. "It's his. Someone dumped it here."

"Someone who knows about the sinkhole," Robin adds. "They did it that night, using flashlights to find this spot. That's what Edgar saw."

He pulls his wet phone from his pocket, thumb smearing the screen. Thank God it's waterproof.

Robin's hand falls over his. "What the hell do you think you're doing?"

"I'm calling the sheriff."

She glares at him. "Are you insane? Mase, this is *your* investigation."

"I'm on suspension. Henderson—"

"Henderson's an idiot!" She waves a hand to the bike. "You think he's going to know what to do with this?"

"It's not like he's gonna cover it up—"

"Mason, this bike means you were right: someone on Swamp Angel Road killed Elliot Stone. We know it's not the Cox family or the Cranston family because of their alibis. We know Ramirez is probably telling the truth about Elliot passing his house. That leaves the Jenkins family, the Andersons, and David Bauer. All of them have already been questioned by your sheriff … you really trust him to go back and get it right?"

Mason says nothing. It's a rhetorical question, obviously. He looks down at the bike.

"Look, you and I both know you're the one who has to do this, no matter how much it pisses of Henderson."

Mason thinks about Eva. He wonders if there's any way he could get a message to her on the Jenkins farm. Warn her of the danger. Or is Eva the danger? Is she on the farm because she's somehow involved in Elliot Stone's disappearance?

"Have you had any luck finding Miriam Jenkins?"

"What? No. Who cares about the Reverend's daughter? We're so close now."

"Why do you want me to do this?" he asks angrily. "I thought you didn't *want* me risking my job. Is this so you can write your perfect redemption story?"

"It's so we can put Elliot Stone to rest!" Her voice echoes in the empty forest. She pulls the stray hairs away from her face, looking up at him. "Like you said, Mase: it's not about the job anymore."

26

Knowing

TINA'S MOANS TRAVEL down the hall, permeating the old farmhouse walls.

Sofia lays in bed, listening in the darkness. The covers have been cast aside because it's so hot in the house; the single window only lets in a gradual breeze and the frogs are so loud outside that it's been impossible to sleep.

Now this. This intrusion of privacy. This personal act broadcast to the entire house.

At least it *sounds* like she and the Reverend are having fun. It's a far cry from the afternoon, after the Reverend caught Sofia and Josh in the calf barn. First, he'd accused his son of playing an *occult* game—and that was bad enough. But then the Reverend had asked Josh where he'd gotten the money for them. Immediately, Sofia knew: the church donations. Josh confessed, and Sofia couldn't help but feel culpable. Would he have admitted the truth if she hadn't filled his head with thoughts of divine forgiveness?

The Reverend had proclaimed the game an affront to God,

assigning Josh to repair the east group fencing while Sofia handled the cow chores for the rest of the day. Face red and sweaty, he'd held each card in his right hand and used his teeth to tear each one in half while Sofia and Josh watched. Between each rip, he spat out passages from Leviticus. In his righteous fury, all the calves grew anxious and ran frantically around their pens, a terrified congregation. The dehorned ones looked like bloody sacrifices.

What really happened to Miriam?

There's no better opportunity to snoop than while the resident patriarch and his wife are sexually distracted. Sofia grabs her cell phone from her suitcase, turning it on. She has a voicemail.

"Hey, it's Candace. I just heard from L'oreal. Guess what? They're putting your shampoo commercial back in full rotation. I'm gonna use your old headshots and shop you around to some studios this week while the ad is playing. Cross your fingers!"

Sofia deletes the strange message and turns on the phone's flashlight function.

First, she gives the bed a thorough examination, checking the mattress for any holes or cuts that might be a good hiding place for something forbidden.

Nothing.

Tina's moans continue, more passionate now.

Sofia tries the dresser drawers; in the stifling summer heat the wood has swelled so it pops and groans. She goes next to the closet, rifling through Miriam's plain-looking clothes, checking the pockets. Nothing.

Tina's moans grow louder and more insistent.

Sofia searches the top shelf of the closet, where there are a number of pink and red and purple shoe boxes sitting in stacks. With shaky hands, she takes one down and sets it on the dresser, opening it up.

Homework. Worksheets, precisely filled out. Math equations

that grow more complicated toward the bottom of the pile. Sofia puts this shoebox back and grabs another. In this one are writing skills worksheets, but near the bottom of the stack they grow into paragraphs with pictures asking for descriptions of certain scenes. Miriam's mother has graded each one, correcting spelling and grammar and writing little encouragements at the top.

Tina's moans of pleasure grow louder, less insistent now and more panicked.

Sofia grabs the last shoebox, rifling through the papers inside, noting the complexity of the math problems—it looks like calculus, if Sofia remembers her college math. At the bottom are more writing assignments, utilizing paragraphs and topic sentences and carefully cultivated research, the work of a high school student. And now the conflict is evident. Miriam has begun to entertain dangerous notions. In one "research" paper, she's written about the geologic composition of bedrock in the Driftless Area. Her estimation of the age of the minerals has been corrected by her mother, who crossed out "millions" and "billions" everywhere they're mentioned.

There's more. In another essay, Miriam talks about helping her grandmother raise cows. She writes in detail how a cow's digestive system works and the best way to castrate the bulls. Tina's red pen suggests a more domestic way of life and gives Miriam a very subjective C+. The tone of the feedback is growing more impatient.

Tina's moans no longer carry any hint of pleasure. She's crying out between thumps as the bed's headboard hits the wall again and again like the ticking of a grandfather clock.

Another essay, this one about Sally Kristin Ride, the first woman in space. Miriam's prose is delicate and beautiful. She writes long, excited sentences that Tina incorrectly marks as "run-ons." And at the bottom, a subjective grade: "F – We talked about this assignment at lunch" with "talked" violently underlined three times.

Tina has grown quiet. The pounding's rhythm speeds up.

Sofia scans the bookshelves. She grabs the state-mandated textbooks for homeschooled children. She pages through them one by one until she gets to sixth grade and finds the missing piece of the puzzle: pictures of female astronauts. Pictures of space and Earth in all its beautiful glory. A world so much more expansive and interesting than the one Miriam had learned here, growing up isolated and alone in the Driftless Area. And Miriam had grasped that bigger world with both hands, refusing to let go.

Every single 12th grade essay received an F and a frantic, impatient message from her mother. It had probably seemed like such a good way to protect their child: teach what you want, keep them away from the temptations of public schooling or, worse, the Catholic school in Fayette. But Miriam had latched onto the lessons her mother tried to skip. She had the mind of a dreamer, and Sofia feels an intense connection to this woman she's never met.

So intense, in fact, that she knows exactly where Miriam would hide her most precious secrets: the only place her parents wouldn't think to look.

Her Bible.

It's sitting on the middle shelf, flanked by study guides and religious books focused on specific passages from the New Testament and coloring books featuring famous stories from the Old Testament. Sofia grabs the Bible off the bookshelf and flips the pages.

There, finally, are Miriam's secrets. Pieces of paper spread out through the book, no more than one at a time so the book doesn't look stuffed. Sofia grabs a piece of paper and unfolds it.

A news article about Sally Ride.

She puts it back and unfolds another piece of paper.

A Wikipedia article about space travel.

She opens another.

An article about how programmers wrote code for the moon landing.

The pounding stops. Suddenly, the house is silent again except for the patter of rain on windows and the chorus of frogs.

Sofia puts the paper back into the Bible and replaces it on the shelf. She turns off her phone and lays in bed, listening to nature's symphony, thinking.

Miriam's space articles didn't come from newspapers, and they didn't come from somewhere in this house. There's no printer in this house. There's just a laptop, and only the Reverend is allowed to use it. Someone printed those articles for Miriam.

Someone who knew her secrets.

Sofia counts her breaths. The frogs stop croaking all at once and she can hear a police siren, distant, echoing. Coyotes answer the siren from somewhere in the valley, their warbling yips and howls building into a crescendo. The sound ignites a fury of memories growing up, a child hearing the sound of predators in the darkness, heart beating hard in her chest.

No.

My name is Sofia. I grew up in a suburb in Chicago.

The house feels unsettled. Sofia's finger goes to her face, gently running across the pimple that's formed on her cheek. She always gets a bad cheek pimple before her period starts. Ever since she was in her teens. It's required a fair bit of make-up magic on acting gigs.

No.

My name is Sofia. I'm a gambler. I work in finance. I hate my life.

She counts to five hundred, then gets up and walks down the hall to the bathroom. She sits uses the toilet, then flushes it and runs the sink. She goes to the little closet tucked in the corner and finds a white container of feminine napkins sitting on the top shelf. Quietly, carefully, Sofia reaches her hand into the container to grab one of the packages. As she does, her finger brushes across something hard and plastic. It's her mother's curious genes that get the best of Sofia, forcing her to grab the mysterious object and remove it to take a better look.

Birth control pills.

Eva feels herself falling out of character. The sound of Tina's cries echo inside her mind. Miriam is in her late twenties. Josh is eighteen. This is why they only have two children. Murder— that's what the Reverend would call this. Tina is keeping a secret from him. Miriam kept secrets from her parents. Josh is keeping a secret from Sofia. The Reverend keeps secrets from his congregation. And Eva … Eva is keeping a secret from them all.

She's not sure whose secrets will be revealed just yet, only that some will. And they will lead to a terrible violence.

SATURDAY

27

Desperation

MASON SITS in his Chevy on the end of Jefferson Street, next to the Mexican grocer, watching the Jenkins family car pull into a space across the street. Out steps Tina Jenkins, wearing a flowing blue dress; she walks around to the passenger's side and helps her mother step onto the sidewalk. Slowly, together, they walk into the cream-colored building that was once a Civil War-era factory.

Mason checks the dashboard clock: nearly 10:00 a.m. Robin's intel is correct, as always. How she's managed to befriend the owner of this crusty old antique shop, he can only guess. He gets out of the car, putting on his hoodie to stave off the rain.

Inside, he's greeted by a middle-aged man and woman standing behind a glass counter. A pair of big ledger-like books sits in front of them, partially obscuring the rows of old pistols laying in a neat row inside the glass case. There's one missing on the top shelf, between a tiny silver revolver and a German Luger with a metal handle. A little sign next to the gun proudly announces that they're still 100% functioning. Mason remembers what

Robin texted him about the shop: *Great place to buy a fully functioning six-shooter that helped clear the Driftless of those pesky natives.* He wonders if the missing gun was purchased by her.

The antique shop has tall ceilings and lots of old rugs underneath the consigned sections. Mason inhales the tangy, moldy scent of old dust. He walks down one of the rows, wondering which knickknacks belong to which local families. There's an old secretary desk with a damaged hutch that doesn't close. Two wooden library filing cabinets that went obsolete with the Dewey Decimal System. A corner consignment full of old tools with wooden handles and rusted, black steel. A glass case full of fishing lures. Old paintings of the Driftless: sloping prairies and twisting blue streams that cut through wide valleys and steep cliffs of exposed rock with beautiful layers and old Cornish cottages with chimneys spewing curls of gray smoke.

"This way, mom."

Mason cocks his head; Tina's voice is coming from the other end of the store, which is much bigger than it looks from the outside. There's two straight aisles down to the other end, and more between them that snake like the Driftless streams between sectioned-off furniture and dressers and mirrors and old sporting equipment and rusted Coca-Cola signs. Mason takes one of the aisles that's filled with bookcases, scanning the spines of old books. A few boxes of vintage comics sit on an old, dirty brown rug. The books along the bottom shelves are all for kids. Toward the top are old hardcovers, all the color of rust and blood.

He needs a prop to give himself a plausible excuse for being here, and most of the old hardcovers are unfamiliar Tom Clancy tomes. But next to the bookcases stands an old sewing table stacked with old board games, his specialty. Star Wars Monopoly—perfect.

Mason weaves his way around boxes of old records in dusty sleeves. He reaches the other main aisle, sees Tina farther ahead with her mother. It's striking how similar they look, right down to the simple dresses whose hems have soaked up an inch of rainwater. Tina has stopped beside an old jukebox, but her attention is on the animal heads hanging on the wall. Rows and rows of exotic animals. Water buffalo and deer and antelope and rams, each distinguished by their unique horns that cast strange shadows across the wall.

Below them are taxidermy mountain lions, foxes, a bear, a pair of wolves.

"Hello, Mrs. Jenkins," Mason says quietly, hoping not to startle her.

Tina pulls her attention away from the animals. "Deputy Taylor, how are you?"

"Sick of the rain." He offers a gentle smile and lifts up the board game. "I think I found a winner."

Tina's light green eyes pass over the box. "You can play that with my husband, if you'd like."

"Does he like Star Wars or Monopoly?"

"Monopoly started as a game that criticized greed," Tina says. She glances over Mason's shoulder. "Mom, don't stray too far."

Mason's mind is searching for a subtle way to get around to the topic of Elliot. To buy time, he nods to the animal heads. "Anyone you know?"

"We used to hunt deer," she says. "My family, not the Reverend."

"They live around here?"

"Don't be stupid," Tina snaps. The harshness of her voice seems to hang eerily in the shop, haunting the stuffy air. "You must know my history by now. And the motorcycle accident. You've been in Carthage too long to not have heard about it."

"Did you ever kill one?"

"One what?"

He waves his hand to the array of animal heads.

She turns to look at him. "Once. It was a lucky shot and I think I lost some hearing in my right ear. Are you a hunter?"

"No."

"You're going to be awfully bored in the winter."

He holds up the board game. "I'll keep busy."

"I'm sure you will," she murmurs, crossing her arms. "Especially across from the strip club."

"I haven't …"

"Mom, please don't go too far!" she calls out. She turns back to him. "Be honest: what do you want, Mr. Taylor?"

He's momentarily too stunned to answer. Where he'd expected a meek submissiveness, he only sees a hardened anger. An elk confident in its stand-off with a solitary, hungry wolf. "I wanted to ask you about Elliot Stone."

"We were home playing UNO the night he went missing."

Mason follows her down the aisle. "Do you remember anything about the night he went missing that stood out?"

"It wasn't raining. Mom!" she calls down another aisle. Wilma is nowhere to be seen. She's slipped down one of the side-aisles and now she's disappeared.

Mason follows her, searching the dim lighting for any evidence of another human being. "Wilma!" The place seems to grow more cavernous the deeper they go.

"Mom! Mom, this isn't funny!" Tina calls out. Her voice has changed to panic.

"Wilma!" Mason calls out. He takes one of the side-aisles to the other end of the building. Rows and rows of antique cookie jars sit on shelves built into the wall. Batman, Santa Clause, Garfield, cats, dogs, racoons, ballerinas and a hundred others watch Mason walk past.

"Mommy!" comes Tina's frantic voice. Across one of the straighter aisles, Mason sees her like a mirror image, their eyes locking for just a moment before she disappears behind an oak credenza. The cookie jars give way to houses and buildings, carefully constructed along a model train track. At least a hundred little structures of all shapes and sizes, quaint and old-fashioned, and on the top row—encased in glass—are carefully preserved model trains.

Mason and Tina meet in the next side-aisle, where they find Wilma sitting in a recliner with a floral design. She's holding a board game in her lap: Apples to Apples. "I found something for us," she announces proudly.

"That's a good game," Mason tells her. "Good for families."

Tina helps her mother up. "Time to go, Mom."

"Shouldn't we buy a game? We always do."

"Mom, stop." Tina grabs her wrist tightly. "We're going."

"Mrs. Jenkins," Mason pleads. "I'm worried Elliot Stone went missing on Swamp Angel Road. If you remember *anything* strange about the evening he went missing ..."

Tina spins back to him, her soft skin flushed a crimson red. "Do you want someone to investigate, Deputy Taylor? Investigate David Bauer."

"... Why?"

"Because he's a *predator*." She gives her mother's wrist a tug, forcing Wilma behind her. The elderly woman cries out in pain. "He drives by our house. He calls us at night and harasses us. I'm sure he broke into our house at least once." A tear slides down her cheek. She puts a hand on her mother's back, pushing her. Mason's memory recalls the violent way Josh handled his injured cow when Mason began to press with questions. When Josh became frustrated.

"Tina. Did David Bauer do something to your daughter Miriam?" Mason asks.

Tina doesn't answer. She pushes her whimpering mother through the entrance, then stops and turns back. She opens her mouth to say something. Mason holds his breath, waiting.

And then she's pulls her mother to the car.

28

Search

THIS ISN'T IN CHARACTER.

Eva is standing in the Jenkins family kitchen, staring at the pictures of Miriam on the refrigerator. A plate sits on the countertop. On the plate is a half-eaten turkey sandwich, Sofia's lunch. But its purpose isn't sustenance. It's a prop and nothing more.

Tina and her mother are in town. The Reverend is visiting the Stone family. Josh is banished to fence repair sun-up to sundown.

Eva goes through the cabinets one by one, then the drawers. She moves to the beautiful credenza, leafing through paperwork and bills and junk mail. The Reverend has a single credit card that tracks his purchases around town. The newest bill is for over a thousand dollars, but none of the purchases seem out of place. Pharmacy, supermarket, hardware store, feed store, Wal-Mart, Lowe's. She rifles through the drawers, finding medical bills. A neurologist for Wilma Jenkins. Physical therapy for Wilma Jenkins. An obstetrician for Miriam Jenkins, five months ago—around the time she disappeared.

Sofia has no reason to be doing this.

But Eva can't pass up this chance. She needs to search this house. She needs to know what happened to Miriam and get out of here.

The Reverend is dangerous.

"Satanism!" he'd shouted in the calf barn, picking up Josh's Magic cards. "Idolatry! Sloth!" It would have been funny, listening to him rattle off whatever sinful words he could conjure, if not for the fiery red face, the volume of his thundering voice, the way his fist squeezed so tight that the veins on the back of his hand looked ready to burst. A fist ready to swing at something.

Eva goes to Josh's room. The walls are covered with jungle wallpaper, with little jaguars and tigers and leopards hiding in the foliage. The bed is unmade, so she tosses the green covers, then searches underneath the mattress, then underneath the bed itself. She checks his dresser, lifting up folded clothes, searching for any evidence of Miriam. She checks his closet, where he's hidden a few comic books underneath a pile of farming magazines. On the wall inside the closet, he's recorded his height almost monthly since he was twelve.

The Reverend's fist had found a target: the bale of straw sitting next to the pallet of milk substitute. He hit it hard enough to leave a gaping hole. The commotion caused the calves to flee to the back of their pens, mooing nervously. Josh had begun crying, apologizing. Sofia had watched in horror as the Reverend kicked at the buckets in front of the feed panels, one after the other, like a spoiled child.

Eva goes to Wilma's room next. The flower-pattern bed is made, the beige carpet clean and vacuumed. It looks unused, right down to the plain pine dresser whose wood has been sealed with a glossy coat of varnish. Eva searches the dresser, finding only Wilma's undergarments and stacks of photos of Wilma, aged, holding up a calf. She goes to the closet and finds dozens and dozens of Sunday dresses. Nice dresses. In one corner of the closet sits a pile of blankets and, sitting on top, a Bible. Eva grabs it, leafs through it, surprised to see highlighted passages and notes in the margins, written in legible cursive.

Eva sets the Bible back in place and searches the other corner of the closet. Underneath a few dirty clothes is a stack of board games. Candyland. Shoots and Ladders. Sorry! Clue. Next to them is a tower of Crossword books, nearly a hundred by Eva's estimate. The books are stacked by date, with the newest on top. The date of the top book is familiar: right before Wilma's stroke.

The Reverend had kicked every single pail in front of every single feed panel. His breaths eventually came out in wheezing gasps and still he found the energy to scream at the top of his lungs. Red-faced, ferocious, and terrifying.

Eva crosses the hall, into the master bedroom. The shades are still drawn and the room is dark. She feels a surge of dizziness, being in here, after what she'd heard the night before. The end tables are mismatched. One of the dressers is made of a dark wood with beautiful, curling curves like leaves. The other dresser is tall, made of an equally beautiful wood only much warmer in color, its grain running like tiger stripes. Eva goes through Tina's clothes hamper, stopping at the nightgown stained with blood. She searches both dressers, both closets. Nothing.

No evidence that Miriam is still alive.

The waste basket underneath the Reverend's end table is overflowing with garbage. Eva pulls out the crumpled papers— old sermons, a few pamphlets for Bible study, receipts from the grocery store and the pharmacy.

Nothing to suggest they are still caring for their daughter.

He'd begun speaking in tongues. Sofia had fallen back in fear, painfully bumping into the feed panels. Josh was ripping up the remaining Magic cards into smaller and smaller pieces, sobbing and apologizing. The Reverend loomed over both of them, eyes wide, muttering what sounded at first like Bible verses but slowly the words morphed into nonsense, as if he was being consumed by some otherworldly force. He spat and drooled as he rambled. The angry tone softened, grew quieter. The Reverend's face changed and the fury faded; he looked *afraid*.

The front door opens and closes with a slam. Tina's voice carries down the hall. Eva glances at the door to the Reverend's room. She goes to the window, is about to pull up the shade when she hears Tina's footsteps coming down the hall. Eva runs to the Reverend's closet and slips between his suits hanging from their hooks.

Tina enters. The soft pad of her feet on the thick carpeting leads to the other side of the room. Metal hangars clang together. "Fuck," she says sharply. "Fuck, fuck, fuck!"

Eva peers between a pair of suitcoats that reek of the Reverend's musk. Tina is standing in front of the oval-shaped mirror sitting atop her dresser. She removes a pair of blue earrings, setting them on a T-shaped stand beside the mirror. She stares at herself, running fingers across her bony bare arms. Whatever has her upset has sapped her will; she leans her forehead against the glass.

Finally, she calls out to her mom. Her voice is shaky. "Mommy, let's get you in the bath."

She leaves the bedroom. Eva exhales. Her heart beats so hard in her ears that she can't even hear them walking down the hall.

"Pray with me," the Reverend had said, falling to his knees before Sofia and Josh. He put his right hand to his heart and closed his eyes. "Pray with me so we can save your eternal souls."

Sofia folded her hands together. Josh, sniffling hard, followed suit.

"Dear God," the Reverend began, "forgive them, for they know not what they do. They mock you with false incantations of sorcery and the occult. You forbade this in Deuteronomy and you made no difference between good and evil, only that you are the one true God and we are your servants. You ask us to dwell on that which is true and honorable, pure and lovely. And we obey. Amen."

Eva peers out into the hall. The bathroom door is closed. She angles closer, breathing deeply, listening to the voices in the bathroom. The water is running. The timed heater is on, humming gently. Tina and her mother are singing a hymn in perfect harmony.

Eva tiptoes down the hall, needles running up her back, anticipating the bathroom door will open at any moment.

"No!" Wilma shouts. Eva freezes, throat dry, heart racing. "Why did he kill her?" she shouts.

"Mommy."

"Why did he kill her!" she screams, her voice hoarse.

Eva hurries to basement door and slips through, closing it gently behind her. Her heart breaks for Wilma. God was supposed to protect her, not let something as trivial as a stroke take the most precious parts of her humanity.

Eva takes the basement to the back door, returning outside. She inhales deeply through her nose, smelling fresh rain and sweet silage and soggy manure. It's time for Sofia's final act. Time for the carefully scripted climax that will force the Reverend to make a choice: reveal Miriam Jenkins, or lose Sofia to the Devil.

29

Love

MASON PULLS onto David Bauer's driveway at 2:30 p.m., timed so he can catch David before the afternoon calf feeding. His car's tires kick a little bit on the gravel. Potholes have developed in places, testing the old suspension. Mason can see David sitting in a rocking chair on the half-painted front porch, the picturesque image of rural America: a man in his early fifties, staring out at a field of winter wheat that he no longer farms on land he no longer owns.

An old milking parlor sits behind David's house. It's empty, in disrepair, the door held shut by a bungee cord. There's still a calf barn and a couple small loafing sheds where heifers take refuge from the rain on old bedding. An overgrown asparagus patch sits next to the oldest loafing shed, behind a wooden fence with a red water hydrant.

Mason parks behind Bauer's blue Dodge Ram. "Afternoon," he calls out to David.

Bauer watches Mason approach, rocking gently in his chair. "How are you, Dave?"

Bauer shrugs. A beer bottle sits on a little white wicker table with a glass surface. Condensation is gathering on the bottle, dripping down the Miller Lite logo.

"Mind if I get out of the rain?"

Bauer motions to the other rocking chair. Mason steps into the shade of the porch and takes a seat. The flowery cushions are surprisingly comfortable.

"I wasn't drunk," Bauer says, apropos of nothing. "Everybody always says I'm drunk. Where do they think I get the money? I barely had enough for a beer and a taco."

The only place in Carthage to get a beer and a taco is the Way Back Pub. Bauer must have gotten into it with someone over there and now he thinks Mason is here because someone called it in. "You wanna confess?"

"I don't need to be drunk to yell at someone."

Mason's fingers pick at the wicker armrests. "Well … did he deserve it?"

Bauer smiles and gives Mason a questioning look. "He called me a child killer."

"Seems a bit extreme."

"I'm not a big fan of swearing." Bauer takes a deep breath. "I didn't hit him. I just stood up for myself. That's not a crime."

Mason thinks about what Tina told him, about the phone calls and the harassment. It doesn't square with the "Gentle David" persona championed by Robin Wells, and neither does whatever went down at the pub.

"Is it a citation or what?" he asks.

"Dunno yet. But I'll clear it for you."

"Really?"

"I'm already on the sheriff's shit list anyway."

Bauer eyes Mason's civilian clothes: a pair of shorts, a simple t-shirt with the Milwaukee Brewers ball-in-glove logo. "So this is a social call?"

"I want to talk about Elliot Stone."

"I already talked about him with Sheriff Henderson."

"Indulge me. How long did he work for you?"

"That long," Bauer says, pointing to the spot on the porch railing where the color changes from a beautiful greenish-blue to a faded, dirty white.

"And you'd never hired him for any farm projects before that."

"No."

"Did the Reverend send you Elliot to paint the porch?" Mason asks, remembering what Robin said about the Reverend, farming his congregants' kids out.

"I asked the Stones." Bauer takes a deep breath. His lip curls into a snarl as the rain picks up, as if it's a personal affront. "They liked to keep Elliot working because it wore him out. Kid was a handful, but he was sweet. I didn't mind the paint getting on my rose bushes."

"So you went behind the Reverend's back."

Bauer nods. "I didn't want any money to go to Jenkins. And the Stones are good people. They weren't always religious nuts. It wasn't until the Anderson boy died on their farm that they turned all holy and got involved with the Reverend."

"Was Elliot acting strange at all? Did you see him talking to anyone else on Swamp Angel Road?"

Bauer's expression hardens. "Why is it you're sitting here, off-duty, grilling me about Elliot Stone when Miriam Jenkins has been missing for five months? Why doesn't that bother anyone except me?"

"Because Miriam is an adult, Dave. She moved away."

"Oh, is that what the Reverend said?" Bauer laughs and crosses his arms. "Must be true, then. God knows the Reverend doesn't lie."

He's a predator. Tina's words reverberate in Mason's memory. "Dave, did you ever have any sexual contact with Elliot?"

Bauer's arms land hard on the armrests. He faces Mason with

an expression of surprise. "Of course not. Why would you think something so horrible?"

"Did you ever have any sexual contact with Miriam while she was employed by you?"

The older man's expression falters.

"Is that why the Reverend and his wife hate you?"

Bauer doesn't answer. Mason leans back in the chair, watching the winter wheat dance in the rain. It runs up to the road, offering a clear view up the gentle slope, toward the Ramirez house. Muddy, unplanted cropland sits on terraces, interspersed with chunks of exposed dolomite, glistening wet.

"You've earned a reputation for being good to your employees," Mason says. Robin has more than a couple stories of Gentle David helping seasonals—loaning money, helping with security deposits, putting in a good word with other dairy operations. He may keep to himself, but almost forty straight years of farm work has put him in the good graces of a lot of Driftless farmers.

"Is that it?" Bauer asks. "Or do people say other things, too?" He doesn't sound angry when he asks it. He sounds hurt. "My first wife worked for me. It was how we met. People say she was illegal but that's not true."

"I didn't know that."

Bauer leans closer. Conviction burns in his eyes. "Miriam wouldn't just up and *leave* that family. She *couldn't*, Mason."

"Tina Jenkins says you've been harassing her family for months now. Calling them. Driving up and down the road. Going down their driveway at night."

David takes a deep breath. One finger absently wipes sweat off his beer bottle. "She's not lying. I call every day, hoping Miriam will answer. I just want to know she's OK."

Mason chooses his words carefully, knowing that David is embarrassed. "Miriam wasn't just an employee."

"I don't know why she liked me," he says, shaking his head. "I knew it would be a problem, me being so much older. But it's so lonely out here, Mason. It felt so damn good to be in love again." He lets out a sigh; his eyes scan the waterlogged crops that used to be his. "I sold all my land. Hired a private detective. The guy couldn't find her, Mason. Not even a trace. He even dug into the Anderson family."

Mason looks at him sharply. "Why the Andersons?"

"Their son, Jon, the one who died," David says. "Reverend Jenkins had his eye on him. Thought he might be a good fit for Miriam, even though she's ten years older. He wanted to marry her off. Then the Anderson boy died and he didn't know what to do with her. I needed a farmhand to help with morning calf chores."

"So she started working for you. And you fell for each other." Mason leans on the unpainted porch railing, staring out at Swamp Angel Road. All these secrets out here, layered in sedimentary rock. "Was it consensual?"

Bauer nods hesitantly. "I second-guess myself now. I thought maybe she'd sneak back if she really loved me, you know? But I think it was real. That's why I've been so worried. She's *disappeared*, Mason." He chokes up a bit. "And I'm worried she's dead."

"I'm sorry, Dave. I know it doesn't mean much, but I believe you."

Bauer wipes his nose on his bare arm, composing himself with a few deep breaths.

"Look," he says, licking his lips. "You wanna find Elliot Stone's killer?" He points west, his finger hovering over the forest just past the Ramirez house. Behind the forest stands the Anderson house, resting atop a sloping hill. "The Anderson property is the highest spot in this little valley. Ryan Anderson's been working on his house every afternoon since his son died."

"The sheriff questioned him …"

Bauer shakes his head. "That family's held onto a lot of pain since their son died, Mason. I ain't saying Ryan Anderson lied to the sheriff, but losing a child makes you lose all sense of your faculties. People do bad stuff they come to regret. Take it from me."

30

Final Chores

SOFIA FINISHES with the last group of calves and takes the pails to the sink. Slowly, methodically, she scrubs each of the pails, disinfecting them and placing them upside-down on the shelf. She wipes her hands on her jeans and stretches her back. The afternoon feeding is done, two hours late. Many of the calves have already returned to the softest piles of bedding, ready to go back to sleep. Above them, fans blow fresh air through the ducts. She's been with them all day, tube-feeding the ones that refuse to eat, changing out the bedding, spreading lime over runny shit, jotting down notes for Josh.

Sofia wouldn't know how to do any of this, but Eva does. She remembers tube-feeding calves with her mother and her father. She knows how much electrolytes to give them based on weight. She knows to insert the tube on the left side of the calf's mouth, letting the calf swallow the tube so it doesn't go down the wrong passage. She knows the liquid should be room temperature. One hand under the jaw. Soft reassurances.

She remembers dancing for the calves and putting on

"dinner shows" with them while her parents prepped milk substitute and fluffed up the straw in the stalls. The last day with her mother was in the calf barn. She'd been solemn and quiet, as if she knew that the car accident was going to happen.

Every day after that was different. Her father was more exhausted, and his smiles wouldn't have fooled even the worst acting teachers. But he never stopped loving Eva. Never stopped supporting her wild dreams and outsized ambitions to be a star.

Failure.

Torn pieces of Josh's Magic cards litter the floor. Sofia sweeps them up into a tidy pile, using the bristles of the broom to get at the straw. Something blue appears underneath a particularly sticky clump. Sofia reaches down and picks it up, examining it with the help of a curious Guernsey calf who's stuck her head through the nearest feed panel.

A Candyland game piece. A gingerbread pawn.

She puts it in the pocket of her jeans, thinking about what Josh said earlier, about how Tina would come here in the afternoon around the same time Elliot showed up. How the three of them would sit on the floor and play games together while the Reverend was out and about. A memory from yesterday morning hits her hard: the way Tina looked at her and Josh at breakfast, the very real smile on her face, as if everything was OK again.

Sofia opens the calf barn door. The setting sun behind rain clouds is a bullet hole bleeding through a cotton shirt. Rain patters on the aluminum roofs of the loafing sheds. A stream of water falls from the roof of the calf barn right in front of the doorway. Across the drive, she can see the cows in the north group taking shelter inside the loafing shed.

Sofia stands in the doorway, searching for Josh. He's been working outside all day, repairing the west group fence in the rain. Penance for his sin. Sofia isn't even sure if he came in last night at all. He wasn't around when she woke up and a pot of coffee had already been brewed for her, already room temperature.

How much longer will he work in the rain? The answer is obvious: Josh will work until his father tells him he can stop.

Sofia walks back to the house. The water on her neck, soaking her hair, infuriates her. She's exhausted, and it occurs to her that she hasn't thought of all the horrible shit in her life all day. She's forgotten parts of her old life and she doesn't miss it at all. She wants to stay here but she doesn't know if she can. She's afraid of the Reverend's wrath because she doesn't understand all the hidden rules of his religion.

They were just playing a game.

What other mistakes will she make? How much harder does she have to work in order to win acceptance? The answer hits Sofia so hard that she needs to stop and lean hard against the exterior of the north group loafing shed. She isn't strong enough to exist here. She's weak. Pampered. And she deserves the greedy life she built in Milwaukee.

Failure.

She doesn't belong here. And it's time to go home.

31

Confession

ROBIN PICKS MASON up at 7:30 p.m. in a shiny black Mercedes. The car is so nice that she initially refuses to let Mason bring his travel mug of coffee until he proves that it's spill-proof. The interior smells like a new car. The black leather seats feel so good that Mason's entire body seems to melt into the cushions. The display looks futuristic: digital speedometer projected onto the windshield, EV mode activated, and a careful analysis of her driving skills to maximize fuel efficiency.

Her dashboard is completely free of dust, glossy and polished.

"Adjust this if you want," she says, pointing to the passenger climate control settings. "Don't touch anything else."

Mason relishes the dry, cool air blowing in through the vents. Red sunlight is streaming in through the passenger window, spilling over his bare arm.

"So you believe David Bauer?"

"I do."

"And you read my story about the Andersons' son?"

"I did. This afternoon, actually." After he woke up, he went through everything one more time. Hoping to find something obvious that he missed. This is the only lead left.

"So what happened after Jon Anderson died on the Stone property?"

Now he sees why she's taking the long route. She wants to test him to make sure he did his homework. Failing this, he wouldn't be surprised if she turned the car around and dropped him back off at the motel.

Challenge accepted.

"Ryan and Tracy Anderson filed a complaint with OSHA. That was when they learned that small family farms are exempt from federal safety regulations. So they came to you and you discovered there were more deaths on family farms in Kane County over the last decade. All of them involved Mexican laborers."

"Poor saps. Takes a white victim to make it newsworthy." She turns onto Cherry Ridge Lane, a road that hews closely to a hill of exposed sandstone with porous vertical holes where ancient sea creatures burrowed, back when the Driftless Area was under a sea. "What happened next?"

"It got hard, financially," Mason recites from memory. "Tracy Anderson took a second job at the Home Depot in Fayette. Ryan Anderson did some contracting work on the side. When the price of milk dropped, they had no choice but to sell the farm to Wilson's Dairy."

"Beautiful," Robin says with a grin. "Not for them, obviously."

"Ryan started calling the farmer suicide hotline every night. Tracy started developing back problems. And then the rest of your story lamented the loss of the good old days when family farms could make money."

"Don't be so crass. Locals eat that shit up, Masc. And so did the Andersons. They literally called me in tears after my story was printed. So when we get there, let me do the talking. If you're right about this ... then we're going to need them to open up."

Cherry Ridge Road twists and turns up a long, steady hill. Trees replace fields of alfalfa plagued with dandelions, and then up on the left is the old lead mine. Its buildings are made of crumbling, cream-colored bricks. A massive structure with a conveyor belt running up to the second story. Cracked windows with frames like rows of teeth. A rusted water tower standing sentry next to a small building that's been demolished by half of a mighty oak, rotten and mangled.

"So that's it," Mason says.

"That's it." Robin takes her eyes off the road as they pass, her hands naturally easing the steering wheel to the left. The car auto-corrects. "You need to understand how important that mine is, Mase. Lead is the antagonist. Lead and greed and racism and desperation. You take all of that together, and you end up with Elliot Stone's disappearance."

"How?" Mason asks.

"I take it you didn't read any of my older stuff. That's OK. I didn't assign it as homework, so you get a free pass." She taps the steering wheel to the pop music playing through the speakers. Mason watches her eyes on the road, sees the way she's stitching everything together in her mind. "I started writing the story. About you. About Elliot's disappearance. Ready to hear it?"

"Yes."

"So when I was researching the lead mine, I went back. Way back to Lead Fever, when miners were flocking to southwest Wisconsin. I came across a letter written by Joseph Street in 1827. He was the new Indian Affairs agent, and he was writing back to his superiors the tension between Cornish miners and local Indian tribes. I'm gonna use the word 'Indian' here because that's how he referred to them, so don't go and think poorly of me."

"Got it."

"So in his letter, he wrote *The Indians have been soured by the conduct of the vast number of adventurers flocking to and working the lead mine of the Kewaunee River.* I remember that line so fucking clearly, Mase, because reading this letter was the first time in my life when I truly realized just how much violence greed can beget."

"The miners were violating a treaty," Mason guesses.

"Oh yeah. Big-time. And the worst part is this letter makes it clear that the miners were *knowingly* violating the treaty, just showing up and digging for lead wherever they fucking wanted. So these little conflicts broke out and of course it grew into the Blackhawk War. Only ended when pretty much all the local natives were eradicated."

"That's no surprise."

"No, no." She laughs bitterly. "You've heard that sob story before. Indians fight back, then Uncle Sam shows up with guns and germs. The point is the lead mine started running, started dumping its pollution. People who worked the smelters got sick all the time back then. Conditions were horrible. There's actually an old cemetery in that forest." She points to the trees on the left side of the road. "Trengrouse Cemetery. Totally overgrown now. Totally creepy. When I was in high school, I took my boyfriend out there and we fucked on the grave of a guy named *Cobbledick.*" She bursts into laughter. "We just had to, when we saw the name. Very classy, though. We had a blanket to lay on."

"Jesus Christ, you were a wild card even back then."

She grins at him. She likes getting a rise out of him, he can tell. "Let's fast-forward. The mine's pretty much dead by the mid-twentieth century. Just a couple dozen jobs left, mostly processing zinc. Worse, you've got government agencies sniffing around all the time now. Back in the 1800's, no one cared about pollution—and if they did, there wasn't much anyone in government was going to do about it. But then the EPA is formed, and this mine is on the top of its shit list. They want to shut it down. Carthaginians erupt in outrage. You know why?"

"Because people need the jobs."

Robin snaps her fingers. "Hell yes. Carthage fights it every step of the way. We need these jobs. Got to preserve these jobs. Pollution? No, no, no. We *need* those *jobs*. So the federal government buys up a bunch of land around here and sets up a grant program to promote dairy farms. It takes a couple decades, but the dairy business is lucrative enough that the lead mine can finally be shut down. Dairy is now officially king of the county."

"Milk prices went up," Mason says.

"Right. Things were good for a while, especially after Starbucks made lattes and mochas the drink of choice in the nineties. But then milk prices tanked. Dairy operations needed to get bigger and bigger and bigger just to eke out a profit."

"And the family farms around here started shutting down," Mason finishes. "And the summers got warmer, and kids started getting lead poisoning from all the pollution at Kewaunee Lake, and Reverend Jenkins started to grow his flock. Is that what you're getting at?"

"I was building tension, if you hadn't noticed. You're mostly right, except you're missing our angle." She turns left on Swamp Angel Road. On one side of the road is a pond, its surface clogged with neon-green algae. A hand-written sign sits next to the road: *Caution: Turtle Crossing!*

"The Andersons," Mason says. He can see their driveway up ahead, where the forest gives way to a field of corn sprouts that run up a long hill. The driveway runs a good two hundred yards, all gravel, inclining to the house and a round-roof barn.

"The Andersons' ancestors fought the Indians," Robin says, "and they lost family members. Tracy Anderson's family worked the lead mine, and they lost family members. Ryan Anderson's family fought in the world wars, and he lost family members. Then it was Tracy and Ryan's turn to make a sacrifice."

"Jon Anderson."

Robin nods grimly. "Tracy and Ryan lost their son in a tragic farm accident at a shitty job on a shitty farm loaded with debt.

Because Tracy and Ryan Anderson couldn't make enough to provide for their son."

"And now Elliot is missing," Mason says.

"It's the Stone family's turn to sacrifice." She makes a circle gesture with her finger. "It's all connected, Mason. That's what makes this story about Elliot Stone so fucking *good*. All these victims of circumstance and greed, so connected and so far apart."

"I thought this wasn't about the story anymore."

Robin sighs. "I know it's gonna sound crazy, but I feel like we *need* to bring Elliot's killer to justice. So someone can break this fucking cycle."

Mason smiles. Robin's the type of journalist who should have investigated him after the shooting of Tramon Perry. She would have never let Mason's resignation be the end of the story. She would have extracted like an infected tooth every single cop who tried to cover for Mason that night.

She turns onto the Anderson family's gravel driveway. It's lined with little bird boxes sitting on wooden posts. Every bird box is decorated differently. Mason counts them—six, eight, ten, twelve. A cardinal pokes its head out of one, cocking its head as the car passes.

Robin parks next to an old Ford F-150. Mason gets out of the car, glancing at the old milking parlor behind the house. It's still in good shape, as if it's just waiting for Wilson's Dairy to close down. The Anderson house has blue aluminum siding currently undergoing a do-it-yourself patch job, leaving sections exposed with weather stripping. Mason remembers the picture accompanying Robin's feature on the Andersons from so many years ago. They were standing in front of their house and the east end's siding had been dismantled. Now that siding has been replaced, all the way to the west end. All that's left is the attached garage, bare with underlayment.

He turns and looks east. He can see the Jenkins farm, the

Cranston farm, and the edge of the forest where they found Elliot's bike.

"Showtime," Robin says, leading him to the front door. She knocks gently on the glass. A moment later, Tracy Anderson answers. She's a full-figured woman, wearing a flowery dress and a pair of gray slippers. She was thinner in the photo. Less gray in her dark brown hair, too. But in the photo, she was unsmiling; now, she looks positively ecstatic to see Robin.

"I'm so glad to see you, honey," she says, giving Robin a hug. She scrutinizes Mason's jeans and t-shirt before shaking his hand. "Deputy."

She leads them inside, through a little porch that's crammed with old children's toys and a chop saw. The toys are covered in orange sawdust. Tracy knows Robin's family by their first names and Robin knows hers, and they get each other quickly up to speed on news. Mason steps into a small living room. To his left is a staircase leading upstairs, and on the steps are folded laundry. To his right are two couches in an L-shape against the far walls and between them is a little end table covered with wrappers of miniature candy bars and crushed soda cans.

A man sits on the far couch. The TV is on, tuned to a TV show Mason doesn't recognize. Ryan Anderson looks a little older than his wife. He has a dark red beard and thinning hair that sits on top of his crown. He's wearing a button-down t-shirt and a pair of faded jeans. A bag of pretzels sits next to him and in one hand is a glass of chalky-looking liquid, too thick to be milk. A protein drink, maybe.

"Have a seat," Tracy says. She sits beside her husband. Mason sits with Robin on the other couch. Robin pulls out her smart-phone and holds it up.

"Remember the drill?"

"Yup," says Ryan. To Mason's surprise, he turns off the TV.

Robin starts a new recording and sets the smartphone on the

arm of the couch. "Last time we talked, you mentioned a trip. Maybe to Alaska."

"Oh yeah, we did that last summer," says Tracy. Ryan gets up and walks into the adjoining dining room. The table is a mess of potted plants, opened mail, and some half-finished fabric project. Ryan grabs a framed picture and brings it back. He's wearing a smile now. "That's us in front of a glacier. You can use it in your story, if you want."

Robin admires it, letting Mason get a good look. Ryan and Tracy are smiling in front of a sprawling field of ice at the edge of a rocky river, clutching each other over their heavy winter hunting jackets. "It's beautiful," Mason says.

"Dirt cheap," says Tracy. "We have a cousin in the area so all we needed to do was get there."

"So things are going well?" Robin asks.

The muscles in Ryan's face tense, maintaining the smile. "Better than a lot of people. Still buying a lottery ticket once a week, though."

"How can you not?" Robin asks. "Jackpot's insane right now. Are you still raising some cows?"

Ryan shakes his head. "I work at Wilson's full-time."

"He's a shift manager," Tracy says proudly. "Good overtime."

"Great overtime," Ryan says. "Every time someone quits, I end up with a sixty-hour week."

"And one less credit card bill to worry about," Tracy adds. "We're still paying down some debt."

Robin nods. She cocks her head in Mason's direction. "The deputy here is investigating Elliot Stone's disappearance. I'm shadowing him a bit so I can write about it."

"Hell of a thing," Ryan says with a shake of his head.

"Does seeing the Stones suffer feel good?" Robin asks.

Mason blinks hard. The question is … *jarring.* Is she so close with them, that she could ask such a blunt question?

"Yes," Ryan says.

"It did," Tracy says, grabbing her husband's hand. He tries to withdraw but she grips it tightly. He gives in. His fingers find hers, interlocking. "But it's begun to wear off."

"Mostly."

"It felt very … fitting," Tracy says, "knowing that they were going through the hell we experienced with Jon. Like justice was being served."

"They never apologized," says Ryan. "For our son." He chokes up a little, swallows hard, resumes his polite smile. "They just said it was a tragic accident and then they moved on."

"Do you think you can ever reconcile?" Robin asks. "With the Stone family, I mean? Maybe come together at some point and share that grief?"

Tracy stays quiet. Ryan shakes his head. "I can't ever forgive them for the sheer negligence that caused my son's death."

"But it wears on you, doesn't it?" Mason asks. The suffering is a cycle and he's been here before. Mason's sitting with the Anderson just like he sat with the parents of Tramon Perry. And their suffering is so identical that it breaks his heart. It breaks his fucking heart to think about the kind of person he once was and the horrible mistake it led to. "The grief feels like a weight that's pulling you under the surface of something dark and suffocating. And all you want to do is let go of all that pain so you can live with the good memories."

Ryan simply nods. Robin gives Mason an encouraging look.

"I murdered a young man," Mason says. He clears his throat, but can't fully stifle the sob that comes. He takes a tissue from Robin and wipes the tears off his cheeks. "Tramon Perry. I thought he was a threat and I shot him while I was on duty. Months later, I visited his family. I sat with them and looked at photos of their son when he was a kid. I watched him grow up as we flipped through the albums. I apologized and you know what they did? They forgave me."

"And you moved on?" Tracy Anderson asks.

Mason shakes his head. "Being forgiven didn't absolve me

of guilt. I'm different now and I always will be. No matter how much pain and darkness lifts from my soul, I can still feel that young man's death deep inside my chest."

Ryan Anderson's hardened expression breaks. He takes a tissue, wipes his eyes quickly, then blows his nose. His wife's hand finds his, squeezing.

"You think forgiving the Stones will absolve them of the pain you *want* them to feel," Mason continues. "You're wrong. Forgiving them is about making your *own* peace. The Stones will live with the pain of Jon's death forever." He looks down at the carpet. "The Perry family calls me sometimes. Tramon's mother asks how I am. I pretend I'm doing better. Sometimes, I don't answer the phone because it hurts so much."

No one talks. Tracy blows her nose.

"I can't force you to forgive the Stones," he says. "But I want you to know that what happened to your son was horrible and he deserved justice."

"Thank you," Tracy whispers.

Mason turns to Ryan. "Your fields give you the best view of Swamp Angel Road. I know you've been working outside on your house, adding new siding. I know your secret, about the day Elliot Stone went missing. You *saw* something, Ryan."

"How could you know that?" Tracy asks.

Robin gives her a warm smile. "Mason's pretty damn good at his job, Trace."

"Please," Mason says. "Who did you see that day?"

They don't answer.

Mason leans forward, clasping his hands together. "Help me right this wrong."

"Across the street, at the Jenkins farm," says Ryan. "I saw the breeder for Wilson's Dairy." The muscles in his face loosen. He looks down at the carpeting. "Steven Brown. I saw Elliot Stone's bike in the back of his truck."

And then Mason is out the door, with Robin at his heels.

32

Act III

THROUGH THE BACK DOOR and down into the basement. Sofia peels off her wet clothes. Josh, true to his charitable and thoughtful nature, must have snuck into the house sometime during the afternoon and brought down two fresh towels. She dries herself off and puts on her clean clothes, brushing dust and basement grime off the bottoms of her feet before she puts on her socks.

She goes upstairs. The TV is on in the living room. Sofia wants to shower, but Tina is in the kitchen and she thinks the Reverend would probably like it if she helped his wife with dinner.

"Do you need help?" she asks meekly.

"Could you peel potatoes?"

Sofia draws the last of her strength to grab the strainer full of potatoes and bring it over to the end of the countertop. Grandma Wilma watches with a grimace. The Jenkins family potato peeler isn't very sharp—it's old, too. Sofia knows this because all new kitchen utensils now have colorful rubber handles and this one is just made of metal. What estate did the Reverend take this from? What life did it have before the Reverend found it?

She peels two potatoes, then cuts herself. She gets blood on the potato's white flesh. Wilma is watching but if she saw the cut, she's not surprised or concerned. Sofia wipes her finger on her pants and peels away the bloodstain. She's afraid if she throws the entire potato away, Tina might notice and reprimand her.

"How are the calves?" Tina asks.

"Good," Sofia murmurs.

"What was that? Speak up a bit." Tina's voice is stern. Sharper than usual.

"The calves are good," she manages in a stronger voice. She decides to do an extra good job on the potatoes, stripping them entirely of skin, even where there are divots and dimples. She wants to impress Tina and it takes forever and her hands hurt from carrying heavy pails all day, but the sight of the spotless potatoes makes Sofia feel good. She places them all into a pot. "What else can I help you with?"

"That's all. You can clean up for dinner."

"Should I call for Josh?"

Tina's eyes dart to the opening that leads into the living room. "No. Josh can eat later."

"I could bring him a plate ..."

"Just go wash up, sweetie."

Sofia glances at Grandma Wilma. The woman's head is cocked, her right eye on Sofia. Sofia walks slowly to the hallway. Her head feels light. When was the last time she had sugar? Days. Freaking *days*.

She takes a long shower, using her own little baggie of travel soaps. The beautiful bathroom is clean, free even of a single shaved whisker on the porcelain sink. Sofia can't see her reflection in the steamy mirror and she's glad. She hasn't worn make-up in days. She doesn't want to see her face in its most natural, raw form. She doesn't want to see herself at all.

She dresses and walks back to the kitchen. Plates of food are set out on the counter: chicken that's been cooked in the oven, mashed potatoes, and limp asparagus. "Come on, Grandma Wilma," Sofia says, helping the elderly woman off the stool and walking with her into the dining room. There are four plates set out with three glasses of water and one can of cream soda. Sofia sits beside Wilma.

"Anthony," calls Tina as she brings in the chicken. The Reverend gets up from the living room couch with a groan but doesn't turn off the TV. He's very interested in this particular show about some Armageddon-style apocalypse. The actors are located inside a bunker of some kind, shouting at one another. Their faces seem to go in and out of focus when they move.

They're not hitting their marks.

Tina, Sofia, and the Reverend pray together. Grandma Wilma defiantly eats her food. Sofia knows better than to eat before the Reverend so she waits, watching with hungry disappointment as he takes both drumsticks. The drumsticks are her favorite because they have just the right combination of flavorful dark meat and white meat. She takes a breast instead, then stabs a few pieces of limp asparagus and puts them on her plate. She foregoes the mashed potatoes, which of course Tina notices.

"Are you sure you don't want potatoes, sweetie?"

Sofia shakes her head. "No, thank you."

"Just take a bit," says the Reverend.

Sofia obeys, scooping a single spoonful onto her plate.

She waits for the Reverend to begin eating. Everything tastes bland, but she's so hungry; she needs to pace herself. She knows she shouldn't finish before the Reverend. She knows he'll take seconds, which means Sofia will need to eat half as fast as him.

She eats slowly, in silence, while the TV blares from the adjoining living room. She times each bite, methodical, matching the rhythm set by Tina. Tina is staring down at her food. She doesn't look at the TV. She's mastered the art of moving her food around to make it seem as if eating each bite is a laborious process.

The Reverend rends meat from the bone like he hasn't eaten in days. He washes it down with red wine in long gulps. He bites through bone and sucks out marrow. Clear juices drip down his chin. Finally, when there's no meat left, the Reverend gets up and goes back to the couch. Grandma Wilma stays at the table. Sofia clears the plates and Tina brings her mother a coloring book.

"No!" Wilma shouts, throwing the coloring book on the floor. Sofia freezes in the kitchen, watching Tina walk past the open doorway to retrieve the book. She returns to the kitchen and sets it on the countertop, then brings the rest of the dishes, tossing them in the stainless steel sink. Her eyes are sad and distant. The character of docile, supportive wife has broken out of the sightline of the Reverend, an actress between takes.

Sofia washes each dish with a scrub brush, her eyes losing focus as she stares at the white suds. Her legs are sore from squatting while she tube-fed calves. Her shoulders ache from pushing wet silage. Her head is throbbing from lack of sleep. And buried deep under these layers of pain is an unmistakable truth:

She will never be good enough to be accepted by this family.

It comes slowly at first. Just a few tears that she can hold back with deep breaths. But then it begins to feel worse, and she has to stop scrubbing the dishes every few moments to gather herself.

Failure.

The line where Sofia ends and Eva begins has disappeared and now they're both afraid. Afraid of their futures and afraid of themselves. Their failures are a cycle they can't break, no matter how many times they try.

Sofia grabs a fresh glass to wash—Tina's—and as she reaches for a towel, she feels it slip out of her hand. She watches in horror as it falls to the floor.

It breaks apart with an incredibly loud crash.

Sofia feels her heart thump against her chest. She begins crying harder, kneeling on the floor and trying to pick up the pieces of glass with shaky fingers. Little pieces slice through her skin with a satisfying pain that penetrates deep. Her hands become maroon gloves. Blood smears the white tile. This is my penance, she tells herself; this is the pain I deserve.

"Oh my," Tina says the moment she walks into the kitchen. "Oh, sweetie, just hold on!"

Through teary eyes, Sofia can see Tina going to the closet and grabbing a dustpan and broom. She wipes her bloody fingers on her pants, sobbing. "I'm so sorry. I'm so, so sorry."

A shadow passes over her. She doesn't need to look up to know it's the Reverend. "It was an accident," she tells him, keeping her eyes lowered. She doesn't want to see his disappointed face.

"It's an easy clean-up," soothes Tina, although the way her voice carries it sounds as if she's talking to the Reverend. "It's nothing to worry about."

"I can't do this," Sofia sobs. "I just don't know what to do with all the things I'm feeling and it's never going to get better. I'm never going to get better!"

She wipes her bloody hands on her pants again, watching a broom sweep up the shards of glass.

"It can be a difficult adjustment," Tina says gently. "And maybe ..."

"Everything will be fine," says the Reverend.

"I have to leave," Sofia says. Deep down, memories of failed auditions stir. "I'm a waste of your time."

Silence. Sofia sniffs in deeply, staring down at thick blood oozing out of dozens of cuts on her fingers. Her knees ache but she dares not get up. She's hit her mark.

"Sofia, it will get better. Please, please be strong," Tina says gently. She uses a dish towel emblazoned with farm animals to wipe Sofia's hands clean.

"I'm trying so hard," Sofia sobs. "But I just can't. I just *can't*. I'm a fuck-up. I'm worse than everyone else. I have … no one I can talk to. No one understands what I'm going through and I'm so *alone*."

More silence. Sofia risks a quick look up and sees, through watery eyes, the Reverend's wife giving him a desperate, pleading look. Sofia returns her gaze to the floor. She listens as the Reverend's heavy footsteps walk to the other end of the kitchen, where the cordless phone hangs on the wall. There's the unmistakable beep-beep-beep … beep-beep-beep, beep-beep-beep-beep of the phone's number pad. The Reverend speaks low into the phone; Sofia can't hear anything over the anxious beating of her heart.

A phone appears in Sofia's cloudy vision. "Talk to our daughter," the Reverend says gently.

Sofia, heart racing, puts the phone to her ear. "Hello?"

At first it seems like a dream, and maybe there's no one on the other end at all. But then a voice manifests: "Hi Sofia." She sounds just as Sofia always imagined. Sweet. Soft. Pure.

Miriam. She's alive.

Sofia accepts the Reverend's hand and gets to her feet. He gently ushers her to the hall. "Have some privacy," he urges.

Sofia glances at Tina for confirmation. The woman nods briskly, her fingers clutched together as if she's fighting the urge to snatch the phone from Sofia's grip. On wobbly legs, Sofia walks to her room. Miriam's room. She shuts the door and sits on Miriam's bed in the darkness. She listens, breathing deep, trying to imagine the woman on the other end of the line. Is she alone, too? Is she sitting in the darkness?

She's alive. That's all that matters.

"I hear you've been helping Josh," Miriam says.

"Yes," Sofia whispers.

"Thank you so much. I love my brother."

"He takes such wonderful care of the calves."

"He has a kind heart." Miriam laughs gently. "I don't know how he does it, honestly. Years ago, we had to put down a calf with my grandmother's help. It nearly cleaved my heart in two."

"I don't know if I could do that," Sofia confesses.

"Me, neither. Maybe my father could find another job for you that doesn't involve livestock."

"But your brother. He's so tired. He can't keep this up alone."

Miriam is silent.

"I want to help him," Sofia says. "I just … feel stuck in this weird place right now. Like I'm trapped between two worlds."

"I know what you're feeling. But listen to me, Sofia: if you pray long and hard, God will reveal the right path for you. If you stay true and believe in his plan, he won't lead you astray."

"How will I know?" Sofia asks.

"You'll feel it in your heart."

Sofia feels more tears coming. She stifles a gentle sob. "W-What happened to you?"

"I … had a very difficult decision to make. But I prayed on it with my father and God led me to the answer. And I know in my heart it was the right answer, even though it was the hardest thing I've ever done." Miriam exhales too close to the phone. "Things don't happen the way we expect. You think you have the world figured out, and then all of a sudden God shines a light on a shadow you missed. A spot in your life you didn't even know existed."

"Yes …"

"And sometimes God loses sight of the Devil," Miriam continues, her voice shaky. "Sometimes, the Devil fools even the best of us, and we don't recognize him when he shows up. We're blinded by our feelings. It takes another person to help us see him."

Sofia closes her eyes. The bedroom is hot; a wet breeze sneaks in through the open window. Goose bumps creep up her neck. She feels a terrible anger course through her.

Stay in character. Just a little longer.

"Do you have kids?" Miriam asks.

"No."

"I have a baby son," Miriam whispers, as if she's both ashamed and proud. "He's my anchor. I don't know what I would do if I couldn't look at him in the morning when I wake up. He makes life worth living."

Sofia says nothing. Eva doesn't trust her to respond.

"What did my mother make for dinner?"

"Chicken and mashed potatoes," Sofia whispers.

"She makes such awful chicken."

Sofia laughs. "The skin *was* rubbery."

"The Reverend likes his food bland," Miriam says. "He likes the *world* bland because he's afraid of everything. My mom … I think she's afraid of herself."

"Maybe I could sneak a little salt into the next meal."

Miriam laughs lightly. "Lord, I didn't even know what I was missing until I got out of that house."

Sofia feels her heart beat faster. "What do you mean?"

"I took a job on a farm for a few years." She laughs. "The Reverend thought toiling all day would be enough to temper my wild side that I got from my mother. But my boss … he sometimes cooked and it always tasted so wonderful. Stir-fry chicken. Pork chops. Meatloaf. It tasted so different from what I was used to. He used all these spices I never knew existed."

"Did he …" Sofia swallows. "Is he the one who gave you all the stories about astronauts?"

"You found those. I guess I didn't hide them well enough." Miriam is silent for a moment. Through the line, Sofia can hear the soft wail of a baby. "I guess the best way to describe it is he gave me freedom. And I learned the hard way that freedom is dangerous."

Sofia's breaths catch in her throat. She can't respond. Even if she could, she doesn't know what she would say. She wants to ask Miriam if she still wants to be an astronaut, but before she can formulate any words, the baby's cries grow louder.

"I have to go," Miriam says. "I hope I helped you a little bit."

"You did," Sofia says.

They hang up.

More than you could ever know.

Eva sits in the darkness, staring at the phone in her hand. It takes every ounce of willpower to control her breathing and keep from hyperventilating. She wipes the last tears from her eyes and goes to her suitcase, turning on her smartphone. She has a few text messages from Hollywood friends, a few voice-mails from her agent, but she doesn't care right now.

The only thing that matters is Miriam.

She turns on the Jenkins' phone and presses the redial button. A phone number appears on the little green digital screen. Eva types the number into her smartphone, using a reverse-lookup database online.

An address appears.

Huntsville, Alabama.

Eva copies the address and sends a text message, then turns off her smartphone and puts it in her pocket, along with her wallet. All she needs to do now is escape. She composes herself, lets her consciousness shift back into the character of Sofia, and steps out of Miriam's bedroom for the last time.

She walks hesitantly down the hallway. Grandma Wilma is sitting at the kitchen countertop, watching with a grim look on her face. Eva walks past her, into the dining room. Tina is sitting at the table, mending the sleeve of one of the Reverend's shirts. She looks up when Eva sets down the cordless phone.

"Did it help?" she asks.

"Yes," Eva says, washing her blood-stained hands in the sink. "*So* much. Thank you."

"And your hair has never felt shinier!"

Eva freezes. She turns to the TV just in time to catch an image of herself on the screen, her beautiful brown hair billowing in the gust of an off-camera fan, the L'Oréal shampoo product sitting in the corner of the screen.

The Reverend, stunned, turns and looks at her.

Eva feels a cold, bony hand grab her arm.

"Run," Grandma Wilma whispers.

33

Hunt

"THANKS AGAIN," Mason says into the phone. He hangs up. "The woman at Wilson's says Steven Brown is still out tonight. She's emailing a log of Brown's insemination schedule with a map."

Robin hits the brakes hard at the next stop sign. It's gotten so dark so fast and the driving rain makes it impossible to turn on the high beams. "What's your play here?"

"I'm going to apprehend him and try to get him to talk without a lawyer," Mason answers. Raindrops pound the windshield so fast and hard that Robin has the wipers on at full speed.

"You think that'll actually work?"

He shrugs grimly. "Rainy evening, plainclothes officer hunting him down, eyewitness testimony … it'll work a helluva lot better than letting Henderson have a crack at him. Turn right at the next road. It's a dead-end but there are two farms that I know for sure raise calves for Wilson's."

"I know you'll think less of me," Robin says coolly, slamming on the brakes so they don't overshoot the intersection, "but this is far and away the most exciting thing I've ever been a part of."

"Here," Mason says, pointing to where the headlights are illuminating a white mailbox up ahead. "Pull into their driveway."

She turns at the driveway next to a row of pine trees. The farmhouse stands near the road. They drive past it, to a pair of barns at the far end where a short row of empty headlocks sits. "U-turn, back to the house, back to the house," Mason orders.

Robin takes him to the house and stops. He gets out, ducking under the torrent of warm rain, and rings the doorbell. A man in his fifties appears in the doorway, looking at Mason with a lot of suspicion.

"Deputy Mason Taylor," he says, flashing his badge. "Did the breeder from Wilson's Dairy come here today?"

"Not sure," says the man. "I was laid up all morning with a back thing."

Mason runs back to the car.

"God damn it," Robin mutters, peeling out of the driveway. "Wilson's has at least twenty farms in this area alone. He could be anywhere."

"The other house is up here on the left," Mason says. Ahead the headlights cut through darkness and raindrops to another farm, tucked back at the foot of a steep hill with exposed rock. The house is old, its white paint peeling, and under the glow of a light in the driveway he can see the rain pounding roof shingles that have curled under stress.

No sign of Steven Brown.

Finally, the email from Wilson's Dairy comes through with a map and schedule. Mason pulls up the schedule, scanning back over two weeks.

There.

"The evening Elliot Stone went missing," Mason says, "Steven Brown was inseminating at the Jenkins property between 6:30 and 7:30. Robin, he was on Swamp Angel Road!"

"I can't believe I never considered the guy from Wilson's Dairy," Robin says.

Mason reads closer. "Brown's notes say he fell behind and took longer than usual that evening."

She pounds the wheel as she suddenly remembers something. "Teddy Cox said he saw a pair of headlights pass his house at around 7:30. That had to be Brown's truck!"

"We assumed the truck was heading west," he says to Robin, "but it was heading *east*. Toward the forest to dump the bike."

They head east, stop at three more houses. Steven Brown has already been there today. Mason feels anxiety charge through him like electricity. He wishes he was the one driving, just so he has a little more control. He hates sitting here, feeling helpless.

Lightning lights up the sky. Rain starts coming down in sheets, forcing Robin to slow the car to a crawl as they reach the end of the road, which terminates at the foot of a steep bluff, a yellow DEAD END sign glistening in the headlamps. "We'll have to turn around …" she says.

"There," Mason points to a pair of metal gates hanging over a barely visible, overgrown road. "That leads south toward David Bauer's property."

"Mase, that's a fucking service road for the electric company. It probably hasn't even been used in—"

"Just go!"

"Shit!" Robin shouts, gunning the engine. The metal bars bounce off the car's bumper with an expensive crack and the tires skid a moment on the wet gravel before finding traction. The car's suspension bounces over potholes but Robin keeps the car's speed steady. The old road takes them to the edge of a steep hill, snaking slightly and leading the car to the back end of David Bauer's old milking parlor.

"God, I hope he's home," Robin says with a laugh. "Seeing a random car flying down the old service road in the middle of a thunderstorm."

"Park here," Mason says, pointing to the driveway in front of Bauer's half-painted patio. Robin does so, but before he can get out, she's already got her door open. He watches her run through the rain, up the patio. David Bauer answers, his shadow obscuring what's no doubt a photo-worthy expression of surprise as Robin hammers him with questions.

Robin returns to the car, her soaked hair clinging to her face. "Bauer says the breeder's truck was here just a few minutes ago."

"Which means the next farm he hits …"

"The Jenkins farm!"

34

Bang

EVA RUNS TOWARD the calf barn as quickly as her eyes will allow in the darkness. Her socks are soaked; every step on the old concrete hurts. Pouring rain hitting the stainless steel roof of the shop garage hammers her eardrums. Water soaks her clothes.

"Josh!" she calls out. She has to find him.

She has to save him.

She reaches the door to the calf barn and swings it open, wiping rainwater from her face. He's not there. He must still be working on the fencing. She runs down the driveway, turning in front of the silo. The cows at the headlocks pull back but the gates are locked, holding them in place. Was the breeder here? Is he still here?

"Josh!" she calls out. Her voice barely carries at all, lost in the pounding rain. Her feet slosh through sloppy manure, splattering her jeans. She looks in the vehicle shed. Not there; the racoon kits' curious eyes glint in the shed's overhead lights. She hurries over to the west group and unlocks the gate, pulling it open. Immediately, a few curious cows wander over. This will be her distraction to make a safe getaway.

But not before she tries to save Josh.

She crosses to the feed shelter, searching desperately along the fence line of the west group. More cows have escaped, black shapes wandering toward the feed shelter, letting out cautious moos.

"Josh!" Eva screams at the top of her lungs.

Nothing.

She needs to escape. *Now.*

Staying close to the fencing, moving just slow enough for her eyes to discern the shadows in the darkness, she makes her way to the compost mounds just beyond the west group. What did Josh do? Who did he kill?

She gets on her knees and claws madly at the wet dirt, wrenching free soft chunks until she reveals the snout of a cow. Fresh. A recent death.

She crawls on hands and knees to the older mound. Heart racing now, she digs and digs and digs until she feels something hard like bone. She claws all around the hard object, aware that she's not just getting dirt under her fingernails, she's getting rotten flesh as well. Rain washes away loose granules, revealing a skull.

A cow skull.

Eva breathes a sigh of relief. Two cows. All this time, it had just been two cows.

"She was my grandma's."

Eva turns. Josh is standing over her, soaked head-to-toe, holding a clawed hammer in one hand.

He crouches down. "My grandma kept her like a pet. I promised to look after her when I took over the cow chores. Then the cow started to get sick. She was suffering. I told my ma and she snuck some money from the Reverend's wallet to pay a vet even though we know stealing is a sin. The vet said it was something neurological and it would only get worse."

"So you did the humane thing," Eva says, "and your grandmother blamed you."

Josh lets out a quiet sob. "My grandma *told* me to kill her. Then she had the stroke and it was like she forgot. Now she blames me."

"Josh, you're a *good* person," Eva says. "You need to get out of here. Away from your parents. Away from this place—"

Something hard hits her across the temple. She hears Josh cry out but she can't see anything, can only feel wet mud splash across her face as she falls over. A strong hand grabs the back of her shirt, twists, and pulls her off the ground, her collar choking her windpipe.

Far away, behind the ringing in her ears and the pouring rain, she hears the Reverend's voice:

"Get the gun."

And then she's dropped unceremoniously in the slushy manure at the end of the north group feed panels. The fetid taste of manure on her lips brings her to; she spits, then opens her eyes. She stands up, head raised, letting the rain wash it off her face.

A pair of dark figures are standing in front of her.

"Who the hell are you?" asks the shorter one. Eva blinks away rain, taking in his frame underneath a thin rain jacket and the shadows along his narrow face. Steven Brown.

"Answer," says the Reverend. He points a finger. "And don't you dare say Sofia. You've lied enough."

"My name is Eva Bauer," she says proudly.

The Reverend lowers his finger, his mouth hanging open. "David Bauer's daughter?"

"Holy shit," says the breeder, running a hand through his wet hair. "What the fuck is she doing here? What the *fuck*?"

"Answer, *Eva*." The Reverend's baritone voice is cold and

calm, carrying between the raindrops as if its heavy wavelengths are perfectly fitted.

"Because your daughter's child is my brother," Eva says, spitting rainwater with triumphant abandon. "He's my brother, god *damn* you!"

"And your father is the Devil," the Reverend snarls. "He corrupted my beautiful child!"

"He's a better man than you could ever hope to be!" Eva screams, so hard that her throat feels shredded by the sharp words. Whatever happens next, she wants him to remember this. "He's the best father Miriam's son could ever have!"

Josh appears at the entrance to the vehicle shed. He's holding his revolver. Eva turns to him, heart racing. "Josh!"

"Josh, kill her," says the Reverend.

"Josh," Eva pleads. "Josh, my father spent every last dollar he had to find Miriam. He cares about her, just like you."

"Josh, she is a Jezebel," says the Reverend, turning to his son. "She has come into our home, pretending to be someone else, infiltrating our family with the intent of destroying it."

"Jesus Christ," Steven says, pacing back and forth. "Jesus Christ, maybe we can just—"

"Steven, shut up." The Reverend points a hand to him. Lightning lights up the sky. He turns to his son. "Do you want Miriam to come back? Do you ever want her to return? She can't do it so long as this Jezebel is alive. *Kill her.*"

"Josh," Eva pleads.

"*Kill her!*" the Reverend shouts.

Josh raises the gun. He turns the gun and points the barrel squarely at his forehead.

Eva raises a hand to stop him. "Josh, no!"

He pulls the trigger. His head snaps back. The Reverend and Steven both cry out—one in agony, the other in surprise—and they both rush to Josh's body as it crumples in front of the skid steer.

Eva gets up and sprints down the row of feed panels, ignoring the pain in her feet as they land on gravel and sharp chunks of concrete. She hears shouting behind her and knows she can't run back toward the house with them following her. She has to lose them.

She turns right at the last remaining silo, her soaked socks slipping on a track of mud, losing her footing.

She takes a deep breath …

And falls into the moat.

Darkness. Sludgy liquid fills her ears and the sound of rain pounding the surface reverberates all around her. Her hands reach out, swimming wildly to keep her body from floating back to the surface. She thinks if she can just stay down here for a few more crucial moments, her aggressors will split up and search the farm in the darkness or, better yet, run to the house for flashlights. That's when she'll make her move: escape across the CRP land behind the feed shelter, across the muddy field where the darkness can hide her all the way to Highway O.

Call the police.

She can do this, if she can stay under just a few seconds longer. With her eyes closed, her ears plugged, her heartbeat seems to resonate everywhere at once. The sludge is heavier than water and it seems to close in and squeeze her body. She reaches out a hand, desperate to grab something, *anything*, to keep her under.

Something brushes her fingers. A branch or a root of something that had been buried in the moat. Eva grabs it, feels its familiarity, and her screams are carried up in bubbles.

A hand. It's a human *hand*.

Her lungs spasm for fresh oxygen. Eva kicks frantically, turning underwater, feeling her foot bump painfully against the edge of a cinder block at the bottom. She kicks again, coming into contact with a chain that must be holding the body down. She rises to the surface, gasping for air, choking on the torrent of raindrops. She clings to the edge of the moat and wipes her face.

The dull, orange light attached to the calf barn illuminates the south end; at the edge of the light, she sees the Reverend's large body disappear behind the burn pile—he's heading around the old milking parlor, back toward the house. Eva swims to the other side of the moat, glancing around the silo. A few heifers have their heads through the headlocks, mooing at the escaped cows on the other side who are eating their soggy silage.

Movement. Eva's head snaps in its direction—it's Steven, walking up the driveway, stopping at the door to the calf barn. He opens it and steps inside.

Something touches Eva's shoulder. She turns, stifling a scream as she comes face to face with the corpse's bloated face. He's floating belly-up, his open mouth filled with water. The chain—she must have kicked it loose from the cinderblock, freeing him.

Eva crawls out of the moat, gasping, feeling the rain baptize her body. There's no time to mourn. She has to escape while she has the chance.

Eva moves to the shadows along the south group's loafing shed, toward the west end of the farm, passing the old silo bases that stand like tombstones.

35

Deliverance

ROBIN TURNS onto the Jenkins driveway. The weeping willow trees' branches dance hypnotically in the rain, their branches like tentacles. Ahead, Mason can see the truck belonging to Steven Brown, parked at the loafing shed just beyond the Jenkins house. He can feel his entire body going numb with adrenaline. A hundred thoughts race through his head but the only one that matters is this:

The dead body of Tramon Perry, the man's eyes staring up at the night sky.

"Park here," Mason croaks, willing his breaths to slow before he can hyperventilate. Robin parks next to the Jenkins house. "Lights off. Stay in the car with the doors locked. And I need to borrow your gun."

"What if Steven tries to flee in his truck?" she asks, reaching over and flipping open the glove compartment. "I won't ram him, but I could move the car—"

"Just honk the horn." Mason grabs Robin's gun: a vintage six-shooter with a sleek walnut handle and nickel finish. He remembers the missing gun from the display case at the antique shop. "This actually work?"

"Perfectly. But Mason." She grabs his shirt, pulling him close enough to press her lips to his. He feels a jolt of electricity course through him. Robin pushes him away. "Be careful."

He gets out of the car, making his way to Steven Brown's truck, checking the dark corners of the loafing shed. The downpour all at once slows to a drizzle. He fights the urge to wipe rainwater from his face, keeping both hands on the pistol while he glances through the truck windows. No sign of Steven, and just as importantly no sign of the tank of bull semen. If he's lucky, he'll be able to catch the breeder unawares and make this easy.

Breathe.

Mason blinks rainwater out of his eyes. He imagines himself walking down the driveway, following the west group fence to the feed panels. If Steven sees him coming, he might have time to hide or run. But there's another option. Mason can go the other way around the enclosure, skirting the corn field, and take Steven by surprise.

And hopefully initiate a peaceful surrender.

Mason creeps south along the back of the loafing shed, his boots sloshing in the muddy buffer strip along the edge of the crops. A crack of thunder hits like a gunshot. The rain picks up, pounding the metal roofs, deafening his ears. From behind the big breds pen, pregnant heifers watch. Mason crouches low when he reaches the compost heap. His eyes search the open space between the west group and the vehicle shed, where soft light spills out across cracked, muddy concrete.

Nothing.

No—wait. He sees a shoe poking out from vehicle shed. Someone lying down? Hurt, maybe? Mason creeps closer, feeling the same numbness in his legs that he felt the night of Tramon's death. Something is wrong.

He reaches the corner of the vehicle shed and inhales slowly, letting his eyes adjust to the darkness. He scans the pole barn across the way. Shadows everywhere, moving around the bales of hay. Cows—they've escaped from the west group pen and now they're everywhere. Something is very wrong here.

He leans around the corner of the shed.

His heart stops in his chest.

"Josh!" he whispers, running to the boy's body and falling to his knees on the hard concrete. He checks a pulse, then lifts the boy's head.

He's alive. Bleeding a lot from a wound right between his eyes that runs up his forehead that half-scalped him. A cut or … no, as Mason gently rubs away dirt, it must have been a gunshot. Self-inflicted? The revolver's tremendous kick-back would explain the near-miss. But where is the gun?

Lightning flashes across the sky, followed by a boom of thunder. The escaped cows bellow stressed moos.

"Help is coming, pal." Mason pulls out his phone and initiates an emergency call, then sets it next to the open gun box where two racoon kits are sitting, rapt by the excitement. One of them hops off the bale of hay and that's when Mason notices: Muddy boot prints turning away from Josh and heading toward the calf building.

He crouches low, exiting the vehicle shed and skulking along the north group feed panels. The first cow jerks her head back but she can't leave—the bars are all locked. Mason's entire body feels as if it's breaking down, eroding in the hard rain. He has to tense his leg muscles just to get them to move.

He peers over their heads, searching the darkness for Steven inside the west group's enclosure.

Nothing.

Mason ducks down and skulks down the row of silo bases, toward the calf barn. He can feel the strain in his leg muscles but as long as he stays low, he has a wall of cow muscle between himself and whatever gun Josh used. Mason keeps his mouth open so he can take deep breaths, swallowing rainwater and righteous fury and atavistic fear.

Deep breaths.

Wet gasps. Numb fingers, clutching the old revolver. There's only one light source ahead to stave off the darkness: a single bulb attached to the calf barn, spilling orange light onto cracked concrete and a pile of green bale mesh beside the silo moat.

Mason takes it slow, eyes on the old foundations of dismantled silos running in a row right up to the last standing silo. The foundations are cracked, overgrown with weeds and trees and discarded junk like tires and strips of metal and old wooden posts. He peers down the row of panels, then slowly rises and looks over the cows, searching the west group enclosure again.

Rain slides off the metal roofs in heavy streams, disappearing into the darkness. Shadows of cows sitting on their bedding under the shelter.

Something moves behind him. He spins, pointing his gun at a black shadow moving toward him, his finger slipping under the trigger guard.

Wait.

It's a cow. One of the escapees from the west group. She and a handful of others have followed Mason.

He turns back toward the calf barn and closes the rest of the distance to the end of the panels. He peers up the driveway. Empty. Maybe inside the building? Or near the south group?

Try the south group first, then double back to the calf barn. Trust Robin to honk the horn if she sees anything.

Mason turns to the moat of manure that runs around the last remaining silo—and stifles a sob when his memory conjures the image of Josh gently warning him about it just days ago.

Wait.

There's something floating in the moat. *Someone.*

He kneels down and gasps in horror.

Elliot Stone.

Mason pulls the body out of the water. Rain washes away manure clinging to the corpse, revealing arthritic-looking fingers frozen in claws, an innocent blue Milwaukee Brewers t-shirt, a pair of stained shorts. The boy's face looks frozen in agony. His eyes are puffy, the skin bloated and dark. His body is mangled, his shirt ripped to reveal a broken ribcage. A chain is locked around the boy's leg, pinching his skin.

"It was an accident."

Mason turns and points his gun. Steven Brown is standing not ten feet behind him, arms out, rain slicker unfurled so he looks almost angelic. Behind him, the calf barn door is caught in the wind, swinging wildly in warning.

Mason's finger touches the trigger.

"Get down on the ground!"

Steven raises his arms. No gun. Mason's entire body tingles with electricity. He carefully takes his finger off the trigger. He can take Steven peacefully. He can do this.

"Why was he here?" Mason asks.

"To spend time with me," comes another voice.

Mason aims the gun over Steven's shoulder, watching the dark figure step into the soft light from the calf barn. Tina. She stops next to Steven, her dress soaking wet, her thinning hair matted to her skull.

"After my husband sent Miriam away," she says over the rain, "Elliot started to visit the farm in the afternoons, when I was helping Joshy with the chores. It made Joshy happy. It made me happy."

"How did he die?" Mason asks.

"He climbed over the north group fence," Tina says. "I was in there, fixing a headlock. Something spooked the heifers and they trampled him. It was an accident."

"I saw it," Steven says. His fingers twitch. "I saw it all, God damn me."

"I panicked," Tina says. "I buried his body in the moat."

"Did the Reverend know?"

Tina shakes her head. Water falls from her hair in waves. "He wrenched her from me, deputy. He didn't even give me a chance to say a proper goodbye to my own fucking daughter. He sent her away forever. I worried … if he learned what happened to Elliot, he might never let me see Miriam again."

"And you hid the bike," Mason says to Steven. "In the forest near the Ramirez property."

Steven nods.

"Why?"

"Because I would do anything for Tina," he says. "I love—"

Then: a crack of thunder. Tina screams and steps back in horror. Steven lets out a gurgling groan, collapsing on the edge of the moat. Mason makes a move to grab him before he falls in, and as Steven turns, the soft light from the calf barn illuminates the hole in his neck.

Too late: another crack of thunder and Mason feels a terrible pain in his chest. He falls over and lands on his back.

Raindrops pelt his face and he thinks finally, here, he's gotten exactly what he deserves.

36

Redemption

EVA'S JUST REACHED the last demolished silo when she hears the gun's report, followed by Tina's screams. She makes her way around the slab of concrete, frightening a handful of escaped cows who begin trotting down the north group's head-locks where a pair of figures stand. The light from the calf barn makes their wet hair shine like halos.

The Reverend and his wife.

Eva reaches down and grabs a chunk of broken concrete from the silo base. She can see the Reverend standing near the moat, pointing the gun at something or someone. Between Eva and the Reverend are a dozen escaped cows. Rain streams down the back of her neck; her entire body shivers uncontrollably.

Leave.

But she can't.

She creeps closer, using the escaped cows for cover.

"I lied for her!" shouts the Reverend. Who is he talking to? Not Eva. He hasn't turned her way, hasn't even noticed the dozen escaped cows making their way down the row of headlocks. "I told the sheriff we were sitting around playing cards the night Elliot disappeared. She didn't have an alibi. I had to protect her, Deputy Taylor."

The deputy. The one who was staying at the motel.

She gives the Jersey in front of her a quick slap. The cow hops forward, pushing into the others, keeping them moving.

"I swear I didn't know the entire truth," the Reverend continues. "And I'm sorry it's come to this. But I have to protect my family."

There's no more time. Eva brings up the cinder block and pounds it against the rear leg of the Jersey. The cow takes off, bumping into her neighbor, and suddenly all the cows are running toward the Reverend and his wife, their hooves clomping on the blistered concrete. Tina's the first to notice. She cries out and steps back, tripping on wet bale twine and falling onto a pile of rotten hay. The Reverend points and fires his gun; Eva sees the orange flash of the muzzle, but nothing except a clean shot would stop an adult cow and it only terrifies them more, causing them to pick up speed as they reach the end of the headlocks.

The Reverend is too big and intimidating for them to trample him, so they turn left and head up the driveway toward the house. Eva is close enough now and all she needs is a second of surprise. She reaches back and swings the chunk of concrete at the Reverend. The concrete block bounces off his chest and strikes him in the chin.

The momentum carries Eva forward. She falls, landing hard on her shoulder, splashing into a puddle, temporarily blinded. She blinks, heart racing, and gets to her knees to grab the chunk of concrete.

But it's gone. And looming over her is the Reverend.

"You corrupted our son," he says, hefting the concrete over his head with his one hand.

Eva, on her knees, looks up at him, blinking away raindrops.

She thinks maybe she can duck out of the way if she times it right. She thinks she can still disappear into the field of corn if she can *just get the timing right.*

The Reverend glares down at Eva. "If God wants you to live, then let him strike me down now. Before I kill you."

His arm tenses, ready to bring down the cinderblock. But then there's a crack of thunder, and another, and another.

The concrete drops from the Reverend's grasp. He collapses, struggling for breath, his face frozen in a look of absolute surprise.

Behind him, laying on the ground with his gun still pointed, is Deputy Mason.

Revelation

A BODY LAID TO REST in a wet cemetery on the edge of Carthage, at the end of a long row of tombstones. A mother stands with a grandmother, one umbrella between them. A boy next to the them, his head covered by a thick bandage. When the casket is lowered, the mother is taken away by police, the grandmother and boy taken by an actress who keeps a litter of racoons in the backseat of her car.

An ex-deputy, lying in his hospital bed. On the little table next to the bed is a game of Battleship.

A journalist, putting the final touches on her redemption story.

A father, standing on the top step of his porch, watching a car pull onto the driveway and park in front of the house. A young woman gets out and that's when he sees for the first time his baby son, swaddled in a white blanket. And he begins to cry.

A boy, finally laid to rest. Mourners gather around his coffin as it's lowered into the earth. His parents are there, and another couple, keeping a respectful distance, there to experience a peaceful closure they never received.

ACKNOWLEDGMENT

WHAT A STRANGE ADVENTURE this has been. First and foremost, I should probably thank my wife and her family for "allowing" me to work (for free) so many hours on the family farm. There's nothing quite like the intense joy that comes with midwifing a calf with your bare hands, or staring down a charging bull, or screaming at the top of your lungs to stop a herd of escaped heifers in their tracks. Also, thanks to my readers Liz and Steph, who gave me great feedback on various drafts of this book. Dear God, there were a lot of drafts to get this one right. Oh! And a special thank-you to Professor Bob McCalliser (now retired) whose geographical expertise helped me nail the nuances of the setting.

I'm immensely proud of this story, and I'm so glad to be a part of the Shotgun Honey family. So a final thank-you goes to Ron Phillips for his tireless work. Indie publishers are the beating heart of literature, and the work they do deserves to be celebrated.

KEN BROSKY is an author of horror and mystery novels, and teaches College English in Wisconsin.

ABOUT
SHOTGUN HONEY BOOKS

THANK YOU for reading **What the Rain Reveals** by Ken Brosky.

Shotgun Honey began as a crime genre flash fiction webzine in 2011 created as a venue for new and established writers to experiment in the confines of a mere 700 words. More than a decade later, Shotgun Honey still challenges writers with that storytelling task, but also provides opportunities to expand beyond through our book imprint and has since published anthologies, collections, novellas and novels by new and emerging authors.

We hope you have enjoyed this book. That you will share your experience, review and rate this title positively on your favorite book review sites and with your social media family and friends.

Visit ShotgunHoneyBooks.com

SHOTGUN HONEY
FICTION WITH A KICK

www.ingramcontent.com/pod-product-compliance
Lightning Source LLC
Chambersburg PA
CBHW011130190726
48289CB00012B/2980